Murderbirds

Unhelpful Encyclopedia Volume 1

MURDERBIRDS
An Avian Anthology

Edited by Mike Jack Stoumbos
Published by WonderBird Press

Cover Design by Ruth Nickle

Murderbirds © 2023 by Mike Jack Stoumbos and WonderBird Press

All rights reserved. No part of this book may be reproduced in any form or by any electronic or mechanical means, including information storage and retrieval systems, without permission in writing from the publisher, except by reviewers, who may quote brief passages in a review.

ISBN: 979-8-9875384-0-1

Cover Artwork © 2023 by Ruth Nickle
Interior Illustrations on page 15 and 24 © 2023 by John K Patterson
All other interior Illustrations © 2023 by Mike Jack Stoumbos

"The Fat Guy's Gotta Die" © 2023 by Martin L Shoemaker
"The Delicious Irony of Dino Nuggets" © 2023 by Z. T. Bright
"Outback Attack" © 2023 by John K Patterson
"Blood on the Wing" © 2023 by Jenny Perry Carr
"Whatever Lola Wants" © 2023 by N. V. Haskell
"Polly Want an Apple" © 2023 by Mike Jack Stoumbos
"An Unkindness" © 2023 by Rebecca E Treasure
"Obsidian Grackle" © 2023 by Desmond Astaire
"Doesn't Belong" © 2023 by John Gleason
"Boneyard" © 2023 by Wulf Moon
"Taking Flight on Bone-Shard Wings" © 2023 by M Elizabeth Ticknor
"Sing Me to Sleep" © 2023 by J. L. George
"Facts that Lead to My Choosing the Hawk" © 2023 by Leah Ning
"Give One to the Soul" © 2023 by Michael Panter
"Felix and the Flamingo" © 2023 by David Hankins
"The Boy He Wove" © 2023 by Ryan A Cole
"Cheer Hawks and a Side of Murder" © 2023 by Crystal Crawford
"Forget-Me-Not and Morning Dew" © 2023 by Yelena Crane
"His Glowing Feathers" © 2023 by Akis Linardos
"Falcon's Apprentice" © 2019 by Jody Lynn Nye

This Anthology contains works of fiction. Names, characters, places, and incidents are either the product of the authors' imaginations or are used fictitiously. Any resemblance to actual events, locales, or persons living or dead is coincidental, with the exception of requested name inclusion by some of this publication's sponsors. Opinions expressed in the fiction content and accompanying biographies are entirely their own.

Table of Contents

"The Fat Guy's Gotta Die" by Martin L Shoemaker	2
"The Delicious Irony of Dino Nuggets" by Z. T. Bright	16
"Outback Attack" by John K Patterson	25
"Blood on the Wing" by Jenny Perry Carr	37
"Whatever Lola Wants" by N. V. Haskell	44
"Polly Want an Apple" by Mike Jack Stoumbos	55
"An Unkindness" by Rebecca E Treasure	64
"Obsidian Grackle" by Desmond Astaire	70
"Doesn't Belong" by John Gleason	83
"Boneyard" by Wulf Moon	90
"Taking Flight on Bone-Shard Wings" by M Elizabeth Ticknor	110
"Sing Me to Sleep" by J. L. George	113
"Facts that Led to My Choosing the Hawk" by Leah Ning	127
"Give One to the Soul" by Michael Panter	133
"Felix and the Flamingo" by David Hankins	141
"The Boy He Wove" by Ryan A Cole	151
"Cheer Hawks and a Side of Murder" by Crystal Crawford	162
"Forget-Me-Not and Morning Dew" by Yelena Crane	176
"His Glowing Feathers" by Akis Linardos	182
"Falcon's Apprentice" by Jody Lynn Nye	196

Acknowledgements

The Communities that Made this Possible

One thing that I love about anthologies is that they are community efforts. In compiling this anthology, I specifically put out the call to education and support networks for emerging authors, a couple of which have been instrumental in my own fiction writing opportunities. A special thanks to Superstars Writing Seminars, Apex Writers Group, Writers of the Future Workshop and Forum, and Wulf Moon's "Wulf Pack."

A few members from these groups gave additional time and energy in the story selection and publication process, in particular, Ryan A Cole, Rebecca E Treasure, N. V. Haskell, M Elizabeth Ticknor, Len Berry, and Megan Higgins.

The cover was designed by Ruth Nickle, also a member of the Wulf Pack.

The Supporters who Made this Successful

Compiling the stories was only part of the battle. We ran a Kickstarter campaign in September 2022 which saw great success and an outpouring of support.

Thank you all for the vote of confidence on this journey. We hope you enjoy the book.

Aaron Thomas ♦ Akis Linardos ♦ Alex Fox ♦ Alex Harford ♦ Alexandra ♦ Alexandros Papadakis ♦ Alicia Cay ♦ Alissa Perry ♦ Amandeep Kaur Uppal ♦ Andrew M ♦ Andrew Still ♦ Anne Larsen ♦ Anonymous ♦ B. K. Wellman ♦ Barry R. Hunter ♦ Beau Dupuis ♦ Ben P ♦ Bess Turner ♦ Beth Lobdell ♦ C&H Stoumbos ♦ Campbell R ♦ Candice R. Lisle ♦ Cat Girczyc ♦ Catherine Weaver ♦ Cathy Green ♦ Chad Bowden ♦ The Creative Fund ♦ Cherise Papa ♦ Cliff Winnig ♦ Cody L. Allen ♦ Colleen Feeney ♦ Cotie Morehouse ♦ Crystal Crawford ♦ Danielle Thompson ♦ Danuta ♦ Darren Lipman ♦ David Hankins ♦ Dead Fishie ♦ Devin Miller ♦ Dione Basseri ♦ Dom Michaels ♦ Don E Ray ♦ Don Treasure ♦ Dylan Humphreys ♦ Eden Winslow ♦ Elizabeth Abowd ♦ Emily Wells ♦ Eric Stallsworth ♦ Francesca Rose Villegas

♦ Fyrecon ♦ Gabriel Casillas ♦ GhostCat ♦ Grace M ♦ Grace & Jason Stewart ♦ Hana Corrca ♦ Isracl Sanchez ♦ J.T. Evans ♦ Jacen Leonard ♦ Jacob Perez ♦ Jade C Wildy ♦ James Powers ♦ James S ♦ Jared Nelson ♦ Jarrod Williams ♦ Jason Harkins ♦ Jason Sizemore ♦ Javeria ♦ Jeff H ♦ Jenn Fir ♦ Jennifer Flora Black ♦ Jenny Perry Carr ♦ Jeremy Carl Reynolds ♦ Jessica Enfante ♦ Jessica Guernsey ♦ Jessica Meade ♦ Jordan Theyel ♦ Jordan, Kimberly, Landon & Evan ♦ Joshua C. Chadd ♦ J. O'Donahue ♦ Joshua Palmatier ♦ Julia V. Ashley ♦ Julie B ♦ Justin Thomas Suits ♦ Kai Delmas ♦ Kat Farrow ♦ Katerina Gratsea ♦ Kellie Hallam ♦ Kelly Lynn Colby ♦ Kennedy Williamson ♦ Kevin A Davis ♦ Kevin A. Fronzeck ♦ Kim CW ♦ Klikke S ♦ Krisla B ♦ Lakea Lin ♦ Laura Cahill ♦ Lauren Nicolette Colie ♦ Leah Ning ♦ Lily Raven ♦ Lisa Kruse ♦ Loukadakis Myron ♦ Lynn Still ♦ Martha E. Pedersen ♦ Megan Higgins ♦ Michael Gardner ♦ Michael Kingswood ♦ Michele Hall ♦ Mike Baldwin ♦ Mike Wyant Jr. ♦ Misty Rowsell ♦ Morgan J. Muir ♦ Mustela ♦ My Shade ♦ Nick Mandujano III ♦ Nina B. ♦ Olivia Schmidt ♦ Paul ♦ Paul & Laura Trinies ♦ Paula Maylin ♦ Phillip Hall ♦ pjk ♦ R. Hunter ♦ R.S. Johansen ♦ RationalStork ♦ Rebecca E Treasure ♦ Richard O'Shea ♦ Robert Brown ♦ Rodechi ♦ Rosamaria Cirelli ♦ Ryan Cole ♦ Samantha B ♦ Sara and Alex Charney Cohen ♦ Savana St. Aubin ♦ Scot Noel ♦ Scott S ♦ Shannon Fox ♦ Shannon L Miller ♦ Shelley Swift ♦ Stace Johnson ♦ Stefanos Gratseas ♦ Steph T ♦ stephenswoodworks.com ♦ Suzanne Gochenouer ♦ Tai B ♦ Talia B ♦ Tanya Hales ♦ Tara Henderson ♦ Terry Ebaugh ♦ Three Ravens Publishing ♦ Tim Jordan ♦ Timothy Hankins ♦ Timothy VanKleeck ♦ Tracy 'Rayhne' Fretwell ♦ Tracy Popey ♦ Travis H ♦ Trip Space-Parasite ♦ Trisha J. Wooldridge ♦ Troy Hooker ♦ Tyler Hulsey ♦ Val S ♦ Veronica ♦ Violet Jijing Covey ♦ Wulf Moon ♦ Yelena Crane ♦ Zachary J.V. Rhodes ♦ Zack Fissel

Introduction

and the origins of the Unhelpful Encyclopedia

First of all, I want to make absolutely clear that this book is a work of fiction, or more accurately, a collection of many works of fiction. It is not a literal encyclopedia any more than Max Brooks's *World War Z* is a compilation of real memoirs or Douglas Adams's *The Hitchhiker's Guide to the Galaxy* can help you hop a ride on an intergalactic cruiser—believe me, I've tried.

The Unhelpful Encyclopedia series was inspired in part by works like *Hitchhiker*, my peculiar love of creature features, and a tendency to tease out an elaborate backstory for every cautionary sign. Most people see "Don't Feed the Ducks" and either obey or ignore it; I dream up killer gremlin-duck fantasies, which could not have possibly led to any conclusion other than a warning sign for the protection of humanity. And yet, out of the hundreds of anthologies I'd encountered, I still hadn't seen anything quite like that.

As someone who grew up on *Twilight Zone* reruns, faded short-story collections, and series with "Star" in the title, I was sold on anthologies in general long before I started writing for them. Of course, as soon as I was published in my first anthology in 2016, I couldn't help but consider the kinds of anthologies I would most want to produce. Several publications later, including a *Writers of the Future* win and a scifi novel trilogy, I had compiled a list of possibilities in journals, a handful of which were filed under the self-indulgent header, "unhelpful encyclopedia ideas."

The final ingredient needed to get this project going came in the form of Zoom calls with authors throughout 2021 and 2022. I was already hosting productivity calls for a few writer-support networks, and I started running my ideas by them as sample audiences. I'd find a way to drop some anthology themes into conversations, and gauge reactions. The most laughs and off-the-cuff story ideas came from three categories: Murderbugs, Murdermice, and of course Murderbirds.

Maybe the reaction to Murderbirds was most encouraging. Maybe, as a bird owner and life-long bird lover I just wanted it to be. Either way, *Murderbirds* came first.

~Mike Jack Stoumbos of WonderBird Press

To Lilith Lavinia Cassidy
for reminding us that power and wisdom pass through us, they don't come from us

CROW *(CORVUS BRACHYRHYNCHOS)*

The Common American Crow, our first corvid specimen, a black-feathered perching bird believed to have sophisticated flock communication, hierarchy, and (sometimes) uncommon intelligence

The Fat Guy's Gotta Die

by Martin L Shoemaker

You gotta understand, I'm a peaceable crow. I'm a Sentry, not a fighter. It's my job to stay up half the night and keep watch while the flock sleeps. So I sound the alarm, and *then*... You want to see fighting? Watch the hens when I tell 'em there's a fox in the field and they have to protect their chicks. They're vicious!

So you have to believe it's not like me when I say it, but it's the truth: the Fat Guy had to die! You see, it was *personal*. He made me a failure in my job.

Oh, I don't think he was one of the humans dressed all in black who snuck up on our roost that night. As fat as he is, he wouldn't fit in those outfits. But he sent 'em, you can be sure of that, to the trees where our flock nested. And wouldn't you know it, it was *my* shift when *they* snuck in.

And I have to say—even if nobody believes me—that I *did* see 'em! I saw the movement of black-clad humans. I just saw 'em too late. Before I could squawk out a warning, one of 'em had his hand over my beak, pinching it shut, and was stuffing me into a burlap sack. I couldn't make a sound as his companions worked through the tree, grabbing one sleeping crow after another. We was sittin' ducks—or sittin' crows, to be precise. The flock never stood a chance... because I let 'em down.

I give my abductor credit: he was a stubborn son of a pigeon! I stabbed him at least four times. I tasted blood! And still he never let go, never let me give a warning.

They didn't get all of us. We were a big flock; and they took none of the nesting hens and chicks. They didn't nab all the cocks either, so the flock wasn't defenseless, but they took more than half.

I only learned that when they released us in the big barn. At least I think it was a barn. I never saw no human building that big that *wasn't* a barn. But there was no livestock in it, no horses or pigs or cows or nothin'. The only other animals I smelled were pigeons and... ugh... seagulls...

Now look... I ain't prejudiced against 'em. There's some good gulls, to go with the stupid ones; and they mostly leave us alone. Oh, they come into our fields and eat our corn, but that's only as they're passing through. Mostly they stay at the sea. If they eat too much corn, we chase 'em off, and they don't put up much of a fight.

But seagulls are *stupid*. And worse than that, they're... they're practically *pets*! They just love it when humans feed 'em, fish and cakes and whatever. They'll flock around and let humans throw 'em food all day long. They put on a *show!* Good grief, gulls, have some dignity!

But I guess putting on a show was exactly what the Fat Guy was after. And gulls are good at that.

I stared at the big metal cages. One filled each end of the big barn, all the way to the roof. One was full of gulls and pigeons. The other was empty, waiting for *us*. Inside it were some wooden bins, posts for roosting, and some stacks of hay.

The guy with the bloodied finger who was holding me gave me a close-up look at the thing as he pulled me out of the bag. I was still taking it all in when he opened the cage door and shoved me inside. He wasn't gentle about it either, and he shouted some of that warbling squawk that humans do. I took a little pride that I had made him suffer.

I was the first crow in the second big cage, but not for long. More black suited humans came up, each carrying a small cage full of birds. Some had four, some had six. There wasn't a brood hen in the bunch, and I noticed some of the older, faster birds were not to be seen. Snap Beak, Long Flight, Two Feather... They weren't around. The flock would survive, but they would be weaker. As for us, I had no guess what lay in store. Not yet.

It took a while to unload everybody, in part thanks to Crooked Claw and Red Eye. They hatched some sort of plan, I was never clear what, and managed to escape their small cage before they could get put into the big one. They flew around the big barn, squawking at all of us. *Escape! Escape! It's your chance!*

I'm a Sentry, I got fast eyes. When Crooked Claw and Red Eye raised the ruckus, I saw my chance, and you better believe I took it. As the humans were looking at those two, they left the big cage door unwatched, and without hesitation, I sprung into the air!

And I wasn't the only one. Fork Tail, Old Lucky, and Snap Beak took their chances as well. But I was in the lead. The humans wised up fast, I'll give them that. The two nearest the cage door were looking up like idiots, but a third one saw that the escape was spreading. He jumped forward to grab the door, and started to swing it shut.

I swooped as fast as I could, and then twisted to fit between the closing bars. And I was free!

Then, just for good measure, I dove straight at the eyes of the guy on the gate, making him fall backwards and pull it open again. All three of the other fugitives got out.

That was when I noticed the Fat Guy for the first time. Like some humans, he had almost no plumage on his big, round head. His jowls hung loose, and his eyes were small and round.

He was dapper. Where the other men in the barn wore grubby black covered with bird shit, *his* gray suit was pristine. It looked like perfect material for nest building, good and soft. Instinctively I wanted to tear it apart. It was baggy to fit his blubbery form... because he was *fat*. Not big! He wasn't particularly tall. But he was round, big enough to make two humans, three if they were small.

He was also in charge. There was no doubt about that. He sat on a stool, just inside the barn door, pointing and shouting something. His look bothered me, the way he stared out at the birds and the men as if he owned all of them. All the other humans stared at him, eyes wide, and jumped at his commands.

Then the Fat Guy looked me right in the eye; and in that moment I recognized my enemy. He was in charge, the rest flew to his tune. *He* did this to us. To me. The Fat Guy rubbed me the wrong way from the start, and it would only get worse from there.

I was so distracted by the sight of my foe that I almost missed another man picking up a big black blanket. I saw him just before he threw it, and I skedaddled out of there. I wasn't going to let them catch me twice. I let out caws of triumph as I flapped straight up toward the rafters.

I looked back as I circled. It was funny watching humans try to catch the other escaping crows. They ran back and forth from one end of the barn to the other, staring up at the swooping birds. *Hello, wings?* I thought. *You think we're stupid? That we'll come down so you can catch us?*

But we were still stuck in the barn just as much as the rest of the flock were. Meanwhile, others were exploring the cage, indulging their curiosity. That was how old Gray Feather found her way to one of the wooden bins, and she started squawking. "Cornmeal!"

That was enough to get the flock's attention. Let me tell you, fear takes it out of a bird. Our heart gets pumping, we get all worked up to fly or to attack, and it just drains us. After what we'd been through that night so far, we were hungry. They weren't happy to be penned up, but they couldn't resist the food.

And me? I didn't even have corn meal! But I wasn't going to let that tempt me into getting caught again. I circled around, looking for an exit. I found… nothing. And even if I'd found one, I couldn't abandon my flock! I could hide up there and look for some opportunity, but I wasn't about to leave.

Then I learned that I wasn't alone. As I landed on a beam, I woke a sleeping pigeon. She opened one bleary eye, looked at me, and said, "Please! I am trying to sleep here!"

Fortunately for me, I speak basic pigeon. Also gull, sparrow, and a couple others. It doesn't hurt a Sentry to know how to talk to other passing birds, just in case they got info you need.

"Sorry," I said. "I just got away from the humans."

She yawned. "That's nice. *I* got away two weeks ago. Now I'm stuck up here." She nodded towards the cage at the other end of the big building, the one full of pigeons and gulls. "At least *they* get fed. You shall have to learn to scout for scraps."

I shook my head. "Great. Just great. Two weeks, huh? How long they had you in here?"

She sighed. "You aren't going to let me sleep, are you? All right, we've been here nearly three weeks." She nodded toward the man on the stool. "That's when *he* had us brought in."

"The Fat Guy?"

"Fat, yes. He's not very tall for a human, but very round. He is in charge of this endeavor."

"I figured that out," I said with a touch of pride. "So what's he want us for? He doesn't… ummm…"

"No, he doesn't eat us. That might make a *smidgeon* of sense."

That was a relief. Humans will eat anything! "But if he doesn't want to eat us, what *does* he want?"

She turned that big wide eye on me. "It's the oddest thing, even for a human. He wants us to attack other humans!"

"What? We're his flappin' army?"

"It makes even less sense than that. He wants us to attack them, but he gets *furious* if we harm them!"

"That makes no sense."

"Since when have humans ever made sense? The keepers collect their trained favorites, carry them out into the meadow, and have them chase humans back and forth."

"Wait," I said. "They take the favorites out?"

"Indeed. It makes no sense. Some of my fellow pigeons…" She dripped condescension. "…are very easily trained. They become the favorites, the 'trusties'. They get to go out on those little fly arounds, where the Fat Guy shouts orders, and they do his bidding. Chase the Pretty Lady. Divebomb the schoolchildren. Flap your wings menacingly." She sniffed. "It's completely undignified, if you ask me."

"So if he's got the ones he needs, why doesn't he just let the rest of you go?"

"The favorites do the outside work. The rest of us are saved for indoor work. They gather us up, carry us to another building, and then unceremoniously dump us down the chimney! They don't care what feathers they ruffle in the process, they just expect us to come out, fly about this little house, and terrorize all the humans there. Then the Fat Guy shouts something, everybody smiles at each other, and the handlers bring them all back here. It was after that incident that I decided I'd had enough. I bit a keeper on the nose! And while he was crying out in pain, I flew away. I've been hiding up here ever since."

"That's crazy."

"I know," she answered. "The Fat Guy is crazy, and there's nothing any of us can do about it. So now would you please leave me alone so I can sleep?"

She tucked her head under her wing, and I waddled away. The Fat Guy was crazy, she said, and I didn't disagree. But it didn't matter if he was crazy or not, he just had to be stopped.

The Fat Guy had to die.

But how? Could I get close enough to peck his eyes out? I couldn't do it hiding up there in the rafters!

Then I remembered what the pigeon had said: there were trusties, birds the handlers... I had trouble even thinking it... Their favorites did work on command. No better than a gull.

But trusties had freedom that I lacked. And freedom was what I needed...

♦ ♦ ♦

When the humans opened the small door in the morning, I picked one out. Which one? Like I could tell? All humans look kind of alike, you know? But I picked one while another one held the door, and I flew down to land on the ground right in front of him. I gave him a side-eye stare.

He stopped, made some human warbling, and crouched down. I nodded, turned the other eye on him, and then hopped a few steps closer.

He reached out his hand. I flinched, but I didn't flee. *I am a friendly crow, idiot human. I'm not dangerous at all.*

He curled his fingers, beckoning me closer. I obliged. Soon his fingers were right in front of my beak. I *had* to peck them—what crow wouldn't?—but I did it gently. Not to hurt, simply to say hello.

That, I assume, was what his noises meant as well: *Hello, little crow.* Then he reached out and stroked my head feathers with one finger.

Worse... I kinda liked it...

Oh, how I hated myself at that moment. I might as well have been a gull.

But my act must've worked. He made more odd sounds, and he held out his hand, palm up. I obligingly hopped into it, and then slowly crawled up his arm and to his shoulder. There... I nuzzled his cheek.

I didn't have my dignity, but I had a sucker.

♦ ♦ ♦

I called him Red because of the big mop of red-orange plumage on the top of his head. Somewhere between a cardinal and an oriole. I don't know what he called me, but I became his favorite. He offered me treats, nuts and cornmeal, sometimes sweet fruit juice. And he taught me simple tricks—or at least that's what he thought he was doing. None of what he taught was difficult, I just had to learn when he wanted me to do it.

Red had a number of whistling calls he could make with his fingers in his teeth. Like a canary or a whippoorwill, he was that versatile. And he began using these to let me know what he wanted from me. A shrill whistle to fly up. A shorter, sharper whistle to return. A trilling up and down to circle. And more. Land. Take off. Walk. And of course, attack, which really meant swoop. The pigeon had clued me in for that, so I knew better than to make a real attack, just swoop and veer. That seemed to please Red. I got extra cornmeal for that.

Soon enough, I was a trusty, allowed out of the big building with Red, who trusted that I would come back from any mission he sent me on.

◆ ◆ ◆

One day Red took me out into the field, and he introduced me to the Pretty Lady, she of the golden hair and the big, fluttery green eyes. She seemed as skittish as a hummingbird. If I merely flexed my wings, she jumped back. Red spoke to her, soothing tones in that strange warble humans do, as if trying to calm her down. Then he turned to me, and he made the strange *shhh* sound like wind that indicated he wanted me to be to relax. So I sat very still.

Then he spoke to the Pretty Lady again, and she moved a little closer. He held out a finger for me to peck at, and I did, but gently. I could see he wanted to show her that I was no threat. And I guess I wasn't, to Red. If the Fat Guy came around… I guess what I would do would scare her, but I didn't care. He was the enemy. She would just be an innocent victim of my vengeance.

But the Fat Guy wasn't around, and Red wanted me to be nice to the Pretty Lady, so I was. Eventually she worked up the courage to lift a single finger and stroke my head.

I leaned into it. It was a different experience from Red's grooming. She had long claws, like a proper bird should have, whereas Red had practically none. So when she stroked, she also dug in a bit, and she got to those itchy spots under the feathers that are especially hard to reach on the back of my head.

If anyone tells you that I cooed like a pigeon, it's a filthy lie. But almost…

Almost…

All right. I cooed. A little. But she had the touch, I tell ya!

The cooing seemed to calm her. She did that teeth-baring thing. On her, it was pretty. I think it meant she liked me.

I nuzzled her cheek. I liked her too.

♦ ♦ ♦

Later came the day when I met the Fat Guy again. Red took me out into a big field overlooking the ocean, and we practiced tricks for a while. And just when I was getting bored, all of a sudden Red beckoned me up onto his shoulder. I accommodated him—damn, that was getting too easy—and he started walking up the hill towards where a group of humans clustered around the Fat Guy. There were a bunch of handlers, some other men wandering around… and a group of children along with the Pretty Lady.

All the other humans stared at the Fat Guy, faces practically trembling—even, to my shame, Red. I don't know why that bothered me so much. Maybe I was coming to think of Red as *my* human, too good to bow and scrape to the Fat Guy.

That might've been why I didn't make my move right then. The Fat Guy had ordered my disgrace, of that I was certain; but he mattered to Red. I sensed that if I picked the Fat Guy's eyes out now, Red would never forgive me. He might… he might not like me anymore.

Damn. Is this what it's like to be a pet? You actually *care* what the humans think? I was disgusted, but I couldn't help it.

So whatever I did to the Fat Guy, I had to do it when Red wasn't watching. Until then I had to do what Red asked. For Red, not for the Fat Guy, I swooped through the air on command. As I did, one of the Fat Guy's toadies pointed something at me.

That almost made me lose control. I'd heard from older Sentries about long tubes humans would point at crows; and when they did, thunder would sound, and lightning would fly from the tubes. And a dead bird would fall from the sky.

The box the human pointed at me ended in a big tube.

I didn't want to believe that my friend Red was setting me up for the kill, all for the sadistic pleasure of the Fat Guy. But just in case, I started to fly away. I had to escape. I would never have my revenge if lightning struck me from the sky.

Then I heard the short, sharp whistle. And again. And again. Red wanted me to return. My… my friend was calling…

I couldn't help it; I angled a wing so I could bank back and take a look.

He was waving me down. Closer to the box and the deadly tube. Making me a perfect target.

I swallowed hard. I didn't trust the Fat Guy. I didn't trust the guy with the box.

But Red had been kind to me. I trusted him. I started back down towards him.

Red bared his teeth in the odd way he did when he seemed pleased. Instinctively I was happy, even as I worried about the chance of a sudden betrayal.

Then he started waving one arm around in a circle and making the warbling whistle. He wanted me to circle around. I did. Curse me for a gull, but I did.

The box with the tube followed my path. At any moment, I expected the thunder and lightning.

But it never came. Red gestured me into a slow spiral downward. And I felt like my trust was well-placed.

Then suddenly the Fat Guy shouted something and waved his arm forward as if throwing something. And as if this were some command, the schoolchildren on top of the hill started running, following the Pretty Lady.

That was when Red suddenly pointed and whistled for me to swoop after the children. He was not alone: other handlers were commanding pigeons and gulls and other birds to descend upon the running children and the Pretty Lady. Other birds followed, taking their cues from these leaders. I had no crow followers, but all those birds made quite a swarm.

Then Red made the clapping gesture that said I was to attack the running humans: to get as close as I dared, and then veer off.

I felt bad. The kids had done nothing to me, and the Pretty Lady was harmless. Like me, they were all slaves to the Fat Guy. I couldn't bring myself to attack the children, even in play. I might make a mistake, or they might fall and hurt themselves. I just couldn't bring myself to scare the little kids.

But the Pretty Lady…

She seemed frantic, as did the kids. They were all running, making loud screeching noises and waving their hands in the hair in the air. It was… Well, it was flat confusing for a bird, let me tell you. All those waving hands were frightening. I didn't know when one might hit me. I didn't know where to go, what to do.

But I had come to trust the Pretty Lady, like she trusted me. An oasis of trust in the storm. I swooped in, hovered by her head, and settled down on her shoulder. And then I nuzzled my head against her cheek. She turned, reached up to me to my head, and stroked it, calming me down.

The Fat Guy exploded in snarling sounds. Some of them sounded almost like a crow. *Caw! Caw! Caw!* Something like that.

Immediately the kids and the Pretty Lady stopped running. It took longer for the birds to settle down, flying back to their trainers. But I didn't fly back. I sat on the Pretty Lady's shoulder, and she petted me.

There, I said it! Are you happy? She petted me. Like a *pet*! Okay?

Eventually Red came up, made noises at me, and lifted me from her shoulder and carried me away. The whole time, the Fat Guy was making loud noises at him and at her. And judging by the glares, at me.

Then the humans did the craziest thing ever. All the kids and the Pretty Lady and the guy with the box-and-tube who had followed them all… They all walked back up the ridge to where they had started. They took up positions like a flock gathering in formation to fly south for the winter. Then they stood there, waiting for something.

Apparently the "something" was a shout from the Fat Guy. Suddenly the humans started running again. The keepers released their birds, and we all took flight once more, diving at their hair and their flailing hands.

This time I wasn't afraid. I saw almost a sort of aerial dance, a performance. They were *supposed* to run, we were *supposed* to chase, that was all what the Fat Guy wanted.

Well, I had no intention of giving him what he wanted. He was the enemy. I know what Red wanted, but I just didn't care. As soon as I flew into the crowd, I found the Pretty Lady, and I alighted upon her shoulder.

This time when she saw me out of the corner of her eye, she stopped, put her hands over her mouth, and made that cackling sound that humans make, the one that sounds like a chicken who just laid an egg. Her teeth were fully bared, and her head rocked back and forth as she looked at me. I worried she might be angry; but again, she stroked my feathers. She wasn't angry, she was pleased. And that was good.

But the Fat Guy… Now *he* was angry! He came running up—well, waddling up, as big as he was—and stuck his face right into hers. He frightened me, and I jumped back off her shoulder, flapping in the air and then circling around as he made loud noises at her.

And she… Her eyes went wide, and I sensed terror. If she could fly, she would've flown away right then, and I wouldn't have blamed her.

Then the Fat Guy turned and made loud noises at Red. My handler stood, elbows out at his sides, and made loud noises right back. I was proud of my human. He wasn't afraid of this petty little tyrant.

Then the Fat Guy went too far. He rolled up a bundle of papers in his hand, and he started poking Red with them while shouting. *Noise! Poke! Noise! Poke! Noise!*

Then he started swatting Red with the papers, over and over. Red didn't flinch. I don't think the papers hurt. But the spirit in his eyes fell. This was some deeper hurt. Some shame.

Like I felt for letting the flock get captured.

I couldn't take it anymore. I launched in the air, and with my most vicious *Caw*, I dove at the Fat Guy's eyes.

If I had restrained myself and hadn't announced my attack, it might've worked. Instead, he covered his head with his arms, and he shouted. Instead of pecking his eyes, I pecked his arms. I pecked and pecked and pecked until he started to run; and then I chased after him, pecking the back of his featherless head. He waddled down the road, but I was faster. He covered one side, and I pecked the other. When he started to wobble to the edge of the road, I urged him on with attacks and squawks until he stumbled over the side, fell, and slid down the ridge into the muddy ditch below.

I realized too late: throughout my attack, Red had been whistling the retreat call, trying to summon me back to him. I couldn't understand! I had done this for him!

But somehow I had made Red's situation worse. When the Fat Guy finally came out of the ditch—assisted by three strong men—he quietly but inexorably marched up to Red. And then…

The Fat Guy didn't shout. He said something in a quiet tone, a very short statement. And then he was done. He turned away, and he said no more.

And Red turned the other way, back toward the barn. He held up his hand, and he made our special whistle. I alighted on his palm, and we walked away.

In Red's stance, I saw only defeat. I had failed him, but I didn't know how.

◆ ◆ ◆

By the time we got back to the barn, Red seemed crushed, barely a shadow of himself. He shuffled slowly and with no spirit. I tried climbing on his shoulder and pecking his face to cheer him up, but it did no good. Whatever was going on, his spirit wasn't in it.

He walked up to the door, and I dreaded what would happen now. I couldn't face telling the flock that I had had a chance for revenge, but had failed. The Fat Guy lived. And worse, I had let down Red, a human they had all come to like almost as much as I did.

But before I had a chance to explain, Red surprised me. He left the big barn door open. Then he went into the barn... and he opened the crow cage, just pulled the gate wide open, and stood aside. He didn't try to block the gate. Instead, he made the whistling sound that meant *fly away*.

The few that were trained to recognize the whistle took wing and flew out from the cage and out of the barn. The rest naturally followed.

Eventually the cage was empty. The only crow left in the barn was me, sitting on Red's shoulder. He looked at me, made some noise, and walked out to the field.

My flock was already dwindling into the distance. Not so far, nor so fast that I couldn't catch them.

But I sat on Red's shoulder, waiting for instruction.

Red looked at me. At last he made the launch whistle, and he pointed in their direction. When I didn't respond, he repeated it.

On the third try, I accepted Red's command. I took flight to join my flock.

I felt like I had flapped halfway to the clouds, when I couldn't take it anymore. I banked a wing, and I turned so I could look back and down toward the barn door. Red still stood there, watching me leave. And I soared, watching him.

And I couldn't do it. I banked further, swooped around, and flew back to Red's shoulder. He made that cackling sound, and he fed me a lump of cornmeal.

◆ ◆ ◆

And that, kids, is how your granddad got into show business. But Red and me never worked for the Fat Guy again. He's dead to me.

About the Author

Martin L. Shoemaker is a programmer who writes on the side… or maybe it's the other way around. His work has appeared in Analog Science Fiction & Fact, Galaxy's Edge, Digital Science Fiction, Forever Magazine, Writers of the Future, and numerous anthologies. His novel, *Today I Am Carey*, was published by Baen Books in March 2019. His novel *The Last Dance* was published by 47North in November 2019 and was the number one science fiction eBook on Amazon during October's prerelease. The sequel, The Last Campaign was published in October 2020.

~~Tyrannosaurs Rex~~

…Chicken *(gallus gallus domesticus)*

~~Apex predator of the Cretaceous period~~

…food source for most other predators, including humans

The Delicious Irony of Dino Nuggets

by Z.T. Bright

Everyone tells me I shouldn't trust Sbogg as much as I do. Especially as my Spacetime Transport Consultant. But they're so damn *likable*, and they always seem to come through for me... eventually.

"Late again, Sbogg," I say when they enter our transport terminal. "One of these days, I'm going to petition to have you change hosts."

The blood of the species Sbogg currently occupies is known to make its parasites—us—a bit fuzzy in the metaphorical head. Sbogg chuckles, a low, slow sound rumbling from the broad chest of their ape-like host. "Sorry, Trinn. I'm here when it matters though, right?"

"Barely," I chirp, flitting over to Sbogg and perching on their shoulder as they take a seat at the console. My own temporary host is a small, yellow-bellied bird, barely tall enough to reach Sbogg's ear. Predator Curators like myself are off-station so frequently—traveling Spacetime while documenting the biggest, baddest creatures across all time in the Universe—so the hosts we occupy on-station are small and economical.

I hop onto the console and peck at a small dish of seeds. This is what I'm talking about: Sbogg might be a bit flighty with some details, but they can always be trusted with the small, personal things. Like snacks.

I nod my head at the monitor. "So, what do you think?"

Pulling up the files I had asked them to take a look at yesterday, Sbogg starts combing through data—obviously for the first time. "That's one badass beast, Trinny. Tyrannosaurus Rex. Apex predator, on a rocky planet with plenty of water, reigning for two million years. Why hasn't anyone cataloged this one before?"

"Well," I say, "there is a small complication with that planet. Take a look about fifty million years later on the timeline."

"Uh, Trinn. That planet's timeline has a sapient."

"Not a very competent one…"

"Trinn!"

"Look, I've thought about it. Fifty million years is a big enough margin of error for you."

"The handbook says the margin of error should be double that."

"Sbogg, I trust you. I know you can land me there at the right time."

Sbogg wordlessly peruses the data, picking through information around the time that the sapients of that planet would exist. They spend a long time, really digging deep into the species qualification criteria that would usually be my responsibility. I don't know what Sbogg sees, but eventually they grunt and nod their big ape head. One of the few benefits of Sbogg's host species is that it makes them more… agreeable.

I know it's technically a gamble for both of us. Our species flies under the radar. Messing with sapient populated planets is dangerous. Exposing our kind to a sapient species is grounds for execution.

But fifty *million* years—As I told Sbogg, I trust them. They've never missed by even half as much as it would take to create any issues with this jump. However, I've also never put this kind of pressure on them…

♦ ♦ ♦

There's nobody I hate more than Chupp. They are the epitome of everything wrong with our society. No actual talent beyond ass-kissing. Mercilessly using everyone around them to get ahead. Needlessly brutal to those they deem lesser, like Sbogg.

"Trinn," Chupp says, the forked tongue of their serpentine host darting toward me menacingly. "Why do you bother with Sbogg? You know they're useless. In fact, I suspect they chose that slow, lumbering host just to mask their natural dim-wittedness."

All of this infuriates me, amplified by the fact I'm perched atop Sbogg's shoulder as we speak. Chupp says all of this *because* Sbogg can hear it.

"I hate you," I say under my breath.

"What was that?" Chupp asks.

"I said I like your shoes."

Chupp looks at me flatly, their footless, serpentine body draped over the shoulders of their Spacetime Transport Consultant who tries to hold in a laugh, unsuccessfully.

"Come on, Sbogg, let's go find a new terminal," I say.

"It's all good, Trinny," Sbogg says. "I've got our coordinates entered anyway."

"If you're sure," I say, clicking my beak in Chupp's direction. "But why don't you ever stick up for yourself?"

Sbogg chuckles. "The more they underestimate me, the easier it will be for me to surprise them. Besides, I know who my real friends are."

The way they say that gives me pause. *The easier it will be?*

"You ready?" Sbogg asks.

In response, I flit into my pod atop the terminal.

Chupp slithers into the pod next to mine, eyeing me smugly. When the lightbridge fires, we'll be sent to our target planets. Me into a parasite residing in the gut of a Tyrannosaurus Rex. Chupp hopefully many, many lightyears away, which would still be too close.

Sbogg winks at me and fires the bridge.

It takes some time for us to gain control of our hosts. We have to learn how their muscles work. Get used to the data flooding their senses. As expected, my first moments inside the T-Rex are complete sensory overload.

But as I settle, I can feel the strength and agility of my beast. My host looks side to side with lightning-fast reflexes. I'm huge. What must be small, thin trees reach about halfway up my body as I stroll through them, brushing them aside as if they are mere blades of grass. Tiny creatures flee from me, but my head darts down too quickly for them, and I am nourished.

Seemingly pleased with our meal, my host struts out of the patch of small trees and onto some hard packed dirt. I scratch the ground, my monstrous, three-toed feet tearing deep gouges into the dirt. I reach my head up to the cloudless, blue sky and… cluck?

Huh. Wasn't expecting that sound. Not quite as intimidating as I thought it would be.

Feeling a bit more control, I test my new body. I stand tall, puffing out my chest. There's something dangly hanging from my neck that I wasn't expecting. Maybe this T-Rex has a strange injury. I can feel my feathers—definitely more than my research had suggested—thick and covering my whole body.

A shadow rolls over me. I look up, expecting cloud cover. Instead, a towering bipedal creature looms overhead. I realize with horror what this means. Sbogg has messed up their calculations, and I've inhabited the T-Rex's closest descendent.

I recognize the creature before me. The local sapient. Human.

I scream, which sounds appropriate from my host, and sprint away from the sapient. But the bipedal creature is too large and scoops me up easily. I thrash about, but I'm quickly tucked under one of the sapient's upper limbs, held immobile.

"Oh, don't worry, Trinn," the creature says in my native tongue.

I freeze.

"It's me, Chupp."

I pass out.

◆ ◆ ◆

As I come to, I'm disappointed there's no moment of blissful forgetfulness. No, I'm thrust immediately into the recollection that I am not in fact a T-Rex, that those small trees really *were* blades of grass, and that Chupp has followed me to this planet. Into the body of a sapient, no less!

Looking around, I realize I'm in a cage. Chupp reclines in the grass, leaning on one elbow, smiling at me like a real creep.

"I hate you," I say.

"These shoes are pretty nice, aren't they?" Chupp says, lifting a booted foot in the air a few inches.

"What the hell are you doing, Chupp? A sapient? Do you have a death wish?"

Chupp ignores my question. "Funny, isn't it? That the fearsome creature you hoped to inhabit would eventually become this." They wave their hand at me. "From the top of the food chain, to being raised as the second largest meat crop by the local sapient. You know, there are about twenty billion chickens on this planet? Most of them in captivity, being bred as food."

"Why are you here, Chupp?"

"Well, I wanted to see how badly that moron Sbogg was going to mess up your calculations, so I had my own Spacetime Transport Consultant comb the data. When we realized where you were going—so close in the timeline to a sapient—we dug a little deeper. Turns out this sapient was a perfect fit for what many of us have been looking for, and you did the work of locating them for us."

"What would you want a sapient for?"

"Oh, Trinn. Don't tell me you don't know. Don't you ever feel…cooped up? Pun intended, by the way." Chupp slaps their knee. "I mean, you're here, on a planet technically off limits. So, to some extent you must agree. We are being restricted from living on the best planets throughout all time in the universe because we're trying to avoid sapients."

"And why do you think inhabiting a sapient will fix that?"

"Ah, not just any sapient. This is not one of the fearsome sapients we have been taught to hide from. This species is just barely sapient, really. For one thing, they've got awful food hygiene practices for their level of technological advancement. It's amazing they've survived at all, really. But it's perfect for us!"

I know what Chupp means. We're parasites. We can inhabit the bodies of any creatures that have parasites within. The more the better. But that didn't tell me *why* Chupp was here, just *how*. "Your point being…"

"There's a growing movement of us that wants to assume control of an entire sapient species."

Oh shit.

"And I'm here to start the revolution, Trinn. I will research this species, and when I return to our station and report my findings, there will be *billions* of us ready to invade this planet."

Not only does this feel… ethically dubious at the very least, it also means I'll be hung up to dry when the council realizes who clued Chupp in on an off-limits planet.

I've got to stop them. But I'm inside the body of a damn *chicken*.

Chupp eventually lets me out of my cage. Wants me to think about joining them. They aren't interested in killing me, though they joke about turning me into something called "chicken nuggets."

"They even make the nuggets in the shape of your beloved T-Rex!" Chupp says with unrestrained glee. "They call them *dino nuggets*. How ironic is that?"

I don't know, actually. I've never been great at understanding what's actually ironic versus wildly coincidental.

Chupp seems to forget about me after a while, focusing instead on researching the sapient.

Chupp knows I'm not a threat. I can't harm them in this tiny body, though I did try to trip them up a few times—humans are surprisingly top-heavy and seem easy to topple. I can't warn anyone—we're out of communication until our timer ends, unless Sbogg were to pull me back early for some reason.

Damnit, Sbogg! This is all your fault. No, I can't blame them. The T-Rex planet was my idea.

I spend my days devising plans against Chupp. After several weeks, my tactics amount to walking around the farm and eating bugs. Somehow, that doesn't seem sufficient.

I decide to spy on Chupp. Day after day, I sneak behind them whenever they are out on the farm. At night, I hop onto windowsills and watch them inside the farmhouse. I'm not really learning much, but the spying is going quite well. Apparently, chickens are very sneaky.

Knowing Chupp's routine, I sneak into the barn one morning before they come in. I hide behind a bale of hay, waiting for Chupp to arrive.

They enter, saying, "So, Trinn, have you learned anything following me around all this time?"

I stay quiet, even though the jig is up.

"I know you're there, Trinn. You're not very sneaky. What do you think? Will you join us? This planet is pretty nice. I'm sure you'd rather be in this body than that chicken."

I don't admit it out loud, but I've been envious. Instead, I say, "You're a traitor. I'll never join you, and I bet nobody else will either."

Chupp grins. "We'll see. Another benefit of having this form is technology. Specifically calendars and calculators. Did you know we only have a few more months here?"

Fear grips me with this renewed urgency. Only a few more months and I'd be in front of the council, with nothing more than the experiences of a chicken to report. Many had been executed for much less than this.

I think of Sbogg and how wrong they were. What had they said? Something like the more they're underestimated, the easier it is to surprise people? Well, Sbogg, it's hard to be more underestimated than a chicken.

But then I remember what Sbogg had *really* said. That it *will* surprise them. Them being Chupp. Had Sbogg known Chupp would follow me? Have they prepared a surprise for Chupp? There isn't really anything

Sbogg can do from headquarters, not without someone here to put their scheme in motion…

It's a thin straw of hope, but I grasp it.

"How many humans are there on this planet?" I ask Chupp, walking close to their booted feet, feigning interest in their plan.

"Closing in on eight billion."

"Wow," I say, remembering something else Chupp had said, namely twenty billion chickens. "So, they really eat a lot of chicken."

"One of their main food sources."

I can *almost* feel the pieces coming together.

"So, what do you think, Trinn? Ready to leave the restrictive policies of the council behind? Or do you want to be the council's tool and turn a better life down for the status-quo? Like Sbogg, rejecting a better way just because it's different."

My tiny eyes widen. "Sbogg knew your plan?"

"They attended some meetings. Turns out they're as stupid as I'd always suspected."

So that was it. Sbogg knew Chupp was looking for a sapient. They knew my T-Rex shared a timeline with a sapient. And they knew Chupp was a leech who would copy our research.

Sbogg must have figured out the T-Rex would eventually become the chicken, one of the sapient's top food sources. *And* that the chicken would outnumber the humans nearly three to one.

If Chupp intends to lead billions of us to take over these sapients, there's a war coming. I'm here to research Chupp's natural enemy: Warchicken, the foe they'd never see coming. Just as Sbogg would like it. After all, what would be more underestimated than a chicken?

"I'll join you," I lie. I'll spend the rest of my time here devising how chickens, the enemy's main food source, could be used against them. "Now let me get a look at those *dino nuggets*."

About the Author

Z.T. Bright is an author in deep (like, really deep) cover as a Financial Planner. He lives in Salt Lake City with his wife, four kids, two dogs, a cat, and some ducks (yes, it's as loud as it sounds). He writes all things speculative and was the winner of the inaugural Mike Resnick Memorial award and a winner of the Writers of the Future Contest.

KELENKEN, ALSO KNOWN AS "TERROR BIRD"
(PHORUSRHACID)

An extinct predatory bird believed to be roughly three meters tall, over 200 pounds, and flightless

...not to be confused with the herbivore, Gastornis, also extinct

OUTBACK ATTACK
A Queensland Crater Story

BY JOHN K PATTERSON

August 21, 2084
Queensland, Australia - 18 km from Queensland Crater

Dennis Longmire cast a nervous glance at the surrounding acacia trees and tall grass, wondering if anything was sizing him up for a meal. With the sun plummeting toward the horizon he would have to stay watchful, and not only for chances to take a solid photo.

Stubbornness alone convinced him to press the dashboard panel once more and check the electric car's battery. Still no juice. Had the safari company even plugged it in last night?

Dennis shoved open the armored door and climbed out. He threw open the hood to check the connection. The battery looked fine, though seemingly a relic from the 2050s. Overhead, he heard the chittering calls of small Pterosaurs, leaving their nests to feast on insects.

The 2067 *GhostCat* Terrain Vehicle met some people's definitions of a tank, reinforced in sheets of carbon-laced ceramic paneling that surely weighed it down. No wonder the battery quit too soon. Kicking one of the wheels, he silently berated himself for cheaping out on electric. He could have splurged on a gas-powered rental, but who needed one of those on a quick drive away from the normal tourist traps?

Not that the New Outback was big on tourism. Everyone was too busy surviving a post-impact landscape where cloned prehistoric fauna had come to dominate. The Land Down Under did have a silver lining, however: it was a gold mine for photographers who didn't mind a little risk.

What was he worried about, anyway? He could run, and he'd made it most of the way to the Archaeopteryx nests. So long as he kept a step ahead of any dinosaurs, he'd be fine.

Dennis took his camera pack out of the trunk. One of the car's unfamiliar alarms beeped, and the dashboard screen returned to life. Had some emergency power kicked in? Dennis's hopes rushed back, but the full display was still blank, save for a small phone icon blinking in the dashboard's center. He tapped it, leaning over the driver seat.

"Auto Seven, we received a power outage alert." The sultry female voice had a light Aussie accent, crisp and professional. "We've got your location. Is Dennis Longmire there?"

"Speaking," Dennis said. "Nothing's chomping on the car, thank God."

"Glad to hear that, sir. But I couldn't find a phone number registered with us."

"Left it at the hotel," he said with a shrug, though she couldn't see him. "I wanted some time away from gadgets. Except my camera."

"I understand, sir. There's a backup reserve for us to stay in touch. The main power is unresponsive, but I can send an armed man with a recharge truck in two hours."

"Two hours?"

"Rolling blackouts. Truck needs to recharge too, I'm afraid."

Dennis pressed his hands to his face, holding back more pointed words.

"Mister Longmire?" said the operator after a moment.

He took a deep breath. "No. I'm not waiting until night. I'd rather walk."

"I wouldn't advise that, sir."

"I run hundred-meter dashes for fun. Ten klicks is easy for me." He glanced over his shoulder. About a hundred yards back, he saw the green road sign with white letters spelling out *New Winton 10 km, Queensland Crater Visitor Center 18 km*. Someone had helpfully added in pink spray paint: *Asteroid-free since 2043*.

"Sir, I urge you to not leave the vehicle," the woman said, her pitch slightly heightened. "Some predators are nocturnal, and a family of Gorgosaurus have been stalking the duckbills east of your location."

"Good thing I'm not here to take pictures of those," he said. "Just the Archaeopteryx nests. They roost in safe areas, and I'm just half a mile away." Dennis scanned the tall grass, kneeling to pull his socks over his pant legs to prevent bugs and snakes from crawling inside. If he was going to reach the nests, he'd have to go before dusk.

"We'll be happy to bring you to the nests tomorrow," the lady said.

"I fly back to the States tomorrow," he snapped. "I haven't had a proper vacation in a year. I spent all week at the sabertooth shelter in Cairns."

"We'd prefer you stay in the *GhostCat*, sir."

"Well, your people should've plugged it in longer. I'll be back soon." Dennis tapped the screen to hang up before she could respond. Predictably, the call icon returned, but he didn't answer. At least they couldn't lock him inside. People should be allowed to take risks. That was how anything worthwhile was accomplished.

The sun's disk had just started to fall behind the hills, lighting the clouds on fire. Dennis could make the best of this, so he fished his camera from its pack and snapped a few photos of the clouds. It was a few decades old, but it would still upload pictures to his private digital drive, where he could tinker with them at his leisure after flying back. For now, all he had to do was enjoy the moment.

Dark silhouettes of acacias formed a breathtaking contrast. Here and there, a few of those small Pterosaurs darted about like bats, catching bugs and showing off their impressive acrobatics to rival any diving falcon.

Dennis pocketed the camera and jogged around the patches of taller grass. Archaeopteryx made communal nests in the acacias growing on hilltops and would start hunting to feed their young at dusk. Dennis hoped he could stay quiet enough to not scare the bizarre little dino-birds.

Some part of him wished he had come armed, or with one of the dino-hunters, who spent their days going after bothersome carnivores. But he didn't have the spare cash to hire one.

Besides, he thought, *Dad was right. You don't have a warrior in you.* Dennis knew well enough to avoid circumstances where he'd have to fight. Combat was simply not his forte. Keeping his distance, on the other hand, was a skill he'd cultivated. He'd be fine. Just a quick ten or twenty minutes at the nests, and back to the car for a nap before the truck picked him up. Stretching his legs would do him some good. No wildlife had shown up yet, except for the flying reptiles circling overhead, emitting those odd clicking calls that didn't belong in the Outback.

He wondered how those calls, voices from a world long vanished, sounded to the first geneticists who made these animals. Cloning long-extinct life had been thought impossible. But once the process was figured out, someone had suggested a prehistoric preserve in Australia, largely as a publicity stunt to raise funds for the main project: restoring the Outback's wildlife, making it as if the asteroid that formed Queensland Crater had never wiped the slate clean.

Naturally, the "publicity stunts" had gotten loose, and the kangaroos and koalas now risked being outcompeted by ancient species. But that was someone else's problem to solve. Dennis could ride the wave and get a couple of gorgeous shots along the way.

He followed a dry riverbed uphill, where he could see trees crowning a gentle swell of earth. Wind carried the whispered echoes of bird calls. Who cared if the rental service was wringing their hands? If they slapped him with a penalty fine, so be it. Dennis didn't go home empty-handed. He wasn't a warrior, but the new Australia was not going to beat him.

This was one of the few places where the Outback still looked like its pre-impact self. Most other locations were smothered in imported plants, another misguided effort to speed along Australia's recovery.

His gaze reflexively snagged on something he thought was a blackened tree trunk, standing about a hundred yards distant and stripped of all branches. He'd read that brush fires would scorch the acacias here and leave their trunks standing tall as the grass regrew beneath them. Except this trunk stood at the edge of a grove, where all of the other trees were quite untouched.

He could have sworn the lone burnt trunk had moved. Just slightly.

Dennis stopped and squinted through the zoom function of his camera, trying to see it in the fading light. Sure enough, it was the curved neck of an animal. A large bird, judging by the eagle-like beak which glimmered against the sunset. A crown of feathers adorned the top of its head, and the animal seemed to be watching him. It remained stone-still except to twitch that large head.

Wasn't there a huge flightless bird in these parts? By now there were more cloned animals than he could keep track of, but a name bubbled up from the fringes of memory. *Gastornis,* he thought. *Wasn't that the name?*

He kept an eye on the bird, nodding to himself. *Yeah, must be one of those.* Gastornis was a member of the so-called "terror birds," but it had turned out to be an herbivore. Carnivorous birds from the same family were confined to southern Australia, thankfully. Still, even herbivores could have quite the mean streak when defending territory or young, so he'd give the bird a wide berth.

Dennis started up the dry riverbed again, passing another cluster of the ever-present acacias. The nesting grounds were less than a quarter mile away. Already he could clearly hear the Archaeopteryx, noting how similar their calls were to the nattering of magpies.

He glanced back where he expected the Gastornis to be. And froze.

The giant bird was closer now. Much closer.

It must have approached when he couldn't see it through the trees, and now it stood still again. It watched Dennis, rigid as a statue. The posture and bulk reminded him of a shoebill, an African bird with a similarly unsettling gaze. But this creature must have stood ten feet tall, twice the height of a shoebill.

How far was it? Fifty yards, maybe sixty? Dennis slowly cursed. He had only looked away for a few seconds. To cover that much ground…

Maybe the Archaeopteryx could wait.

Don't run. Don't give it a reason to chase you. Fear slowly overtook his initial confusion. Dennis backed away, keeping the bird in sight and looking over his shoulder as he turned around. It didn't move, except for the head tracking him.

He had been face-to-face with the sabertooth cats in Cairns, but always with them behind bars. The violence of nature seemed so distant before now. Animal attacks happened to other people, but not him.

Stupid. You stupid idiot. You should've stayed in the car. The bird's head kept following Dennis as he backed up far enough for the grove to come between them again.

Hell with it, Dennis thought. The bird couldn't see him now, and he decided getting a headstart with running outweighed the risk of provoking it to chase him. Gastornis ate plants. He'd probably just wandered too close to its nest. Still, that giant beak could do some damage. Dennis had seen photos of hikers' remains, after they met the variety of terror birds that ate meat. There wasn't much of a body left.

He broke into a dead sprint, gravel slipping under his feet and nearly toppling him. The huge bird gave chase, its shadow lengthened by the sunset and crossing his own.

Dennis's heart went into overdrive, pumping adrenaline-laced blood. He kicked his legs hard to buy some distance. Other than the bird's heavy feet slamming the earth, it pursued him in silence.

Get to the car. But would even the car be safe? Could it stand up to that beak? Something told him he wouldn't live long enough to find out. A loud *clack* sounded behind him once, twice. Was the bird snapping that giant pickaxe of a beak after him?

Dennis dashed through tall grass, straight to the car. He could see its shape just through the stalks.

The towering form of a second terror bird loomed over the dead vehicle.

Waiting for him.

Dennis glimpsed black feathers shining in the fading light, and harsh gold eyes tracking him behind a bright beak. He spun around at the edge of the dirt road, nearly falling. The second bird strode toward him on gigantic black legs, but Dennis was already back on his feet, blurring past the car and running back up the road.

Now he heard two sets of clawed feet pounding after him.

Ten kilometers to town. Six miles. No way he could make that distance.

A bridge. He'd crossed a metal bridge that spanned a ravine, just a little ways past that graffiti-stained road sign. The bridges here had metal grating, to try and discourage wildlife from crossing. That could buy him some time. If he could get across, he could slow the birds down. Then he could double back to the car and lock himself inside.

Were terror birds supposed to be marathon runners? Maybe they couldn't run as fast as emus or ostriches. Some silent warning gently poked at conscious thought: the birds weren't catching up or falling behind. They kept pace with Dennis. Like they wanted him to run.

He passed the road sign, coming to a bend in the road. Dennis's drumming heart leapt. He was almost at the bridge. He barreled on, ignoring the fire in his spent lungs and fatigued muscles.

Vegetation gave way and showed the bridge, almost before he realized it was there. Dennis shot across to the other side, heard his pursuers' footsteps fall behind, slow, and stop.

Tall metal posts to either side of the bridge sported weak LED lights, and moths had started to flutter around them. A huge broken branch lay next to the road, nearly as long as he was tall. Dennis decided it was better than nothing, skidding to a halt to grab it.

Turning around, he finally got a good look at the terror birds. Their black feathers shimmered with a hint of iridescence. Those bright yellow beaks were as long as his arm, sharp as axe blades. The coloration suggested an absurd image of giant toucans. Their legs looked too powerful even for beasts of that size, wrapped in exaggerated muscles. Four great yellow eyes glared at him with pitiless hunger.

One bird planted a cautious foot on the bridge, its body jostling as it adjusted its stance. The vestigial wings unfolded from its bulky torso, flapping up and down. Blue-and-white feathers emerged from under the black as the plumage spread out. The animal took another deliberate step forward, and its companion followed.

Both animals raised their beaks skyward, not vocalizing but snapping with that same unsettling *clack* he'd heard earlier.

They were coming. That burst of exertion left his lungs and muscles burning. Town was miles away, and help wasn't coming for hours. He had a multitool in his pocket, but the knife blade was laughably insufficient to gut a terror bird.

He held the branch up in case the birds charged, brandishing it like a knight gripping a trusted sword. Or maybe a caveman with a club. At least he had a chance to go down fighting, warrior or not.

Foliage rustled, just to his left. Something kicked him hard in his side, throwing him clear to the road's opposite edge. His head struck the ground, and he rolled as lights burst in his vision. He coughed, trying to get wind back in his lungs. Lightning seemed to have struck his flank, and he realized ribs must have cracked.

The shape of a third terror bird strode out of the brush next to him, silent as death. He folded into the fetal position, closing around his fractured bones. He'd lost the branch.

The first two birds stepped off the bridge, opening their beaks to give off a sinister hiss. They circled him, framed against the fiery clouds overhead. They had set a trap for him, had herded him into a killing zone like some panicking prey animal.

He couldn't force his body to rise. Dennis was a helpless kid again, paralyzed in a nightmare as monsters clawed through the closet door.

Where was the branch? All Dennis had was the multitool and his camera, still in his pocket. The third terror bird and its companions surrounded him, each one about five yards away. They stood there for a moment, the three heads lowered and evaluating him.

Every breath hurt as he reminded his arm to move, and time itself crawled slower. Could he at least snap a picture of his killers, and show what happened to him? With a trembling grip he drew the camera from his pocket and pressed the shutter release.

The resulting white flash seemed so feeble, but the birds faltered in their steps. With his fingers shaking, he had to try several times to activate the flash again. Then he pressed it a third time. A fourth. Each of the birds took a step back, shaking their heads. When Dennis could see the pupils, they had contracted to pinpoints.

They hadn't closed in yet. Now was his chance. Back on his feet, he broke into a clumsy run along the road's edge, faltering as his boots snagged on roots or stones. He could still try to get back across the bridge, into the car, and hope he could get in touch with the rental service.

Except he was going the wrong way. He'd gotten turned around when the bird kicked him. Dennis tried to double back and collided with a wall of muscle and feathers. The camera tumbled out of his hand.

He heard fabric ripping, felt molten metal pour down his back. One of the beaks had hooked into his flesh. Dennis screamed as he collapsed backward, scrambling away from the giant bird.

His fingers found something rough and jagged in the grass. It was the branch he'd picked up earlier. Anger welled up from somewhere deep inside Dennis, washing over the fire in his ribs, the pain in his shoulder, dampening both.

Not without a fight.

Tightening his grip on the branch, Dennis launched back to his feet and whipped around. He attacked the creature that had bitten him, slamming the limb against the top of its head. That bloodstained beak opened in an agonized screech as the monster jumped back.

He swung his improvised club again, connecting with the thick neck of another bird. The wood shattered against iron-hard muscle. He'd knocked a few black feathers loose, and his target stumbled back from the impact.

The bird he hadn't hit took a half-step back, cold and cautious as it sized him up. The other two glared. Some distant piece of him knew he was just gripping half a branch now, and they hadn't retreated.

Dennis was going to die.

Under the enraged hissing built another noise. It sounded like a revving engine, racing up from behind. The acacias around him lit up with unsteady white light. Something heavy crashed along the road, headlights jumping and throwing shadows through the darkening forest.

A truck.

One terror bird, the one he'd hit on the neck, darted its head forward. The beak struck his pained side, hitting the cracked ribs. New fire ripped into him. A high-pitched cry tore from Dennis's lips as he spilled on the ground.

The bird rushed him, pinned Dennis with a heavy foot over his thigh, pressing down with so much force he was sure his femur would snap.

Dennis didn't know how the multitool got into his grip, but there it was, his hands working to pry out the knife blade. He screamed through the agony of leaning up far enough to reach that black demon's foot, and drove the blade in between the long, clawed toes.

It was the bird's turn to scream, that anvil of a foot lifting away and taking the knife with it. The other birds lowered their giant heads and screeched at the approaching vehicle, as if to challenge it.

A cloud of thick dust billowed ahead of the truck as the driver hit its brakes, just before the bumper slammed one of the birds. The impact toppled the giant avian backward. It rolled with the momentum and stood back up with uncanny agility, before it sped off into the forest. The leader's two cohorts shot off after, disappearing into the dark.

Only now did Dennis start to realize how much it hurt just to breathe. He lay there on the ground as someone leapt from the truck's driver side door, a tall man in a coat that reached his ankles, gripping a massive rifle.

"Better cover your ears," the driver said. "Stay down."

Dennis obeyed, trying not to faint from the lightning shredding his nerves as a gunshot boomed across the forest. He could feel the shock wave jolt through the ground. Another two reports from the rifle, and then he felt the frightened silence of the forest afterward.

"Did you get them?" said a female voice from inside the truck.

"Not a chance. They're too fast. But it'll scare 'em away for a minute. Get him in before they come back."

In spite of the agony, Dennis fought to rise, feeling gentle hands help lift him under the shoulders. He gasped as the motion tugged at the wound on his back. Someone opened a door for him, and he clambered into the back seat, gritting his teeth as warm blood soaked his shirt, fighting to hold back his tears.

Once the door shut, the truck lunged off, speeding down the road toward New Winton.

"All in a day's work," the man muttered. Only now did Dennis notice the American accent.

Dennis held his side, trying to minimize the hurt of breathing with cracked ribs. The woman had climbed into the back next to him, a blonde in her early twenties. Pretty, but too young for him.

The burly American had set his rifle in the passenger seat. He might have been in his late fifties or early sixties. With his hair still dark, it was hard to tell. He slapped the steering wheel with a callused hand. "I *told* them the Kelenken were encroaching north. Why the hell does nobody listen to me?" With a shake of his head, he glanced back at Dennis. "You must be Mister Longmire, right?"

Dennis coughed, tasting dust in his mouth. "I'm the moron, yes."

"Well, at least you're admitting it," the girl said, flashing a bright grin at him. "Marie Larkwood."

"Good to meet you. What did he call those things? Kelenken?"

She nodded. "*Kelenken guillermoi* is the full name. Biggest bloody terror birds we know of. Not supposed to be this far north, but…well, looks like that info's out of date."

"So, not Gastornis?" Dennis said.

He regretted asking. The girl's smile disappeared into a stare of withering contempt. "Someone needs to hit you up the head with a field guide, mate. Gastornis has white and green feathers. Doesn't look anything like Satan's Toucans back there."

The truck lurched, and a new stab of pain accompanied every bump. Dennis was just glad to be alive. "Noted. Are you guys the New Winton rescue crew, or something?" he said, clenching his teeth.

The man barked a harsh laugh. "Kinda. We're the volunteers who got out here fastest. Marie here's a vet assistant. She and her mom can patch you up at the field hospital." Without looking away from the road, the man reached over his seat, extending a hand toward Dennis. "Clyde Marshall, freelance hunter."

Dennis shook his hand, surprised Clyde kept a gentle grip. "I bet you've gotten a lot of dumb tourists out of scrapes before."

"A few. It's part of the gig. Hell of a lot better than finding a corpse when I get there."

"Did the rental service call you guys?"

Grinning, Clyde looked back at him. "Oh, that reminds me. They'll retrieve the *GhostCat* tomorrow. If we found you alive, I was supposed to give you a message. They said it kinda colorful, but…"

"I'm not getting back my security deposit, am I?"

"Nope," Clyde said.

"That's fair. Just wish I'd held onto my camera. You think the photos will upload from here?"

Marie laughed. "Still not much signal out here. Sorry, Mate."

Figures. They came to a smoother stretch of the road, almost a straight shot back to town.

"I saw you fighting those birds when we drove up," Clyde said. "Most of the time, folks just curl up, and the birds pick at 'em until they're dead. But not you. You put up a hell of a fight, Mister Longmire. That's something to be proud of."

Dennis tried to shrug, wincing as his motion tugged on the laceration along his back. "Looks like I can be a warrior, after all." Even through his pain, that alone was worth a smile.

About the Author

John K. Patterson is a lifelong lover of fantasy and science fiction. A self-trained author and artist, Patterson is the creator of the Queensland Crater and Arrivers universes. Fueled mainly by coffee, he channels his imagination into stories featuring aliens, dragons, wizards, dinosaurs, the undead, and on occasion all of the above. He lives at the roots of Pikes Peak in Colorado Springs, CO.

Gyrfalcon (Falco rusicolus)

The largest breed of falcon, typically residing along arctic coasts, whose regal appearance and demeanor command the respect of many royal (albeit lesser) humans

Blood on the Wing

by Jenny Perry Carr

With a flick of the wand, Addy would prove he was worthy of training. The raven-haired teen focused on the white gyrfalcon, the most prized of all falcons, as it circled the barren, rocky coastline, free and solitary, gliding on the icy wind. His duties as apprentice, if you could call him that, required fetching unusual items for the peculiar sorcerer Elzanore, and today, the item was alive.

"What're we doing here anyway?" Henry, Addy's best friend, scratched his head while wrestling three rustic twig cages with one hand.

Addy yanked Henry behind a lichen-encrusted boulder, out of the bird's line of sight. "We need to catch that raptor."

"Then why'd you have me bring *three* cages?"

Addy furrowed his brow. "Stop asking so many questions. All your talking isn't helping."

Elzanore's shadowy castle stood sentry over the wintry hills above, watching them, passing judgement on his deceit. A building couldn't see, could it? He shook his head to clear away any doubt.

Addy aimed the gnarled rosewood wand at the gyr. He'd show Elzanore. Addy had watched him work his magic. How hard could it be? Point a stick, say a few words, poof.

Addy mimicked Elzanore's motions and incantation. "Aranak. Zolinak. Rhan."

The snowy feathers blurred overhead then split into two. Addy grinned and puffed his chest. His skill would impress Elzanore, especially when he delivered three birds. He waved the wand again. Three falcons hung on a gust of wind.

Then four. Five. Six.

Addy's eyes widened.

Seven. Eight. Nine.

What had he done?

The biting wind shifted, and the gyrfalcons dove, targeting them, grazing their heads with razor-sharp talons. Shrieks pierced the wind. Wings blasted frosty air upon them, their wingspan nearly as wide as Addy was tall.

"Ow!" Henry shouted as a bird dug its claw into his scalp. He dropped the cages and ran through the dried grass. A crimson streak painted his cheek.

Addy batted away the attacks, ducking as each falcon swooped at him. Gashes and punctures stained his arms and hands red. The pain was worse than anything Addy had experienced before. They had to get out of the open.

"Do something, Addy!"

"I know, I know. Take cover there." Addy pointed to an English oak tree near the beach, bleached white from years of sun and salt.

The birds pursued, matching their preys' moves. Their alabaster wings were hard to distinguish from the clouded sky, if not for the red-tipped feathers, tainted with the boys' blood.

As they ran, Addy waved the wand behind him, shouting the incantation again. Maybe he could reverse the spell. An overhead *whoosh* proved him wrong.

Nine birds became eighteen.

"Blasted!"

The falcons seemed to double again and again and again until the horizon swirled with a blizzard of pale feathers. But that couldn't be. Elzanore had turned one animal into three, each with a third of the life-force, but no one could make a sky full of gyrs out of nothing.

"Make it stop." Henry cowered against the trunk, which provided no protection from the onslaught.

Addy's middle churned like the sea, waves of nausea washing over him. "I'm trying."

What was that slowing spell Elzanore used? Maybe it could stop the gyrs long enough for him to reverse the duplication. He racked his brain, searching for the incantation, and gripped fistfuls of hair. Addy sucked in a breath. He remembered.

Addy spun around and stood firm, jaw set, facing the gale of raptors. The falcons glanced off him, beaks gouging holes in his cloak and skin as they passed. Addy stood fast.

"Ergin. Lugrin. Ferio." The wand vibrated in his hand. He could feel the power coursing through his arm. It worked.

Henry screamed as the raptors dove at him with greater speed, far beyond their natural abilities.

How had Addy gotten it wrong? He hadn't slowed them at all. They were faster than before, mere blurs streaking across the sky of pale ghosts.

Talons sliced through air and skin. The gyrs pursued with murderous intent, attacking each other as they swooped at the boys.

"Run!" Addy shouted and grabbed his friend by the elbow, tearing him away from the oak tree.

The falcons would surely kill both boys if they stayed in the open. The sea air tousled Addy's hair. He took a deep breath, and the smell of the beach filled his nostrils. Addy eyed the waves crashing along the coast, the only place to escape the attacks.

"There." Addy raced toward the shoreline.

Maybe he could buy them some time to reach the water, push the gyrs back. Addy pointed the wand to the sky and shouted an incantation, remembering Elzanore's spell to create a gust of wind. A blast of air erupted from him, but it only ruffled the gyrfalcons' feathers as they sped through the sky.

As Addy's stride hit the sand, he stumbled to his knees. His grip loosened in the fall, and the wand tumbled to the ground.

Henry yanked him up. "Let's go."

Addy grabbed for the wand, out of reach behind him. "The wand."

"Leave it."

The boys trudged knee-deep into the frigid water and dove into the surf. The salt stung his open wounds until the chill soothed and numbed. The falcons continued to strike, their talons reaching below surface. Addy sucked in a breath and descended into the murky brine, risking his life in the icy waters rather than face the angry claws and sharpened beaks.

The ocean, like a frozen weight on his chest, made each breath harder to take. He took as deep a breath as he could and held it for dear life. Addy disappeared beneath the waves again. Claws ripped at the water, churning the sea like a shark feeding frenzy.

Addy desperately struggled to stay under. His lungs burned, begging for air.

Beside him, Henry went limp and drifted down into the blackness. Addy reached for Henry, inches from his grasp, as he slipped lower beneath the sea. Addy's chest screamed for breath.

What if magic could create air, like the wind spell? Without the wand, he was powerless. Above was the air Addy desperately needed, but below, his friend faded away. He had to try. Addy concentrated on the wind spell. He focused on the words. *Spuria. Darnum. Havairum.*

Effervescent bubbles formed and swirled around Addy. They coalesced into a pocket of air that enveloped his face. He inhaled a wheezing breath.

He jack-knifed down and kicked his legs, driving him into the deep. Addy strained to reach Henry, then snatched his friend's shirt with an iron grip. He hoisted him up and powered them toward the circle of light above.

The two boys surfaced and took gasping breaths.

Addy patted Henry's cheek with a freezing hand. "Stay with me."

Henry nodded, pale as the feathers choking the sky.

"You okay?" Addy shouted, holding his friend above the waves.

"We're not gonna make it, are we?"

Above the cacophony of screams, from the boys and falcons alike, a familiar voice boomed from the shore. Addy dared a peek as he bobbed in the icy waves, thankful but dreading what he would see.

Elzanore strode toward the water and stooped to retrieve his wand. The grizzled sorcerer's emerald robes billowed in the wind. His long, ashen beard brushed against the sand. He stared at the sea, at the boys, and shook his head. The raptors flew around him like a tornado of feathers but never inflicted harm.

Elzanore beckoned them with a lone curled finger.

A lump formed in Addy's throat. He wasn't sure what he feared most, the falcons or Elzanore's disappointment.

Addy swam to shore, towing Henry who was too weak to swim, and collapsed onto the sand. Somehow, Elzanore's presence stopped the attacks.

Elzanore *tsk*ed, low and slow, over and over again. "When will you learn, boy? Patience has never been your strong suit, and mischief the norm."

The boys stood shivering, soaked to the bone and covered in sand and blood. As they panted with effort, each breath hung in the cold air.

Elzanore regarded the wand in his hand. "The wand is not nearly as important as the sorcerer's willpower and control. The wood merely focuses the energy already present."

Elzanore brandished the wand, waving it with grand gestures, and murmured magical words.

"Ortune. Variune. Karoo."

The whoosh of beating wings fell silent. White feathers stained red fluttered to the ground in the still air, like falling snow.

Elzanore tucked away his wand in his robes and picked up the carcass of the only gyrfalcon that lay on the ground. His baritone voice rumbled in Addy's chest. "In your carelessness, you nearly killed Henry and yourself. And now this noble bird is forever gone, murdered by your insolence."

His words pierced Addy's heart. He had tried to do good, to prove his worth.

Elzanore's voice echoed across the crashing winter surf. "All you have proven is that you are most definitely not ready for training. For your penance, and to recognize the enormity of your misdeeds, you must gather every single feather and bring them to me."

Addy's shoulders hunched forward, and his head drooped. Bloody feathers surrounded him as far as his eyes could see. In shame, dragging his feet, he began gathering the stained feathers and contemplated if he would ever regain Elzanore's trust and respect.

Elzanore held up a crooked finger. "One more thing. Clever thinking, creating the air bubble. Patience, Addy. Soon we'll explore your natural talents."

About the Author

Jenny Perry Carr is group vice president of scientific services for a medical communications company by day, budding sci-fi/fantasy/horror writer at night, which sounds much like the beginnings of a superhero's bio. But alas, her only superpower is remembering random facts, like the human body contains trillions of microorganisms that outnumber our own cells by 10 to 1. She has a PhD in molecular neurobiology from Yale University which influences much of her speculative writing. She's a Minnesota native living in North Texas with her husband and currently working on a sci-fi trilogy.

Blue-Footed Booby *(Sula Nebouxii)*

A marine bird, marked by ~~somewhat ridiculous~~ highly elegant blue feet, whose elaborate mating rituals and unique parenting make them a prime subject for psychological curiosity

Whatever Lola Wants

by N.V. Haskell

The tapping rose above the pattering of rain against the hotel room's glass sliding doors. Heidi wished it was only the storm, but the insistent repetition stifled that hope. Her fingers trembled on the curtains. She knew better than to look. Pedro—the manager who had brought her on to replace him—warned her before he'd joined most of the tourists in the evacuation. If Lola knew anyone was here, she'd try harder to get to them.

Plus, Heidi suspected Lola was responsible for what happened to Jose. Poor Jose. They'd discovered him only an hour before the planes left for Quito. There were defensive wounds on his arms. His eyes gouged.

Dead.

They'd put his body in the freezer when the storm hit. Nothing to do until the Policia could get to them. But this freak storm was causing more than one problem.

Heidi's finger trembled as she pulled the curtain back a few centimeters. Rivulets of rain cascaded down the glass doors. She followed them down to where a pair of yellowed eyes with large black irises stared at her. Lola's bright blue feet peeked from beneath her brown and white body. The blue-footed booby gazed up hatefully; large beak opening and closing as if spewing curses.

According to Pedro, this wasn't the first time Lola's attitude had resulted in violence. He'd lifted his eye patch, revealing the scarred maw beneath, to prove it. He had been at the hotel for nearly a decade and claimed to have named Lola after an old American showtune he liked to sing.

Heidi yanked the drape closed. But it was too late. The large bird quacked loudly. The tapping intensified, followed by a round of thuds that shook the doors as she hurled her body against them.

Heidi backed away, scurrying from the empty hotel room. After taking a moment to collect herself, she headed up the stairs to check on the remaining guests. There was the Johnson family—forced to cancel their flight back to the mainland after the husband, Kurt, contracted the norovirus two days before the storm hit—and the Sweeneys, an older couple interested in birds, and two Ecuadorian women. Heidi and the remaining staff members who lived on the island had chosen to ride out the storm at the hotel.

Heidi considered moving everyone to the ground floor, but with the Booby threatening violence at the lower windows, she thought it best to leave everyone where they were. Unfortunately, the thunder and crashing rain were louder on the upper level. Frighteningly so. A pungent stench wafted through the hall, reminding her that the Johnsons had yet to allow a room clean.

Ellen and Don Sweeney had arrived from Toronto the day before the storm hit. Heidi offered to return them to Quito and refund their money, given the unusual storm barreling toward them. She'd promised to give them discounted accommodations for another time, but they'd adamantly declined. The islands had been on their bucket list for years and with Ellen's recent dementia diagnosis, they were getting in as many trips as they could.

Heidi was determined to check on all the guests to make sure each of them were doing as well as could be expected under the circumstances. Don opened the door after the second knock. Sharp blue eyes and a friendly smile complimented his gray hair and matching beard. He always greeted her by name, with a warm and friendly disposition. She wished more guests were like him. Behind him, Ellen lay napping on the bed.

"Just wanted to make sure that everything is okay," Heidi asked. "Can I get you anything?"

With a glance behind him to his wife, Don stepped out into the hall. "I was wondering if there were any quieter rooms? The noise up here has made it difficult to sleep. I ended up giving her meds last night, and she's still struggling to wake up."

Heidi bit her lip, considering. If she gave them a room that looked at the pool rather than the ocean, Lola might not bother them. At least Heidi hoped Lola wouldn't—the bird was hard to predict. "There is an interior room that might be quieter."

His shoulders relaxed. "I'd really appreciate it."

"I'll send for your luggage around two, is that alright?"

After Don vanished inside their room, Heidi pulled out the walkie-talkie and spoke to the front desk to arrange the move. Next, she checked on the Ecuadorian women. They were lively and easy to deal with. Their only request was for more towels and to have their mini fridge restocked.

Heidi stood outside Suite 224, steeling her nerves and her stomach. The odor was strongest here, but thankfully, she didn't hear the rounds of vomiting that had echoed down the hall three days ago. Lisa, their teenager, had been spared from the illness, and had managed a few solo hikes while her parents suffered.

Heidi had kept them stocked with water, soda, soups and crackers. This morning Caroline Johnson had ordered three breakfasts of pancakes, fruit, and yogurt. Their room faced away from the storm, making it slightly quieter than the others on the top floor. But the odor…

"Is everything alright?" Kurt Johnson asked. He stood with the door partially open, blocking the view into the room. A pungent stench crept into the hall, mixed with the salty breeze that swept in from their open balcony door. Perhaps they were trying to rid the sickness from the air. It had to have been difficult for them over the past several days. At least with them being on the upper level, Heidi didn't have to worry about Lola who had, so far, only lingered around the main floor.

"What does she want?" Caroline called from inside with the same disgusted tone that tainted every word she spoke.

Heidi forced a smile. "I was just seeing if you needed anything."

Mr. Johnson opened his mouth to say something but promptly reclosed it and swallowed. His voice was halted. "Nothing right now, thank you." He shifted uncomfortably as Lisa said something muffled. "Uh, would it be possible to get some sushi or fresh fish?"

"Fish?" Heidi asked. While they had plenty on hand, it was an atypical request from anyone recovering from a stomach bug. "Any fish? I can ask—"

"Nothing canned!" The teenager's voice rang clear this time. "Fresh fish. Surely, you must have something. We *are* surrounded by water, right?"

Caroline nudged Kurt out of the way, keeping the door at the same opening. She had a pinched, exhausted look on her face, covered deftly with obvious irritation. A tight headband secured her hair away from her face. "It can't be that difficult. The ocean is right there." She gestured broadly to the balcony doors. "Just send up some fresh-caught fish."

A nagging sensation settled in Heidi's stomach; something wasn't right. They'd been difficult since they stepped from the plane and insisted everyone cater to them, but Heidi's patience was worn thin. Yelp review be damned. Plus, the internet was out anyway. They'd have to wait to post until they left.

"I'm not sending anyone out in this storm just so you can have fish." Heidi's tone was firm, and she met Caroline's eyes without flinching. She continued before the irritating woman could counter. "Furthermore, we have a policy about keeping the patio doors closed during storms—"

"But we've been—"

"—and allowing our cleaning staff to properly tend and check the room every three days. This is now the fifth day that you have refused the staff." There was an odd noise from the room, stifled quickly. That sense of un-rightness swelled. "What was that?"

Caroline placed her hand against the door. "What?"

"When would the cleaning crew be coming by?" Kurt asked.

Heidi tried to peek around their shoulders, but they leaned together to block her view. "An hour or two."

"Fine," Caroline said. "I suppose the room needs a good cleaning, definitely the bathroom. We'll be ready."

Without another word, the door shut in Heidi's face. She rubbed her neck, imagining unleashing Lola on them, before heading to the lobby downstairs. There was an unpleasant scraping that echoed through the halls from the front doors.

Heidi shivered at the sight of the blurry white and brown figure assaulting the doors with its beak. Slightly smaller than Lola, with feet not quite as vibrant, it had to be Luiz, Lola's mate.

Great. They'd both gone crazy.

"Room 224, that mean woman, rang a minute ago. They want to be moved to a suite downstairs." Sylvie said, casting furtive glances at the front doors.

Heidi frowned, leaning against the desk as the bird pecked again. "We almost got rid of them, didn't we?"

Sylvie chuckled. "Damn stomach virus." They stared at the frantic bird. "Do you think it'll be safe to move them?"

Heidi sighed. "I'd rather move them than fight with them. Any update on the storm?"

"Should be past us by morning."

"Not soon enough," Heidi said, already thinking about what the cleanup would look like and how to get the Johnsons past Lola and Luiz. She'd put a call out to the rangers for help, but the storm had held everyone in place.

"Have you ever seen them act like this?" Heidi asked. Sylvie had been working in the hotels on the islands for the better part of ten years.

"Twice before, but I've never seen them both this upset. Usually, it's just Lola. She's always been temperamental. Before she met Luiz, she attacked anyone who got too near her nest. Pedro and I had just started here then." She winced. "It was a big lesson."

"And the other time?"

Sylvie glanced at her. "When Luiz got trapped in the shed beside the pool. No one knew he was there, and no one knew how violent she could get. We lost a good man that day."

"Lola's killed before?" The hair on Heidi's arms stood up.

Sylvie nodded. "About five years ago. Wild animals. What can we do?"

"They did nothing about her? What about the park rangers?"

"She's being studied by more than one research team for her unusual behavior. The Boobies are normally so docile and easy going. Besides, we are on the Booby's land. These islands belong to the birds, lizards, and tortoises more than us. Once Lola gets what she wants, she settles down. Until then, well…" Sylvie nodded to the doors.

Heidi drummed her fingers on the desk as Luiz pecked at the glass rhythmically. "So, what do they want?"

◆ ◆ ◆

The move went smoothly. The Sweeney's appreciated the quieter accommodations and didn't care about the lack of view. Heidi promised to upgrade them when the storm cleared and asked them to keep the curtains drawn.

She moved the Johnsons to the only suite on the ground floor, but Sylvie reported that the family had acted stranger than usual when they moved their luggage. The girl had zipped up her hoodie and drawn it tight over her head, crouched over her stomach. Once they received the new room key, she and her mother had practically sprinted downstairs, where Lisa had then barricaded herself in the bathroom until the staff left.

Luiz had abandoned his tirade at the front doors and the tapping on the lower windows had gone eerily quiet, almost as if the birds were changing tactics. But that was ridiculous. Heidi knew birds didn't think like that. Certainly not the adorable Blue-Footed Boobies.

Still, Lola's behavior had caused Heidi to question everything she knew about the birds. She had planned to work here another year before applying for positions elsewhere. French Polynesia would be nice. She'd never heard of murderous birds there. But she'd never heard of them here before, either. Speaking of hearing…

Where *was* Lola?

The rain pelted the building as Heidi opened the room she'd been in earlier. Everything was as it had been, though there were streaks and small feathers pasted against the glass where Lola had thrown her goose-sized body against it. Darkness had fallen, the sky and sea lit occasionally by a distant flash of lightning. She shivered again. After nearly three days of their noise, the birds were too quiet. Maybe they'd finally grown tired and gone back to…

"Oh, shit…" Heidi said. A dawning understanding made her curse her shortsightedness.

As she darted from the room, a woman screamed—the old lady. Ellen's yell came again, accompanied by a familiar tapping against glass. Robert's voice was low and reassuring. Their door flew open when Heidi knocked. Ellen's eyes were wide and she trembled in the doorway.

Ellen glanced over her shoulder. "It's attacking the windows. Startled me."

Heidi's hopes that the interior room would go unnoticed were dashed. Lola paused her assault, golden eyes flashed before settling on Heidi through the smeared glass.

"She's been at it for an hour," Don said, placing a reassuring hand on Ellen's shoulder. "We thought about offering her some of our—"

"Everything alright?" Kurt Johnson stood in the hall. His eyes shifted from Heidi to Lola, and he inhaled sharply. He stepped backward and cleared his throat.

"What's going on?" Caroline came up behind him. "The screaming…" She gasped when Lola hurled herself against the glass again.

Heidi turned. "Do either of you know what these birds might be after?"

Kurt looked at his wife, but she pursed her lips and crossed her arms. "Of course not. How could we? I'm not sure what you are insinuating."

"I heard something earlier, from down the hall," Ellen said, looking at Heidi. "It sounded like hoarse quacking. Like a Booby making its presence known."

"You know what they sound like?"

She smiled. "Ornithology is my passion. It's why we are here."

"Are you sure it wasn't from outside?" Heidi asked, watching the way the Johnsons exchanged glances. Lola ceased her assault, waddling away from the windows and out of sight.

"It was down the hall. We both heard it," Don said.

Heidi's face flushed hot. She turned on the Johnson's. "The Blue-Footed Booby is normally a trusting bird with no interest or natural fear of humans. But Lola is not like the other birds."

"What do you mean?" Caroline's voice trembled.

"Most of us avoid her. She's attacked staff members who got too near her chicks. And we suspect her in at least two fatal attacks. Tearing out their eyes with her sharp beak." Caroline paled and clutched her husband's arm. "I can't imagine what she would do if someone was stupid enough to steal her chick. But they'd certainly have it coming."

"Lisa!" Caroline sprinted down the hall, her husband close at her heels. Heidi raced after them.

There was a crash followed by a girl's scream. Rising above that was the beating of the rain and Lola's furious, hoarse quacking.

The door to the Johnson's room flew open. A slim adolescent girl with a gray hoodie pulled tight around her tried to escape, but a flush of brown and white five-foot wings slammed the door shut. From inside the room, Lisa's screams changed from panic to pain.

Caroline threw the door open. Lisa was curled over her knees, one bloody arm covering her head. Her other arm struggled to cradle something against her belly. Lola rose a few feet in the air and dove on the girl's back while the rain sailed in through the sliding door. Luiz perched in the doorway, rocking from one foot to the other, seemingly waiting for an opening.

"Mom!"

Caroline dashed forward, shielding Lisa and taking the brunt of the bird's assault.

"Give it back!" Heidi yelled, ducking beneath Lola's wings as she whipped around for another attack.

Lisa wailed and shook her head. "It's mine! Tell her it's mine, Mom!"

Caroline cried out as an angry beak ripped a chunk of hair from her head. Her headband sailed across the room.

"She'll kill you both," Heidi said.

Kurt rushed into the room. He'd stolen a lamp from a hallway table and raised it clumsily overhead. Luiz launched from the patio doorway, colliding with the man's chest. The lamp crashed to the floor and broke. Kurt landed beside it. Lola quacked and dove again at Caroline and Lisa.

Heidi stood just inside the door, momentarily stunned. This would be a terrible Yelp review, no matter what happened now. She could see the hotel's four-star status falling with each lost feather and drop of blood.

A hoarse quack, followed by a shrill whistle, came from the hallway. Ellen held an open can of sardines in one hand and dangled a fish in the other. Don stood behind her, poised to pull her from the room at the first sign of danger.

Luiz paused in his assault. He tilted his head, beak slightly open to taste the air. His forward-facing yellow eyes focused on the fish. He waddled toward the door, passing Heidi while she leaned away. Ellen tossed the fish, and he swallowed it whole.

Lola landed on an upturned table, beak raised high. Caroline and Lisa scrambled toward the door. But Heidi blocked their way.

"Put it down," she ordered.

Tears streaked Lisa's cheeks. Chunks of her hair were torn from her scalp and the sleeves of her hoodie were ripped. Her lower lip trembled with a look of disbelief.

Caroline released Lisa's hand and wrenched open the hoodie. Inside was a white-downed chick roughly the size of a small hen. Luiz squawked. Heidi swiped the chick and crouched down with it as the teenager and her mother squealed and ran.

Heidi placed the baby gently on the tile as Lola landed before her. Lola's head tilted, her eyes glittering in the thin light as she stared at Heidi. The rain had stilled outside as the silence stretched taut.

Then Lola's head dipped. She nuzzled the chick, who waddled toward her. Luiz landed beside them, his beak tenderly inspecting each wing. Heidi took a breath and leaned back on her heels.

Ellen suggested using the canned sardines to lead the birds down the hall and out the front doors. Sylvie and Heidi opened the doors as the three of them—six, if you counted the birds—exited the building.

The rain had turned to a light drizzle, with stars peeking through the dark sky. The storm had passed.

Early the next morning, the rangers arrived, escorted by the Ecuadorian National Policia. The Johnsons were held and interrogated in a small room until, after Heidi explained what had happened with Lola, Interpol was called. The Policia had been called when they'd discovered Jose's body, but after significant questioning of herself and the staff, they determined there were no guilty parties on the island.

"Lola didn't kill Jose," one officer finally stated. "We arrested Pedro, trying to get out of the country late last night with over eighty baby giant tortoises stowed in his suitcase."

"He couldn't have killed Jose," Heidi said, but doubt settled in her chest. "There was another man a few years ago. And what about his eye?" Could it all have been lies?

"Pedro killed Jose when he discovered him stealing the tortoises. Apparently, the first victim was his partner. After some disagreement, Pedro lost his eye, and his partner lost his life. He confessed last night. Said with the Booby's attitude, it was easy to convince people Lola was to blame. But we've been investigating Pedro for years."

Heidi looked at the Rangers talking with other staff members behind the counter. "But Sylvie said—"

"They were part of the investigation. Lola just helped by distracting everyone."

Heidi bit her lip, feeling foolish. "What will happen to the Johnsons?"

"The girl broke about half of our rules. If they'd tried to get the chick on a plane, not that they could have succeeded, they'd all be in jail right now. Most likely, they'll be extradited and banned from ever returning. Plus, they'll have to pay a hefty fine." He sighed, shaking his head.

Heidi almost felt bad for them, but not quite. "And Lola?"

He smiled. "Lola, Luiz, and their chick are already back along the rocks with the other Boobies. They've quieted down for now." He paused; his nails scratched at the stubble on his chin. "There was one odd thing though."

"What?"

"Pedro swore that he didn't gouge out Jose's eyes. He said they fought, and he strangled him, but he never went for the eyes."

◆ ◆ ◆

It was late afternoon. The Johnsons were gone, along with the Rangers, Policia, and Jose's corpse. Heidi stood beneath a clear sky and surveyed the damage around the pool. A quack startled her.

Lola stood several feet away, cocking her head curiously and examining Heidi with discerning eyes. Heidi froze as the large bird waddled forward. Her sharp beak nudged Heidi's leg twice before she gazed up and squawked again.

With trembling fingers, Heidi reached tentatively down and stroked the bird's head. "You're welcome," Heidi whispered.

Lola snapped her beak, causing Heidi to leap backward. With a satisfied look, the Blue-Footed Booby made one last quack before turning and waddling away.

That evening, Heidi applied for a transfer to Tahiti.

About the Author

N.V. Haskell is an award winner of Writers of the Future, featured in Volume 38. Her works have appeared in Deep Magic ezine and The Last Line. She writes speculative fiction and is only slightly obsessed with non-European history and mythology.

N.V. can be found at Comic Cons or Renaissance Fairs donned in her favorite costumes, reading multiple books at a time, running badly, travelling, or teaching yoga. She lives in the Cincinnati area surrounded by old souls, a rescue dog with a large personality, an indignant cat, and too many squirrels. After many years in healthcare, N.V. continues to be stubbornly optimistic, believing that there is goodness in this world if we dare to look for it.

Parrot

Solomon Islands Eclectus *(Eclectus roratus)*

A brightly-colored, clever, personable, and vocal breed of parrot with a bright red head and maroon and blue body, who subsist on a diet of nuts, fruits, and (given their long lifespan) the lives of their owners

Polly Want an Apple

by Mike Jack Stoumbos

With few exceptions, the most infuriating and potentially lethal thing the bird did was scream.

She weighed a little less than a pound and stood maybe a foot tall when she fully stretched, from the tip of her scarlet head down to the last blue tail feather. And yet, the vocal cords on that tiny parrot hit me harder than any fire alarm. The shriek would have inspired banshee mythologies, had banshees originated in the Solomon Islands.

Despite the risk of hell-raising wails, this bird remained my coworker, often sitting on my shoulder while I typed away early in the morning or deep into the night.

I called her Lutra.

On most occasions, Lutra seemed to know better than to scream while in arm's reach of a human. Across the house was bad enough. In the same room could set me ringing for several minutes. But from my shoulder, the high-pitched cry of the Solomon Islands Eclectus was an instant migraine, more effective than a close-proximity airhorn.

The best strategy for preventing eardrum destruction was keeping her entertained. She generally appreciated screens and music, or even the sound of my voice. She would go through cycles of stretching, preening, and napping, but would also begin fidgeting—bobbing from foot to foot or starting to tap her black beak against my collar—as a fair warning of impending boredom. Giving her things to pick through and climb on tended to occupy her bird brain for long stretches between my having to feed her treats.

Lutra called every treat, "Apple."

True to stereotypes, Lutra also loved crackers, the crust of French bread, celery sticks, and almonds—she and I both ate impressive amounts of almonds. But, unlike the others, "Apple" was lodged deep in her vocabulary. In addition to the nonsensical screams, which might one day result in one or more of our deaths, she had developed a knack for yelling only a few words. Among them, "Hello," "Lutra," and "Apple," each impressively loud in their own right, like declarations from a town crier or intros from a circus emcee. I admit, they were difficult to ignore and quite startling when otherwise alone in one's office, but hardly the stuff that inspires violent anecdotes and urban legends. Usually.

On the night my work-desk cache of almonds ran out, she began employing the request far more liberally. I could be clacking away, completely in the zone, then the word "Apple" would insert itself into a sentence. But I held firm. I couldn't give in to every request, and I figured I had fifteen to thirty minutes before she shrieked. Of course, when I did not provide any alternate treats—whether cracker-shaped apples, celery-shaped apples, or actual-apple apples—she decided to explore and investigate for herself.

Though not exactly pristine, my desk was not messy enough to inspire ants. *Cluttered* fit the bill, and my workspace gave her opportunities to sift through the many pens, several empty water glasses, at least two notebooks, and dozens of sticky-note reminders she could bite right through. She also knew where I usually kept the bag of almonds, now empty.

I was, as I said, in the zone, and couldn't be deterred by picking up the bird and placing her on my shoulder. However, this time, when she climbed down my arm, she didn't make her rounds on the desk but remained on my wrist. I hoped she'd remain there—after all, she weighed less than a pound—and at least permit me to finish my current task.

No such luck. After a second's hesitation to tease me with false hope, she planted her little raptor claws directly on the keyboard.

Now, I don't know what she did—because I've never been able to duplicate it—but something about the keys she pressed in a particular order created a host of new symbols well beyond the standard QWERTY.

"Lutra," I chided, picking up the distracting bird to hold her away from my laptop.

Knowing she'd been addressed, she responded dutifully with, "Apple?"

In two words, we'd struck a contract. If I procured some kind of apple, she would leave me to my productivity.

I set Lutra on the arm of my desk chair—where she would often sit content—and hustled out of the office and into the kitchen. There, I grabbed the nearest treat, a marbled Honeycrisp apple, from the fruit bowl on the counter, silently praying this might sate her.

Running back up the stairs with paring knife in hand (as parents and teachers cautioned me never to do), I called, "All right, Lu, I've got your apple."

I should have guessed she would climb off the armrest in my absence. Despite having wings, this parrot rarely flew unless startled or traveling directly to her cage. But she had two gripping feet and a beak, which had helped her up from my armrest and onto my desk.

Yet again, she'd made her way to the keyboard.

"Lutra!" I said again when I saw her through the door. At the time, I'll admit, I chiefly worried about what I would refer to as "birdily fluids." Clearly my imagination was lacking.

Her red head and black beak bobbed up and down, accompanied by the clicks of keys, until I set down the apple and scooped her up. The fact that I was still holding a knife in my other hand was purely coincidental, but it would make any reprimand seem more threatening.

I could see that no mess had been made on the keyboard, and my documents were all thoroughly backed up. The whole affair would have passed with a sigh and a chuckle—but then I saw what she had managed to type.

Now, I'm familiar with those *smash your forehead into the keyboard* memes, but I'd never known a key-smash to produce so many different non-Latin symbols. Hell, they weren't even Greek characters or anything I recognized. I might have had more luck looking up the alien glyphs from *Predator* or *Stargate*. Not only that, but in a few hops on the keyboard, Lutra managed to change font and color. The largest of the twisted circle figures appeared to be pulsing green.

"What the hell?" I wondered.

"Hello, Lutra!" Lutra sang in reply, apparently pleased to be perched on my fingers yet again—or having spotted the apple.

I was leaning forward to take a screenshot, when a jet of lightning shot out of the system. Seriously, lightning, straight from the back of the console across the room. Fortunately, it went away from me and the bird—both flesh-and-blood mortals—but it summarily fried our printer where it sat on the shelf against the far wall, over six feet away.

Luckily, the printer didn't burst into flames, and, if I'm honest, being charred to a crisp barely decreased its value. Still, one doesn't expect indoor lightning from laptops. One also doesn't expect it to strike twice.

"Holy—" was all I could get out before the second bolt launched, this time at the floor, where it printed a squiggly, twisted circle, much like the growing green glyph on my screen. I might have come up with a better description if I hadn't ducked for cover under my desk—which is more of a table and doesn't have a solid back.

Lutra flapped during descent but didn't let go of my fingers.

When the circle on the floor whipped up, not a jet of flame, but a genuine indoor tornado, Lutra let out a "Wooooow!" halfway between R2D2 and Owen Wilson.

I covered my head, averted my eyes, probably exclaimed an obscenity or two, and debated the likelihood of being smote on my way out the door.

Then the room filled with smoke—crimson smoke—that stung my nose like hard-boiled eggs soaked in expired Tabasco.

I found myself coughing and sputtering, which put the *canary in a coal mine* image in my head and made me do the one thing I could think of to protect the parrot.

I slipped her under my shirt. Not the first time, don't judge. But there's only so much you can expect from a cotton blend T-shirt when it comes to purifying air. I stood, ready to race out of the room, call 911, wonder what had gone wrong with the smoke alarms—but the smoke was already beginning to clear and providing a whole new kind of terror.

The figure first appeared in silhouette, standing on the singed carpet of my office, at least seven feet tall, not including the horns coming out of the forehead.

"Oh my God," escaped my lips—unplanned, unhelpful.

A deep voice replied, "Hardly."

I gasped, which inspired more coughing. I curled forward, and Lutra hunkered against me while I sputtered.

Smoke continued to settle, falling back down and into the floor, some appearing to coalesce into the otherworldly being, taking form as his lower half. Like Lutra, he had a red face and black eyes. Apart from the forehead horns and smoke-for-legs, his form was mostly human from the waist up. The goatee looked gnarled and twisted enough to be charred tree-bark more than hair, aside from which he was hairless. Though slender and wiry, this one wasn't ripped like the average shirtless summons of

Hollywood, but somehow seeing the lines of his ribs made him much more frightening.

My feet could have been cemented to the floor for all the movement I managed out of them.

The bird on my hand, still in my shirt, rang out, "Hello!"

I don't know if this startled the demon—do demons get startled?—or if he saw the knife in my hand—*paring* knife with a three-inch blade. Either way, he reacted.

He thrust forward one palm, and, though he didn't make contact, a surge of force smacked against my collarbone and neck and drove me back. My shoulder clipped the bookshelf en route to drywall but seemed not to damage the books—priorities. The wave knocked several pens and one apple from the desk, which rolled on the floor until it hit my toe. Apparently, my feet dangled just barely off the ground.

The choke-hold pinned more than choked, so I was able to get a few words out. "Okay! Letting go." I held the negligible knife out and away from me, then let it fall. "Let's talk."

Not my most eloquent speech, but it did the trick.

The demon lowered me to the floor, my back sliding down the wall, shoulder blades smarting.

"And this," I said, revealing the parrot, who still appeared relatively unruffled, "just a bird. Not a weapon."

"Of course not," the voice boomed, harmonizing with itself in a manner I would have found cool in any other circumstance.

Current circumstances involved mental images of human sacrifice or torture or at the very least being dragged into some hell dimension. Perhaps I was being too pessimistic: maybe this would be one of those invitations to go on a portal fantasy quest or maybe an alien encounter from one of the *Childhood's End* overlords. My optimism seemed to be misfiring. At least I wasn't dead.

"No disrespect intended," I tried, "but why are you here?"

The demon raised an eyebrow. Though he didn't have pupils, I was pretty darn sure his gaze flicked to my open laptop, whose screen was still dominated by a pulsing glyph.

Gesturing an open palm between his unholiness and the literally smoking laptop, I relented. "Okay, yes, that. But that was an accident."

"The letter is the law," the demon said, like this was casual information.

"Okay." Inhale, exhale, try to not to faint. "What does it mean?"

"The arrangement of the symbols is clear. You summon my person to your shrine for one purpose," he explained, which, if I took away the horns, smoke, and painful slamming against walls, sounded downright genial, if a bit dramatic. "We are under contract for an exchange of a favor, a wish…"

Whole-body dread moved like mercury through my veins.

"…for a soul."

Shit. I didn't say that out loud. I didn't dare speak and accidentally trip the *you already made your wish* switch. *Shit—double-shit—on a shit-sundae.* I looked down at Lutra, little red-faced bird standing pretty as you please on my fingers, who had managed far worse than I ever could have anticipated. Killing me would have been bad, but damning my literal immortal soul?

And it's not like the wish would work. I'd read too many of these stories; I knew that any wish to a crossroads demon or a djinn would come back to bite you long before the soul entered the equation. So where was the loophole? Had the paring knife been an actual threat? Or was I pretty much screwed because I failed to follow a simple *no pets on keyboards* policy?

Speaking very carefully, I asked, "What kinds of clarifying questions may I ask before making my… request?"

The demon threw back his head and roared. Maybe he'd read the stories in which the pathetic mortals had outsmarted his kind and was equally prepared.

He spent the better part of a minute howling and hooting to himself, clutching his emaciated sides.

Lutra imitated his laughter—thanks again, bird.

Shaking his head and grinning, the demon said, "No, mortal. I have no contract with you! I am here for the red-breasted beauty whom we both serve."

I could have protested any part of that explanation, but I echoed, "Serve?" However, I couldn't deny that I was literally carrying the parrot and had been out fetching her a treat when this snafu started. Sudden relief flooded me; I'd dodged a bullet of the ultimate existential dread.

Recognizing the spotlight, she said, "Hello, Lutra!"

"Master Lutra." The demon gave a formal bow, demonstrating how flexible one can be with smoke for legs. "I am Ahtram'Nesredep—or just Ahtram, if you prefer—humbly at your service, ready to receive your wish."

I couldn't be sure if I was spelling the name correctly, and it sounded like it came out of an online djinn generator, but I couldn't care about that at the moment. The rest of the pieces were falling into place—any powerful being who finds someone like me imprisoning their master under a T-shirt and holding a knife is bound to assume ill-intent—but one important factor cured me of my brief relaxation. "Wait! Wait, you're going to take her soul?"

"Of course," Ahtram said, somehow less frightening now that I thought of him by name. "It is the nature of the contract. I provide something that the mortal could not obtain for themselves, and in return I claim their soul upon death. Such a time-honored tradition must be maintained."

Up until that moment, I'd never considered the possibility of a parrot soul and the threats that might befall it. Besides, I knew that in Lutra's life, pretty much *everything* needed to be provided to her. Once again, my brain went to loopholes.

Ahtram drifted closer. "Master Lutra, what is it you desire?"

"Wait!" The stalling tactic was artless, but I needed time to think. "You—um—can you give her a list of options? Some way to select the right thing?"

Ahtram seemed annoyed and might have rolled his pupilless eyes.

"Maybe we could call in a bird translator," I said. "Does your service include that option?"

Then Lutra asked, "Apple?"

Shit. No chance to intervene. My parrot had sold her soul for an apple.

Ahtram narrowed his eyes at her, then turned his head toward my laptop. He brought a hand up to stroke his solid goatee. Then he requested, "A moment," and vanished.

The smoke remained, the ring on the floor remained, and Lutra remained unharmed on my hand. "What the…"

Ahtram *poofed* back into the room, this time wearing spectacles and carrying a clipboard. "Master, I must apologize," he said, his deep voice still booming but no longer harmonizing with itself. "The corporation you requested is—as the phrase goes—above my pay grade. I am afraid it has been tied up in too many contracts already, which are not in my power to undo. Perhaps you would care for a different entity, one less restricted?"

Lutra reprised, "Apple."

"I see." Ahtram sighed. With a flick of his wrist, he erased the summoning glyph from my screen. "As I cannot provide your request, our contract is void. I bid you a good evening."

He began to swirl the smoke around him.

"Wait!" Maybe that wasn't smart, but I had to know. "That's it?"

"Yes," the demon said through the smoke, "unless you want me to clean up your office."

"No!" I yelled, heart thudding in my chest. "I can do that myself."

The demon vanished, leaving a charred ring in my carpet, a few bruises that would heal, and a printer whose warranty had expired anyway.

Both Lutra and I would live, thanks to a logo on the back of my laptop and her favorite treat.

"I don't know whether to be mad or impressed," I remarked, seeing as she somehow undid most of the damage she had caused.

I set my parrot back on my shoulder and crouched to collect the apple that had rolled onto the floor. I was reaching for the knife when, having gone too long without a treat, the bird let out a blood-curdling shriek, right in my ear.

Did that hurt worse than being slammed against the wall? You bet your soul it did.

About the Author

Mike Jack Stoumbos is an author and educator, living with his wife and their parrot in Richmond, VA. He is a 1st-place winner of the Writers of the Future contest and the author of the space opera novel series THIS FINE CREW.

Find his publications and newsletter at MikeJackStoumbos.com

Raven *(Corvus corax)*

The second of our corvid installments, the raven, is larger than the American crow and so widespread throughout the northern hemisphere that many cultures have developed mythologies and folklore around them, especially in association with death

An Unkindness

by Rebecca E Treasure

The summer we went hunting dead relatives, the ravens haunted me.

We left on a Sunday before sunlight crested the plains, pulling out of the driveway to set off on an adventure—taking advantage of the sparkling new car, an unfamiliar luxury. Usually, a cousin would visit, but this summer belonged to the road. The stench of the gold sedan Mom won for selling beauty products teased at my nose, sharp and hard. In my lap, a borrowed CD player spun drums and synth into my headphones, just below the volume where Mom would tell me to turn it down.

We lurched forward and Dad slammed on the brakes as a garbage truck roared down the road.

"Close one," he said, chuckling.

The giant wheels growled past my window. The thought of what it would feel like to be ground underneath those wheels—to be crushed and broken and smeared like so much crunchy peanut butter—consumed me. I closed my eyes against the sick intensity, the fascinating reality of the feeling.

When I opened them, a raven swooped past my now-moving window.

Then another.

And another.

Sleek and glistening, oil slicks with feathers and beady eyes not quite meeting mine. They cawed, drifting into the distance. I mentioned them to my parents, but Mom said, "Your father is driving," without looking up from the multi-state map neatly marked with our lengthy route. Dad chuckled something about my imagination.

I didn't mention them again.

♦ ♦ ♦

When I was nine, my aunt died. Mom picked me up from school early. I got called in from swinging on the tall playground swings. Mom wore this look on her face. Like every muscle in her face had tensed all at once, like her eyes were trying to claw their way out of her face, like her spine sizzled with electricity and pain.

♦ ♦ ♦

Meandering south from a mile high down toward where a river split two countries, we hit every dying mainstreet and ghost town for hundreds of miles around.

Death dominated our drive. We scoped out abandoned cemeteries in towns only inhabited by edifice and worms. Mom's grandmother died from an ectopic pregnancy here, Dad's great-uncle installed the first phone lines here. Untended graves overgrown by sage and juniper pine, dusty greens becoming death's perfume. Would my gravestone still stand in a century and more? We stopped in two-room libraries in one-stoplight towns and flipped through microfiche looking for death and birth announcements. I imagined my name in those sepia tones, a bland description of a brutal end.

Everywhere we went, the ravens followed.

In the roofless rafters of an old barn, on the tattered red awning of a hometown diner, on a sagebrush leaning over the cracked concrete of a hotel pool. No one else seemed to see them, hear their empty caws, but I couldn't escape them.

The certainty in my gut grew. Every semi we passed on the highway caused my jaw to clench, my eyes to water, my breath to quicken. I'd stare, horrified, fascinated, at the black and gray wheels with tread as wide as my hand. Stare and wait for the inevitable.

One of these trucks would kill me.

The ravens were an omen. A warning. I hoped the fact that only I saw them meant my parents would live. I tried to convince myself it was okay. At fourteen, I'd lived something of a life. I'd seen pain and hurt, caused and been both.

I didn't want to die most of the time. When I did consider dying, family ghosts came to mind—one particular uncle, a second cousin, a great-grandfather. Deaths by their own hands stayed mine. Those wounds still scarred our family. Dead ends, in the end, leaving the living with no exit but revisiting the path already trod.

But I knew, down to my toes, that one of those trucks would careen into our lane and send that brand new car spinning across the graying grass. Or cross the yellow line and hit us head on, crunch us like a soda can. I watched the ravens circle wherever we went and waited for death.

Pueblo. Roswell. Carlsbad. Our family adventure continued, tracing deaths back into the distant past while the promise of death clung to me like maggots.

I kept not dying.

♦ ♦ ♦

When I was eleven, my grandmother died. Mom wore that face when she came in from a church meeting. "Who?" I'd asked, and she told me. The old woman who had stacks and stacks of romance titles cluttering low bookshelves throughout her house, who always gave me wafer cookies out of a clear jar on an otherwise empty counter. They tasted like sugar and shards of glass. Mom and I had cried together in the kitchen, then went and bought a box of those cookies.

♦ ♦ ♦

We reached a border town flattened out by politics and heat. The roofs reflected the desert sun in hazy waves, like the roads and sands. Even the cactus shimmered, squat and pressed upon.

We visited a house that screamed of wrongness. I sat on the ash-dusted couch and watched television shows I'd never be allowed at home, braced for death. Deaths on the screen bounced off me like plastic balls in a fast-food ball pit, inconsequential compared to my own short future.

The phone rang. A raven screamed.

When Mom came in from outside, the phone clutched in her hands like the limp body of a dead child, I knew.

"Who?"

"Not now."

"Someone died." Mom didn't react except to hug the phone closer. "Who is it?"

"Not now!"

"Just tell—"

"No!" she screamed at me. In the echo, she whispered, "Go to bed."

I went. In the dark, I inhaled second-hand cigarette smoke wafting through vents and listened to coyotes howl and tried to figure out who had died. And why she hadn't told me. Outside the window, ravens cawed gently into the sandy dusk.

They hadn't been for me. They'd been a warning.

White Sands. Grandma?

Alamogordo. My best friend?

Four Corners. A family friend?

I begged Mom to tell me until she broke down in tears and Dad lost his temper, which never happened. I sank into angry, furious, bitterness, the music up louder than allowed, echoing into my ears. The ravens swarmed our car like flies on a piece of long dead meat.

We trundled up the spine of the continent toward home. Every semi that passed grumbled a mockery.

Not you, they said.

But who, my soul shrieked in response.

We descended into my hometown, gray and lifeless under a shroud of ravens. What empty space sunk while I was away? Who did I mourn without knowing their name? Face after face, name after name, connection after connection formed and shattered and reformed in my mind as I tried to fathom the loss of someone I loved, must have loved deeply, or Mom would tell me. This new death already consumed my very soul, my every waking moment, and my dreams.

We unpacked on a Friday. Not until Sunday did Mom finally sit me down with our family pastor. Mom blinked reddened eyes at the pastor, still refusing to see me.

Through the gauzy gray curtains of the pastor's office, the ravens cawed, almost drowning out the pastor's words. "Your Mom didn't know how to tell you. Your cousin killed himself last Sunday."

The ravens vanished. Silence and cold avalanched me, buried me alive.

We'd met as kids, browned alongside crappy apartment pools, fished in cold mountain streams, sucked on lollipops in the filth of our grandmother's home. When his mom died in a drunken car accident, we'd played together on the plush carpet of the funeral home. He visited my family every summer. Dropped out of school at twelve to do an adult's work herding sheep in his town of eighty people in the far north. He would have been visiting but for our road trip.

And I hadn't even thought of his name.

If I had, would it have been someone else?

I'd thought of distant relatives, old friends, people I barely knew, but not him. The ravens mocked me all along. He'd died when I saw the first black wing. Not only would I live, but I would live with the knowledge that when I considered those I could lose, those I would grieve, those in my heart, he hadn't been there. They had gone, but they would never leave me.

Mom reached out a hand to comfort me.

I screamed, reminiscent of a raven.

About the Author

Rebecca grew up reading in the Rockies. After living many places, including the Gulf Coast & Tokyo, she began writing fiction. Rebecca's short fiction has been published by or is forthcoming from Flame Tree, WordFire Press, Galaxy Press, and others. She is an Associate Editor at Apex Magazine, a freelance editor, and a writing mentor. She juggles children, corgis, a violin studio, editing, and writing. She only drops the children occasionally.

Great-Tailed Grackle *(Quiscalus mexicanus)*

A small black bird with a long black tail, often mistaken for a crow in appearance, but markedly more elaborate in vocalizations

Obsidian Grackle

by Desmond Astaire

SAN ANTONIO – *President Victoria Woodhull survived an assassination attempt today at approximately 1:14 p.m. shortly after disembarking Air Force One at Randolph Air Force Base, Texas.*

In a joint statement, the White House and the Pentagon said that one Airman with the base's 902nd Security Forces Squadron has been detained in connection with the death of a Secret Service agent assigned to the president's security detail. The Pentagon did not name the Airman but did say the service member is currently undergoing evaluation by the Wilford Hall Medical Center Inpatient Psychiatry Flight at Lackland Air Force Base.

Neither agency revealed the homicide's connection to the assassination attempt, citing the ongoing investigation.

◆ ◆ ◆

Day 1

It shouldn't be possible to fall asleep while marching, but I could do it a few paces at a time. All thirty-two of us in Flight 496 spent ridiculous amounts of time in Basic Training practicing marching in formation, stepping in endless circles around the parade grounds. Between our drill sergeant's hypnotic bellow of *"One, two, three, four!"* and San Antonio's blistering heat, I could even catch a few split-second dreams while my feet worked on autopilot. Thus, I wasn't entirely sure at first if I was dreaming or actually hearing the birds talk to me.

Chirp-chirp-chirp-chirp-chirp, screeeee, screeeee, blip-blip, blip-blip, chirp-chirp-chirp.

The big 'ole black blackbird's screeches and clicks sounded artificial. Robotic. Like a dial-up internet modem, but coming out of a living creature. I made the mistake of turning my head to birdcalls, lost my pacing, and marched right into the guy in front of me.

No, no, no, no, no, oh crap*!*

The unholy shadow of U.S. Air Force Staff Sgt. Jeremy Reynolds swooped in on me as I recovered, and the brim of his drill sergeant's Smokey Bear hat bounced off the side of my head as the flight and I continued forward perfectly in step. The outward composure required of me did not reflect the *please-just-kill-me-now* regret seizing my chest.

"Hey, crazy! Hey, crazy! What in the holy name of Hap Arnold are you looking at, Trainee Dawes? What's more flippin' pertinent than the back of your flipping fellow trainees' head while marching in the *position of attention?*" Staff Sgt. Reynolds screamed. His breath smelled so impeccably minty that my stomach lurched. It took everything to keep my face locked forward so that I didn't dare look away again.

"Sir, nothing, sir!"

"Then you must have *brain damage*! I didn't realize that *left-right-left* was going to be such a hardship for your handicapped sensibilities, you useless sack of numbnuts. Are the recruiters sending *brain-damaged* trainees to join the world's finest Air Force?"

"Sir, no, sir!"

"Flight, *halt*!" Staff Sgt. Reynolds called. The formation came to a crisp stop, and the drill sergeant propped himself inches from my ear to whisper at me. Drill sergeant whispers were far worse than screaming. "Trainee Dawes, why are you here? If you want to get washed out, just say the word, and I'll make it happen right here, right now, no problem."

"Sir, no, sir! I'm here because I want to serve my country, sir!" I said.

Then the screaming resumed. "How about you start serving your country by mastering the simple act of *left-right-left*, you oxygen-wasting son of a *America's Got Talent* reject! *HUA!*" Staff Sgt. Reynolds hollered so loud that the entire flight's boots shook.

"Sir, yes, sir!"

"Trainee Dawes, step out of formation." I did. "Place your head between your legs." I did that too. "Now say 'pop.'"

"Pop!"

"Louder, so Jesus can hear you!"

"*Pop!*"

"Do you know what that sound is?" Staff Sgt. Reynolds asked.

"Sir, Trainee Dawes reports as ordered: That's the sound of me pulling my head out of my ass," I said.

"*HUA!* So now, please ex[*cac-cac-cac-cac*] to me why you are *[blip-blip]*ing up my *[screeeeee]* formation, Trainee Dawes!"

Stress's adrenaline assured me I was awake, but I could've sworn that bird had just chirped over top the goliath voice of drill sergeant Staff Sgt. Reynolds.

"Sir: I'm confused at what you said, sir!" I said.

"*Holy [cac-cac-cac-cac]!* How many canteens of water have you had today, Trainee Dawes?" the drill sergeant demanded.

I tried to blink the salty sweat out of my eyes to see the bird behind Staff Sgt. Reynolds, sitting on the steaming blacktop a stone's throw away—large, slender, and obsidian black with neon yellow eyes. The great-tailed grackle—very common to the Lackland Air Force Base area, I would later learn. It looked right into me. Beckoning my attention. *Demanding* it.

"Sir… um—"

I couldn't focus on anything Staff Sgt. Reynolds said. Something emanated from that stupid bird like a magnetic radio wave, shooting right into my head. It twisted my vision, and the ground shifted under me until I had no choice but to grab Staff Sgt. Reynolds's arm for support.

"*Goddd* flippin' bless 'Merica!" Staff Sgt. Reynolds yanked another uniform out of formation. "Trainee Moussa, escort Trainee Dawes to sick call, and do not come back until he is rehydrated, miraculously healed of brain damage, or declared *[wheeeeeee]*ing *dead*!"

This is when I first learned of the obsidian grackle.

Day 8

The best duty assignment to get during Basic Training was "KP duty"—kitchen patrol. Sure, it meant working in the dining facility for fourteen hours straight, but we could eat as much as we wanted, and the drill sergeants didn't mess with us because they were too busy harassing the flights coming in for meals. Thus, no one would notice if I didn't come back inside right away from taking trash to the dumpster.

When I got outside, one of those robot-voiced grackles sat perched on top of the dumpster lid. I'd seen them more and more over the last week. I swear they were following me. This one was waiting for me to come outside. It didn't fly away when I got close. It wanted me to come closer.

"Hey there, fella," I said. "I need to get this trash in there."

The bird cocked its head, and its yellow eyes glowed fluorescent. *"Cac-cac-cac. Blip-blip, blip. Wheeeeeee. Cac-cac-cac-cac-cac."*

I felt tipsy suddenly, and it made me chuckle. "You sound like a computer."

"Wheeeeeee. Cac-cac-cac-cac-cac." The grackle ruffled its feathers in what I thought might be irritation.

"Are you trying to tell me something?"

"Cac-cac-cac-cac. Blip-blip."

The grackle leveled its neon irises at me and beamed the invisible, magnetic bridge into my mind. The connection pummeled me on the forehead and paralyzed my body in the most hypotonic way, multitudes stronger in power than the experience on the parade field. It drowned out anything else around me. And then I could see something in my head. Letters. Numbers. Hazy at first, undefined in my mind's eye.

"Cac-cac-cac-cac. Blip-blip."

"'4b?' I don't know what that means," I mumbled. The black bird flapped its wings in a radiant outburst, and it jumped sense back into me. "Okay, okay!"

I regained the use of my hands and pulled out the notepad I was required to carry. I began writing the letters and numbers I heard in the pings, clicks, and whirls of the blackbird's call. The alphanumeric series scribbled in pen at the end of the bird's vocal volley read "4b696c6c."

I looked back to my grackle for any answer, but before I could ask, the dining facility backdoor swung open and clattered against the brick wall.

The bird startled and launched into the air.

"Dawes, what the hell are you doing? The dinner flights are about to come in. Let's go," Moussa said.

"Yeah… Sorry," I said, watching the bird escape into the distance.

4b696c6c. I could see and feel it with absolute clarity, yet I had no idea what the code meant. The crackle left me only with an undeniable sensation that it was a message delivered to me.

This is when I first learned the obsidian grackle was talking to me.

◆ ◆ ◆

Day 27

The M16 rifle is a gas-operated, closed rotating bolt, semi-automatic rifle. It fires forty-five to sixty 5.56-millimeter NATO rounds per minute. It has a maximum effective range of 3,600 meters, with a point target range of 500 meters and an area target range of 600 meters. Do not point the barrel at anything you do not intend to shoot, maim, kill, or destroy. Keep your finger off the trigger and the safety on until you are ready to shoot. Treat all weapons as if they were loaded.

These were weapons specifications we were required to memorize and recite before rifle qualifications on the range—attention to detail, respect for the weapons system, so on and so forth.

I understood the fundamentals of shooting the rifle well enough: line up the front sight with the rear sight and slowly squeeze the trigger with the pad of your finger.

The pop-up targets were the problem. When they'd jump up, I'd flinch and squeeze too hard, throwing off my aim. I'd missed nine of the twelve so far, and Staff Sgt. Reynolds was not happy. The drill instructors weren't allowed to torment us while we were operating live weapons, but I could feel the frustration radiating off him, enough for me to stress even more. A few more missed shots, and they would recycle me backward a week or two in Basic Training or kick me out altogether. I wouldn't survive that.

And then, wouldn't you know it, one of those great-tailed grackles chose now—of all moments—to come over and harass me.

The bird perched itself at the end of the firing range—abnormal because normally the gunfire would scare off any wildlife within earshot. I tried to ignore it, focusing downrange where the next pop-up target might jump.

"*Screeeee!*"

The grackle's screech surprised me, and I accidentally pulled the trigger. My shot hit a target square center mass, and it toppled over. *Perfect* timing.

"Finally! Nice shot, Trainee Dawes!" Staff Sgt. Reynolds hollered. "Whatever you did, do it again."

"*Chirp, screeeee, blip-blip, blip-blip.*"

I glanced over to my blackbird. It dipped its head to me, yellow eyes pulsating like a traffic caution light. I could see the letters and numbers in my head again, like my mind was automatically translating the bird's voice into alphanumeric code.

53686F6F74.

I put my attention back on the firing range and readied my rifle.

"*53686F6F74!*" the grackle screeched.

Okay, bird, whatever you say.

I pulled the trigger. Another perfect shot and the pop-up target toppled over.

"*53686F6F74!*"

Another target down.

"*53686F6F74!*"

Again.

"*53686F6F74!*"

Again.

"Holy mother of Moses, Trainee Dawes just decided to become a sharpshooter," Staff Sgt. Reynolds screamed. "Keep it up, and you're on track for the marksmanship ribbon!"

I emptied the magazine and slapped a new one into the rifle. Before releasing the bolt forward, I looked over to the bird and gave it a nod. I don't know if it could hear me, but I whispered "thank you" anyway. I owed it.

This is when I first learned to listen to the obsidian grackle.

Day 93

Most of my flight left Lackland Air Force Base for their tech school after graduating from Basic Training. The Air Force assigned me to the Security Forces career field, and that tech school was just a few blocks from the Basic Training dorms. My bus—a whole five-minute ride—left Flight 496 last, and I swear I saw tears of pride blossoming in Staff Sgt. Reynolds's eyes as we loaded up.

"See you in the field, crazies. *HUA!*" he said right before the bus doors closed.

Security Forces served as the Air Force's ground combat force and military police service, so the Security Forces Academy taught us many weapons and fighting skills, including rifle fighting techniques—using our rifles as striking devices. But since practicing with seven pounds of bayonet-equipped steel was a terrible safety hazard, we ran drills with pugil sticks.

The foam-padded staff could still pack quite a wallop if wielded right, though.

A great-tailed grackle circled overhead one hot morning during rifle fighting practice, cheering me on with wild screeches and screams.

"*4B696C6C! 4B696C6C! 4B696C6C!*" over and over again.

Eventually, it became a distraction, and my sparring partner landed a solid slash right to the side of my head. I suppose the helmet provided some protection, but the crack and flash of light overtook me.

The next thing I saw was half my class and an instructor standing over me, beckoning me back to life. Their faces blurred in and out of triple vision.

"Can you hear me, Defender?" the instructor said, his words echoey and distant. "Can you tell me your name and rank?"

"Airman Basic," I muttered. "Andy Dawwww—" I rolled onto my side and upchucked my stomach contents onto the grass.

"Yep, that's a concussion," the instructor said.

I could still see the shadow of the black grackle gliding its circle around me in the sky, keeping its yellow eyes on me, still doing its job and broadcasting its message.

Which I could hear clearly now. Through the disoriented vision, the pain shooting down the skull, and sloshing nausea, I honed my ears because I could listen to the bird differently now. The letters and numbers were replaced by plain English words in the same tone and pitch as the bird's robotic clicks and screeches.

"*Kill! Kill! Kill!*"

This is when I first learned to understand the obsidian grackle.

Day 110

Graduation day from the Security Forces Academy meant that we had crossed the threshold from being students to becoming active-duty Airmen. The next day, we'd all ship out to our first duty stations to start the rest of our lives, carrying everything we owned in the duffels across our backs. The last eighteen weeks of military indoctrination had been a fiery crucible designed to stress-test us until collapse, but we'd survived it. I'd survived it.

That night being our final night together, my class stuck our brand-new stainless-steel Security Forces badges in our pockets and celebrated at the base bowling alley with cheap beer and greasy pizza.

The news was ablaze about worldwide protests against the Saudi Arabian War. Apparently, something like 150,000 protesters had gathered in Washington, D.C., alone that day. "Blah, blah, blah," we spat back at the TV. But when President Woodhull came on-screen to make her statements, we cheered and toasted our pint glasses to her. Chances were that within a year, we'd all be deployed somewhere in the Middle East chasing down terrorists in the name of the Red, White, and Blue. "Bring it on," we said in our drunken stupors.

I did a shot with some girl, and we exited the bowling alley shortly after that for a smoke break—nothing like nicotine to chase down the booze. A great-tailed grackle sat atop the dumpster fence, waiting for me.

"Awww, come on, man, not tonight," I protested. "Can you give me a minute?" I asked the girl.

"But I thought we were coming out here for some privacy," she said.

"Just give me a minute!" I snapped back, and she sulked back inside.

I clicked my lighter several times—missing the cig several times thanks to the Earth's balance being off—until my smoke ignited. "Alright, just kidding. Whatcha got for me?"

"Kill the dragon! Kill the dragon!"

Something about the grackle's tone sobered me up faster than nature intended. This message felt different. Complete. Whole. Final. My smoke fell out of my mouth, but I couldn't bother picking it up.

"What the hell?" I asked. "What the hell's 'the dragon?'"

The bird flipped its head up several times, motioning behind me. I turned and saw the bar TV through the windows. The news replayed President Woodhull's remarks on the Invasion of Saudi Arabia campaign.

"Kill the dragon! Kill the dragon!"

I don't remember the rest of the night. I only remember those words echoing over and over. My first duty station was Randolph Air Force Base thirty-five minutes away, and I transferred there the next day with a good hangover. They had great-tailed grackles there too. I saw the big black birds a good handful of times over the next year, just frequently enough to never let me forget. And they never said anything new.

The message never changed after that night at the bowling alley. It was always the same for the next five months, and it always seemed to show up alongside a mention of the U.S. president. It seemed conspicuously obvious.

Kill the dragon.

This is when I first learned the intent of the obsidian grackle.

But when the time came to "kill the dragon," would I be able to pull the trigger? What kind of mission did these obsidian grackles have me on? And, of course, the most obvious question: What if I was making this all up in my head?

I'm not. But what if?

♦ ♦ ♦

Day 256

The Security Forces life at Randolph Air Force Base was more mundane than I imagined. I was one of the new guys, so all I did was check IDs at the Main Gate.

Twelve hours a day. Two days on, one training day, two days off. Rinse, repeat. Days, weeks, months.

Thankfully, my obsidian grackles were always there to keep me company.

There was a short time after I got to Randolph that I considered the talking blackbirds might have been a figment of my imagination, maybe hallucinations from the stress of basic training and tech school. I almost went to see Behavioral Health about it. Almost.

But my grackles appeared again shortly after I started working the graveyard shift—consistently delivering the same message but catching my attention at the correct times to keep me out of trouble with my sergeants. It couldn't be a coincidence. I even came to think of them as my good luck charm.

There were more grackles than usual flying around the base today. Today was my first presidential security detail. No complaints about working a twenty-hour shift; I always presumed it'd also be my last.

The Secret Service took the lead for presidential visits to the base, but my squadron—along with local law enforcement and FBI—would provide the extra security framework for a smooth visit. President Woodhull was in town to visit San Antonio for her re-election tour, so of course, she made time to shake the hands of veterans corralled behind a barricade along the flightline. Since the Security Forces Squadron had to be on duty for the distinguished visitor event, the consolation prize for us high performers was being paired up with interagency counterparts. That day, I got to work at a long-range observation post on top of one of the Randolph Air Force Base towers with a Secret Service Counter Sniper Team member.

My flight chief escorted me up the tower and introduced me to Stan.

"This is one of the 902nd's star performers, Airman Dawes," the flight chief said. "He's on track to get an M-4 designated marksman slot, so we thought he could shadow you today."

Stan did not extend a handshake. Stan seemed uneasy.

"Good to meet you," Stan said. The flight chief left us, and the countersniper eyeballed me. "Just do me a favor and keep your weapon on Safe and your barrel down, okay?"

"Sure thing," I said.

Stan didn't say much as he set up his gear and dialed in his scope. Some guys were just intense like that. Stan seemed to have a lot on his mind. I'd never met a Secret Service agent before. Maybe they were all like that.

Before too long, a single great-tailed grackle took its perch with us on top of the tower.

"Kill the dragon! Kill the dragon! Kill the dragon!" it screamed at me.

It was almost time. I was chatty and nervous, and I didn't care now if it made Stan uncomfortable.

"What are you zeroed in for?" I asked him, just out of occupational curiosity.

"200 meters," Stan said. His face reacted as soon as the sentence left his lips as if he had just disclosed classified information. Weird. "For close-quarter threats," he backpedaled.

"Cool," I said. Priming the rifle for that close of a distance didn't make sense, but I played it off like I was just happy to be there. Stan seemed to relax at my naïvete.

"Here, take a look," he said, handing me his spotting scope. It was nicer than anything we had in the unit, so I entertained myself by measuring out different points of the flight line. I noted that the barricades where the president would first shake veteran hands were almost precisely 200 meters out from our position. But I still noticed Stan texting on his cell phone out of the corner of my eye. I noticed because it was a flip phone, not a smartphone. Like a burner. The kind you threw away when you were done.

Air Force One landed some time later. My grackle didn't fly away from the noise of the Boeing 747. All the pomp and circumstance unrolled as planned, and before we knew it, President Woodhull was halfway from Air Force One to the barricades. I flipped on the M68 close combat optic on my rifle and discreetly looked down it to make sure I could see the red dot. The battery looked good. M9 pistol on my hip for backup. Ready to engage.

Stan looked at his flip phone one last time before putting it in his gear bag. He closed the bag up, and it flopped over, showing its front side. On it was an assortment of velcro patches—not uncommon for guys in our line of work to collect, but one, in particular, grabbed my attention. An exhale of relief ripped out of my lungs, and I almost had to turn away to collect myself before tears exploded from me. God bless those beautiful grackles.

Stan's nametag velcroed to his bag itself was not abnormal, but some of the consonants and vowels popped out at me most conspicuously.

"Wow. That last name's a mouthful," I said. "What is that, Polish? How do you pronounce that?"

Stan didn't look away from his scope. "*Druhs-gone-ski*. Drzazgownski. Everyone calls me 'Dragon' for short."

My eyes panned over to my obsidian crackle, and it screeched and thrashed its wings in a massive display of victory. I gave it a final nod. Of appreciation, I guess? Hindsight is very much twenty-twenty, but the grackles had always been diligent. Now I understood. Perfect hindsight. Clear direction.

President Woodhull was a half-dozen paces from the barricades. She already had her hands out to greet the first veteran. I'm sure Stan didn't think I noticed, but I watched him shift the safety off his rifle with his non-shooting hand.

"Hey, kid, do me a favor," Stan said. "My radio battery died." It hadn't. I could still hear unintelligible bits of radio chatter spilling out of his earpiece. "Can you go down and get another one out of the black suburban?"

I unlocked the safety of my hip holster, tightened my grasp around the pistol grip, and flipped the thumb safety back to "fire"—very slowly so Stan couldn't hear the clicks. He was so hyper-focused on his scope that I doubt he'd even realize if I needed to chamber a round. Stan was sweating profusely, exhaling hard out of his nostrils. It was Texas hot, but not *that* hot.

"Sure thing, man," I said.

"Kill the dragon! Kill the dragon!"

"And could you get rid of that *[screeee]*ing bird while you're up?" Stan asked.

I pulled my pistol out of the holster and leveled it at the back of Stan's head.

"Absolutely."

This is when I first learned to obey the obsidian grackle. Surely, you must believe me now. Doesn't it all make sense?

About the Author

Desmond Astaire is an award-winning speculative fiction storyteller from Central Illinois, where he navigates the journey of life with his wife and son. In his other life, Astaire is the senior enlisted leader for a military public relations unit, supervising the training, development, and operations of multimedia content creators. His first publication was "Gallows" in 2022's *Writers of the Future Vol. 38*, for which he received the L. Ron Hubbard Golden Pen Award.

Emu, Ostrich, Cassowary

(*Dromaius novaehollandiae, Struthio camelus, Casuarius*)

Three distinct species of flightless bird, all from different locations but often closely associated with one another

…one of these is often considered the deadliest bird on earth

Doesn't Belong

by John Gleason

It wasn't the prettiest part of the continent, but the hot and dusty plain had been home for a long time. The rainy season brought plenty of water. There was food and shade provided by the many trees, making it the ideal place to build nests. As Emu took in the sight, he gave thanks for everything the plain held, giving life, providing a home… as long as you belonged, and that was the problem. The flock standing on the shore of the lake, the ostriches that Emu had been watching, did not belong. They were recent arrivals, intruders really. Emu wished they'd leave. The plain was his home and that of his flock. It had always been that way.

As a species, emu aren't tolerant creatures. Living together with other birds wasn't something they wanted to try, but even though they outnumbered the newcomers five to one, the emu were intimidated—as ostriches were three times their size. If nothing was done about this infestation, would the time come when the emu would have to look for a new home? Where would they go? Would there be food and water? What if there were predators? Who would protect them? Something had to be done about these damn birds!

"The plain is fine just the way it is," Emu said to himself. "It's always been that way." Emu knew he needed to seek the help of his friend, Cassowary.

◆ ◆ ◆

Cassowary was relaxing under the shade tree in the glade. He heard Emu approaching from a distance but waited to say anything until the visitor stepped into the clearing. The glade was surrounded by a stand of trees with a stream that cut through the center. In addition to shade, the trees provided plenty of berries for Cassowary to eat when he wasn't running down a more prized delicacy, such as a desert rat. Beyond the trees was a panoramic view where every animal who lived on the plain could be watched.

"Emu! How unexpected, but always nice to see you." Cassowary had a good idea of why Emu had come. "Can I offer you a drink, or some berries?"

"Nothing to eat thank you," Emu said, stepping up to the stream, "but I would like some water. The climb up here makes me thirsty."

"How many seasons have you lived on the plain," Cassowary asked, "and you get parched at such a small walk?"

Emu ignored the jab and continued to drink. The water tasted better, sweeter than anyplace else on the plain. He took another swallow, stood up and admired the view. Cassowaries had lived above the plain and in this glade for many seasons, it'd always been that way. They didn't take it through force or intimidation, they just—claimed it. Every animal who lived on the plain knew if they had a problem, they could climb the hill, talk to Cassowary, and it would be taken care of. As far as Emu could remember, no one had ever disagreed with a decision Cassowary made—ever. No one complained that it wasn't fair. He was pondering this when he realized he'd been asked a question. "Huh? I'm sorry, what did you say?"

"I said I'm a little busy right now," Cassowary repeated, leaning over to pick up a berry and swallowing it whole. "If this is a social call, could we do it another time?"

Usually at this kind of meeting, Emu spoke respectfully, in soft tones. But this mission called for a more direct approach, and he blurted out, "I want you to murder the ostriches," a little louder than usual.

Cassowary blinked twice, looked down at the ground, picked up another berry, and swallowed it. "Is that all? And what has the ostrich done to deserve this?"

Emu took another quick sip, shaking the remaining water off his beak before continuing. "Ever since the ostriches arrived, they've moved into our area, strutting around like they belong there. My flock can't go anywhere on the plain without running into one of those *buttfeathers*, eating our food and smelling up the place."

"I can see you're upset, but I don't allow that sort of language and you know it. I have chicks nearby who don't need to hear that," Cassowary said before returning to the subject. "So, after all these seasons, you haven't found a way to get along with the ostriches? Have they done something to you?"

Emu continued his tirade. "They don't belong here. You know that part of the plain has belonged to emu for as many seasons as anyone can remember. It's always been that way."

Cassowary mused a moment before answering. He found that taking a pause was often helpful to a visitor who was upset or nervous. "I believe two of the ostriches are adolescents, another is a chick," he said. "You want them killed too?"

The technique wasn't working with Emu, who shouted, "They don't BELONG HERE! You need to make them go."

Cassowary said nothing as he crossed over to the water. Keeping his back to Emu, he took a drink, longer than he needed, then straightened up and looked out at the plain. "You seem... determined."

"I'm sorry if I overstepped," Emu said, almost in a whisper, "but there is no compromise, and the solution is so obvious." Emu wanted to say more but he knew repeating himself wouldn't do any good, it'd just make him look dumb. He tried to get a read on Cassowary, to guess what he was thinking. If the answer was 'no', he wasn't sure what his flock could do.

"I see your point, my friend," Cassowary went back to the nest and settled into it. He nodded slightly, giving Emu hope that he hadn't made a fool of himself. "You do make sense. Should we allow the plain to become a dumping ground for any straggler or riff-raff who happens onto it?" Emu smiled and shook his head.

"Do we have a right to rule our land to the benefit of all, ensuring their safety and long life?" Emu nodded enthusiastically.

"If loathsome creatures aren't wanted, shouldn't they be made to keep on moving? And if they don't, we must motivate them to leave?"

Emu couldn't contain himself. He slapped Cassowary on the back saying, "Yes, yes, yes. I knew you'd understand."

It took Emu a minute to calm down. Cassowary waited, smiling and nodding. Then he leaned in close and whispered, "I'll find a solution, but I need time to think. Come back tomorrow and I'll let you know what we're going to do."

♦ ♦ ♦

The following morning, after bragging to his flock how he was able to show Cassowary the wisdom of his thinking, Emu began the short hike up the hill to the glade for his meeting, proud with himself for thinking like a leader. He'd taken charge and suggested a plan of attack. In the past, Emu had been in awe of Cassowary, even a little fearful. But now, surely, he'd be considered a peer, one who stood on equal footing, ready to consult or give advice. He was prepared for that challenge and continued to think about all the good things that could come to the plain. All this came to a crashing halt as he stepped into the glade and saw Ostrich drinking from the stream.

"Oh, there you are," Cassowary said, reclining on the nest, stretching out his wings in the shade of the tree. "Look who stopped by this morning. He said it was a social call, but I asked him to stay in light of what we discussed yesterday."

Emu could barely get the word out. "Dis…cussed?"

"You know, about the plain and how you felt about your flock having to share it with—what did you call him? *Buttfeather*?"

Rather than taking a deep breath and considering the situation, Emu's newfound confidence encouraged him to respond too quickly. "Never cared for their kind since they turned up here," Emu said flatly, keeping his eyes on Ostrich. "You keep telling everyone that you escaped from something called a…circus? Is that really what happened or did someone just dump you in the hills because they didn't want you either?"

Ostrich didn't bother to look up, casually taking another drink. He swallowed, shook his beak, and stepped out of the stream. "Oh no, we escaped. But what can I say? They couldn't catch us because we run faster than anyone else, and when we reached this wonderful place, we stopped running."

Emu kicked at the dirt, eyes darting to Cassowary. "We've shared this plain for more seasons than you can know. We've helped each other, respected each other. We know how to be neighbors, AND how to stay out of each other's way! Now these buttfeathers show up and take over. Well, they're not wanted!"

Ignoring Emu entirely, Ostrich turned his gaze to the plain. "There are aspects of this place that are similar to where my flock came from. It's called 'Africa'. Open land, good water, a climate perfect to raise a flock—

at least that's what my ancestor told me before we escaped. This is like the home he described, the one that was taken from him, so we decided to settle here and be the good neighbors you value…"

Emu was incensed at the casual way Ostrich described the situation. He wanted to knock this buttfeather to the ground and kick him down the hill, then watch as his whole flock beat it to anywhere else. "You're not wanted." His tone turned threatening. "And you don't belong, so it doesn't matter what you *want* to become."

Ostrich watched as Emu worked himself into a state of anger and frustration. Still, he kept his manner calm, which taunted the other bird. "You think you can run my flock out of here? Our presence isn't a crime."

Emu could no longer contain himself. Futilely flapping his wings, he jumped toward Ostrich and screamed, "If it were up to me, it would be!"

"But right now, it isn't!" Cassowary interrupted, "It's up to me, and I'm not going to let this get out of hand." He arose from the nest and approached Emu, bowing his head so it was slightly lower than his friend's. "We don't have to argue or get worked up. I promised to find a find a resolution, and I have."

Embarrassed at the unnecessary show he'd put on, Emu smiled at his friend. Anger drained from his system, his expression turning from disdain to smugness. This pea-brained *buttfeather* and his kind would be gone soon, and things could return to normal. Emu relaxed and took one deep breath, then another. In that moment he became so complacent he didn't notice the claw swinging toward his head.

Cassowary extended his middle talon mid-stroke, the claw tearing into Emu's face just below the beak. A bloody gash opened across Emu's throat as Cassowary ripped apart the esophagus and blood vessels. By the time Emu registered the pain, Cassowary had stepped back to avoid the splatter. In shock, his vocal cords in shreds and unable to speak, Emu fell over. The two other birds watched as he bled out.

"I was so tired of his whining and that never ending crap about how *'this is the way it's always been'*," Cassowary said, kicking the carcass. Satisfied that the bird would say no more, he looked up at Ostrich. "We're not going to have any issues, are we?"

Bringing himself up to his full height, a good two feet over Cassowary, Ostrich shook his head. "Are you kidding? We're fine," he said, looking at the dead bird. "He never saw it coming. But won't the rest of the emu flock be a problem? Won't they notice when he doesn't come back?"

"Doubtful. They're not that bright. It wouldn't occur to them that I killed him. And even if they did, they'll never come here. This one was their leader, and as you can see," Cassowary said, kicking again, "he wasn't very good at that. They'll never know."

"But there's still a flock."

"The emus may have ten or twelve eggs close to hatching. I've got the dingos going in tonight to take care of that, after they drag this one into the tall grass and… make him disappear. A few will stay, but without a leader, most will scatter looking for another place to live. In three seasons, maybe less, that entire section of the plain will be yours."

Ostrich nodded and left the glade. He took his time walking down the path, gazing out at that small part of the open area where they'd lived, keeping to themselves—but no more. Now, they could wander to any part of the plain they liked, and no one could do a thing about it. When he returned to the shore where his flock lived, the young were playing in the water. One adult remained in the nesting area, keeping an eye on the eggs that would soon hatch. The two greeted each other with short nods.

"Everything go as you'd hoped?"

"Yes. We won't have to be bothered with those damn emus again. This is our place now."

"And the cassowary?"

"For now, we exist together, but I don't trust him. We'll wait; five seasons, maybe more, then we'll deal with him," Ostrich said looking back on the plain and the glade in the distance. "The cassowary doesn't belong."

About the Author

John wrote his first story in the 6th grade, a vampire tale for a class publication. Worried that the theme might not be appropriate for a parochial school newspaper, the nun in charge of the class changed the lead character from vampire to martyr. That was the first time he had to deal with an editor. When not working as a broadcaster for a satellite radio service, John likes to dabble in acting and, of course, writing. He and his wife Niki live in Colorado with a pit bull named Frank.

Bearded Vulture *(Gypaetus barbatus)*

closely associated with extraterrestrial sapients

Lammeravians

A carnivorous bird with an unfeathered head, known for circling dead and dying carcasses

(for Lammeravians, see above)

Boneyard

by Wulf Moon

Captain Wanju "Blackjack" Bratawoolong worked his jutting jaw left and right, grunting under the force of positive G as his flight suit constricted around his abdomen, keeping the blood in his brain. His sleek two-man Assault Raptor sliced through the sky, bright as a silver saber, the words *Big Stick* stenciled below the pilot canopy in stygian black. The Raptor arced toward the upper atmosphere of Primor Five, leaving the landed transport ship with its troops far behind. Wanju blinked away tears to see the console—he hadn't used his eyes in six years, and the readouts shimmered like the heat haze rising off the dunes below.

"Just jerked from the cooler, blind as wombats at high noon, and they've already got us on ops," he said into the communicator. "Somebody screwed the 'roo."

Wanju's normally verbose second in the gun turret made no reply; Gunnery Sergeant Seamus O'Har was probably as grog-headed as Wanju from the thaw. Post cryonic disorientation, that's what the textbooks called it. Punch-drunk, that's what the Rangers called it. Dead man walking, that's what they called the unlucky bastard that had to go from immediate cryo thaw into a hot drop zone.

Wanju eased off on the yoke. The planet's horizon came into view with that familiar curve that only appeared at these altitudes. He spoke a command; a holosphere of O'Har appeared over the console. "Okay, listen up. Situation called for a birdie briefing, accent on *brief*. As you probably guessed, we've got unidentified *xenoi* on Primor Five; this is a meet and greet. Orders are to buy as much time as possible to pull troops from cryo; negotiate the return of poached ore; and serve them SC's official eviction notice."

Wanju sighed. Stellar Command's Brigadier Karenina had given him just enough conditions to start a war. He wanted nothing of it. Wanju was a warrior, descended from Aboriginals that had migrated across the stars to New Sidney. He had no desire to see another bloodbath where he had to tag the bodies of young men and ship them home.

"Why'd we get this mission?" O'Har asked. "Sounds like another soup sandwich."

"Hitch up your panties, O'Har. We're rangers of the One Hundred and Seventy-Fifth Airborne. When is the situation *not* as jacked up as a football bat?"

O'Har crossed himself. "When we're dead and buried."

"Got that right." *And if we fail today, men will die for the title deed to a sandbox.*

Wanju's bloodshot eyes still burned from cryo. Tears spilled, nearly blinding his vision. "Hell, gimme a sec." He touched the release on his helmet's gilded visor. It whisked up. He spoke a command. "Retract right glove."

Seams rippled and fabric crawled back like starfish appendages into the wrist ring. Wanju rubbed away matter and wiped tears from his eyes. He called out a thermostat adjustment on his suit—a multi-purpose flight suit, battle armor and environmental control unit, standard issue by Stellar Command to their Rangers of Interstellar Peace. The Rippers, as they called themselves, referred to the battle control armor as their BCs.

"That's better." He sealed the visor, tilted the Raptor's yoke; the wings yawed in response. He gazed out the tinted canopy. The land below baked under the glowing forge of Primor's sun as it spilled molten light across the red sand. The planet was an endless sea of sand, dune lapping upon dune, crested waves seeking some forgotten shoreline to batter their souls against.

"Ready to rumble, Sergeant. Weapons status?"

The Raptor shuddered; a thunderclap boomed. Mach One.

O'Har fingered the weapons console, eyes gleaming. "Stingers and bloodhounds primed and hot. Weight is heavy in the belly—you hiding Christmas presents in there, Blackjack?"

"Something like that. What about the cannons?"

"Plasma cannons cocked and the juice is boiling. Ready to rock."

"Roger that. *Big Stick* is up to bat. Just keep your didgies off the trigger unless I give the order. The carrier is covering us from any party crashers above, and Brigadier Karenina is pulling the slab from the cooler in the transport below. Let's hope we don't have to fire up the grill."

O'Har lifted a trembling hand. "Hope those slabs can shake the cryo-tremors before this thing gets hot, or we'll be in deep doo." He punched up the targeting system. "Whatever happened to the good old days when you could just shove a friggin' flag in the ground and shout, 'I claim thee for the King of Spain'?"

"We had one. Our discovery satellite. I'm sure the *xenoi* vaporized it the moment they arrived."

"Yeah, well Command would've logged rights to this dung heap with the Andromeda Consortium."

Wanju touched a sensor; a surveillance holo hovered to his right, fresh from the carrier in orbit. "Must think they can bypass interstellar mining regs with an older rule."

"Which one's that?"

"One my father taught me. *Possession is nine-tenths of the law.* What troubles me is the size of this operation—never seen squatters with equipment like this. You can bet we're both holding a straight flush, and we're wondering who's got the ace."

◆ ◆ ◆

Wanju and O'Har stood on a butte, highest in a scattering of monoliths that rose like broken teeth within the maw of a sand-swept valley. Behind them perched the Raptor, a sleek titanium falcon standing guard over her aerie, her silver wings stretched for preening, glinting in bloody sunlight. The ablation skin covering wings and fuselage displaced the remaining heat from hypersonic travel, hissing in irritation.

Destination was the valley floor, but the squatters had stipulated that any craft within a five-klick radius of their operations would be *bone crushed*. Weird translation. Fine by him, Wanju didn't want to risk sucking sand into the Raptor's intakes. Good way to get stranded.

With visors locked, air whispered through regulators at the base of their helmets. The chambers on their backs thrummed, augmenting supply by stripping nitrogen and oxygen from the thin atmosphere around them. The chameleon skin of their BCs lit with shades of silver that mimicked the sides of the Raptor's hull.

"Move out," Wanju said through the comm. Their BCs shifted to mottled patches of rust red and burnt orange, matching the cracked stone of the butte they crossed.

They came to the precipice. In the distance beyond the valley floor hunched a great wall of stone that stretched from horizon to horizon. To the far-right blossomed red ochre mushroom clouds—mining rigs at work, chewing and clawing at the base of the cliff, angry crabs ripping apart a carcass.

Wanju glanced at the blank combat team vid screens within his visor—a panel running down the left side. Only one was lit up. O'Har's image stared back at him, emerald eyes glittering under wiry copper brows.

"Feels like I'm standing naked in a church on Sunday," O'Har said. "Why leave the protection of the Raptor, Blackjack?"

"Part of the terms. I tried to counter. Squatters sent a transmission back that they wouldn't meet if we refused to pull away from our 'wing.' Want a face to face, measure us up. Prefer it that way myself." He paused. "How many species use the term *wing* for an assault Raptor?"

"Hell if I know." O'Har raised his arms overhead, stretching. "The comm was in Beck's Universal?"

"Yep."

"Figures. No clues till they're damn good and ready."

"They'll be tipping their hand soon enough. As soon as we see what's in it, I'll wire Core."

"Better be leaving their *wing* if we have to leave ours."

Wanju peered down the precipice; it was going to be a long drop. Wanju kicked dust and pebbles over the ledge, marking wind direction. "Dry as a dead dingo's donger, this place."

"Yeah, and hot as hell—gonna tap the reserves on our BC's."

"Then let's go have a Captain Cook, mate. Sooner we get down there, sooner we get back."

Wanju stretched out his arms. He focused on an icon in the control bar at the top of his visor. It dropped to center, expanding into translucent neon-blue lettering.

PROPULSION MODE
Lock BC Arms?
YES NO

As Wanju focused on YES, baffles in the arms of his BC stiffened, locking horizontally.

GAUNTLET FINGER CONTROL
YES NO

He focused on YES, flexed his fingers, felt a rumble in the wrist exhaust ports of his BC.

"Have a rage," Wanju said, jumping over the precipice, white vapor trails spurting from his gauntlets.

"Hooah!" O'Har said as he jumped.

They descended to the valley floor. Clouds of sand belched into the air, enveloping them in rust-colored haze. They struck the slope of a dune. Both men's legs buckled, pitching them forward.

"Jee-zus!" O'Har cursed, flat on his face in the sand. "We need more time to warm up! We're supposed to have twenty-four hours to thaw. This is bullshit, Blackjack." He rose, dusting himself off.

"Got caught with our pants down," Wanju said. "Roll with the punches, Sergeant."

"Just did, dammit."

Wanju proceeded down the ridge of sand, climbed to the top of the next dune. He scanned the crests, the troughs between each like rows of undulating serpents. A dune ahead seemed more sandstone than sand—the remnant of a crumbled mesa. Should hold firmer footing, certainly was the higher ground… as long as you didn't look at the stone battlement in the distance. Wanju cut across the dunes, O'Har following. He scrambled up the table of stone, walked to its center.

"Drop a signal canister."

"Affirmative."

Wanju watched as O'Har reached over his shoulder, came back with a palm-sized disc, hurled it toward the dunes. It skipped, landed, and shifted from bright silver to branding-iron red. The air snapped and crackled as it projected a conic field, repelling the breeze.

"Pillar of cloud by day, pillar of fire by night," O'Har murmured.

"O'Har! I'm impressed—you do know your holy book."

"I'm Irish, remember? Irish know the Bible like the back of their hand." O'Har paused, flipped his gloved hand palm to back, back to palm. "Which side was that again?"

"Heh-heh. About right."

The signal canister ignited. White tendrils of titanium chloride spewed from its top, intertwining, expanding, writhing up the projected field. The column filled, a whispering frost-cloaked djinni, dwarfing the men as it lifted its hoary head above the butte, challenging any onlookers to come.

Two did. Twin yellow sulfur comets streaked from the top of the distant cliff, growling in fury.

"We got company, O'Har. Look sharp."

Metallic scintillation burned a trajectory across the dunes, straight for the signal pillar.

Wanju turned up his visor magnification.

Amidst the shimmering distortion of rising heat thermals, two hovercycles came into focus, riders perched on the seats. Their bodies were armored, but the heads were bare. A tall mound sloped back from their foreheads, a globose casque, resembling some grossly oversized Brazil nut covered in flaky scales. Rust-red plumes quivered at the crown of their casques, slicked back by the wind, resembling long feathers dipped in clotted blood. The eyes were enclosed by silver goggles, lenses black as the abyss. Their mouths were hooked scarlet beaks, and their hands and feet were bare, had the look of sun-bleached driftwood.

"Christ," O'Har hissed, tracking the creatures himself. "Lammers."

Wanju squinted. The image magnified in response, focusing on one of the creatures as they skidded their hovercycles to a stop, spraying red rooster tails of sand into the sky. The distance read one kilometer as the crosshairs locked. The digidrive in his helmet whirred, scuttling through exabytes of data.

Identified. The external view dropped into a view box at the bottom of the visor. Across the center of his screen, a three-dimensional creature flickered before Wanju's eyes, rotating slowly, red neon marking vital organs. Its armor superimposed over the image, red crosshairs flashing across optimal target points. Tacticals on the weapons they were packing lit up as well.

ALIEN SPECIES:

Lammeravian.

Wanju glanced to *TRANSMIT*, selected *CARRIER*, selected *CORE*. Core: the artificial intelligence processor that contained all data on current diplomatic status with alien species—which ones had Concordat treaties, which ones weren't in the club but might one day become allies, and which ones the Rangers were allowed to kick butt without reprisal. In the interstellar field away from base, Core was top brass.

The comm sputtered in Wanju's ears. "Ugly buzzards."

"Aww, they're just baby chooks, mate. We can handle 'em."

"Don't look like chicks to me, Blackjack. Look like vultures on Harley sleek riders."

"Give 'em a chance. Gotta find common ground."

"That's why you get paid the big bucks. Me, I just squeeze the trigger. Baby go boom."

"Eyes up. I'm off to the bush to find me a boomerang."

"Come back?"

"Scanning the library. Watch my six."

"Roger that."

Still waiting for updated orders, Wanju searched his drive on Lammeravians. He'd never dealt with them before. He scrolled through the data. Two castes—both matriarchal—one composed of fanatic zealots that believed all sentient beings should be converted to the worship of their bone goddess Xilha; the other composed of ruthless warriors that believed the universe should be cleansed of all races except Lammeravians.

"Knew a sergeant who ran into them once," O'Har said. "Damn murderbirds. They do child sacrifice. Eat their own firstborn—believe the first hatchling carries away their power to conceive if they don't take it back into their bodies."

"Huh."

"It's true! They don't eat flesh—got some whacked out digestive system. Strip the meat off the body, drop the bones down their jaws whole! They eat *sentients*."

"Then you have nothing to fear, O'Har."

"Very funny, sir. Just scan for it. We've got time. They dismounted. Still got a half-klick to cover."

Something did sound familiar. Wanju searched the data.

Lammeravian: human term for the aliens, derived from their birdlike physiological similarities to the lammergeier, also known on Earth as the bearded vulture, (Gypaetus barbatus), but unlike vultures, these birds have feathers protruding from the head and neck, thus the...

~*Scroll, scroll, scroll.*~

Once thought to prey on living creatures, researchers at the end of the Twentieth Century discovered that lammergeier feed almost exclusively on bones. Stomach cells secrete an unusually strong acid that dissolves bone calcium, thereby liberating the protein and marrow fat. This food provides a higher energy value than the same weight of flesh. Lammeravians utilize similar physiology...

~*Scroll, scroll, scroll.*~

Lammeravians have no cemeteries; both castes believe that by ingesting the bones of their dead, they honor the dead by sustaining the living. The Council of—

O'Har's voice crackled. "Nasty bitches, aren't they?"

"As bad as the rest of us, I'd guess."

"Scanner says they're females. Maybe I can hook us up."

Wanju grimaced. "Cork your bunghole, Sergeant."

Wanju resumed reading, noting an important biologic. Lammeravians were similar to the lammergeier bird in another area—they could breathe thin atmosphere, like that of Primor Fi—

INCOMING STELLAR COMMAND TRANSMISSION
AUTHORIZATION: NEDT1004785

Flashing red letters, glaring at Wanju from the upper toolbar grid of his visor. His eyes were still tearing, blurring vision at awkward moments. He cleared the lammeravian data from the screen. Class over.

He focused on the number seven in the authorization code. Didgeridoo moans cycled against his eardrums, his own personalized security check. The code was authentic.

"Receive transmission. Text *only*."

S.C. ORDERS:

Commence negotiations as brigade preps for battle. While Lammeravians spurn ISBC Mining Rights, imperative you record citation of ISBC Code 73. Stellar Command holds mining and possession rights to Primor Five; demand surrender of rutile ore, refined and unrefined. Lammeravians remaining on Primor Five after one planetary rotation from time stamp of citation will be considered enemy combatants and treated accordingly.

Following mission, return to transport to lead your company under command of Brigadier Oksana Karenina.

AMN approved.

"Acknowledged. Message received. Captain Wanju Bratawoolong out." Wanju took a sip of stale water from the tube to his reclamation cache and gulped. He had a good hunch how this day would go down. "There it is. We're on AMN. Core's wiring orders to Karenina as we speak."

O'Har whooped. "Ya-hoo! *Any Means Necessary*. I'm tired of being shut up in that friggin' frigate! Let's go fry some chicken!"

"Stow it, O'Har. Negotiations first. Got to try to be friends before we spill their gizzards on the sand." He paused. "It's the civilized way."

The Lammeravians were close. As they loped, each spun a segmented spear in their left hand, making a sound like a twirling boomerang going in for the kill. They clicked the extended talons of their right, adding an irritating tempo, like marrow-sucked bones clattering in the wind. And then at odd moments, they craned their necks and barraged them with raucous shrieks. It created an unsettling rhythm that transmitted through the receiver in Wanju's helm and raked across his eardrums like ghostly fingernails.

"Bloody balls!" O'Har said. "That tune freaks worse than bagpipes. These chickens are pure dark meat! We're gonna end up shish kabobs if we have to lay out those terms to *them.*"

"You know procedure, O'Har. We state our terms, they state theirs. If we're lucky, we walk away in peace. If not, we walk away under truce. And if that doesn't work, first to blow the other's head off lives. Hang on a tick—receiving greeting protocol now. Follow my lead, and we'll both keep our bones in our pack."

"Affirmative," O'Har said. "Just watch out for those horns on their shoulders. Guy told me they look short, but they can lash out like flails, open like jaws. They're razor sharp, titanium hard."

"Nice accessories," Wanju said. "Now move to left flank and do nothing, I repeat, *nothing* without my order. Got that?"

"Loud and clear, Blackjack."

GREETING PROTOCOL:

Aggressive hand gesture.

A hand appeared on Wanju's screen, displaying the finger positions.

"Heh. You're gonna love this one," Wanju said.

"What? We gotta shake the birds' tail feathers?"

The Lammeravians leapt onto the edge of the sandstone slab.

Wanju brought both gloved hands forward, balled into fists, middle fingers extended toward the heavens. "Smile for the cameras, O'Har."

O'Har grinned from ear to ear. "The Rippers' Salute! Flipping the birds with *the bird*. What's the gesture correspond to in their society? We telling them we think they're number one? Or that we want them to bear our children?"

"Says it has no correspondence in Lammer gestures," Wanju said. "They know its meaning in our society. Appears anything but a strong insult would convey weakness."

The Lammeravians froze, serpentine tentacles spilling from each of their shoulders. The horns at the tips opened into jaws, snapping with all the power of a startled eel. Railing screeches vibrated through their wattled necks and out their clacking beaks.

"Seems we got their attention," O'Har said.

"At least they didn't advance. Core says it's a good sign."

"What next?"

"We wait for their response. Communication, O'Har—it's a two-way street."

The Lammeravians jabbed their spears in the air, beaks snapping, tentacles gesticulating wildly, ending with the jawed tips pointing between cuisses covering their thighs. They rattled dangling plate armor tassets that covered their crotches.

Wanju chuckled. "I believe they just said, 'Bite me.' Yep, Core confirms."

"Didn't need the translator to help with that one, Captain. Now what?"

Green phosphorescence danced across the right of Wanju's visor. "*Crikey*. We fire at them, they fire back. Close as we can without hitting each other. Sear one of them, and we've got trouble."

"You show me yours, I'll show you mine," O'Har said.

Wanju focused on the icon for his thermal plasma sidearms; nine-millimeter muzzles swiveled within small domes on each shoulder of his BC. The air filled with a quick, high-pitched whine as a mix of methane and hydrogen gas heated within shielded cylinders in the backs of their BCs. A magnetic 'bullet' dropped in place, ready to contain and compress whatever density of the superheated gasses the operator specified. The soldier dialed in the specs on his targeting, determining whether the ordnance became a plasma bullet or a plasma bomb.

"We go first," Wanju said. "Switch to manual, tight radius. You target the left one, I got the right. Bullet in the sand—this is a warning shot, O'Har. *No liquidation.* Core says two meters in front of their feet will account for the melt. Use your right sidearm only. Sights up."

"Check."

"On my mark."

"Check."

"Three, two, one, FIRE!"

The bullets spit from each man's right shoulder muzzle, neon blue pearls suspended in magnetic containment—

Radiant bolts thumped the sand in front of the Lammeravians' feet—

A thunderclap boomed—

Wanju and O'Har rocked back from the shock wave—

Sand spurted into the sky, raining across the Lammeravians' bodies.

As the cloud settled, the Lammeravians stood before a small crater of crackled glass, their armor coated in red chili powder dust.

"Top that, ladies," O'Har said.

The Lammeravians' pliant beaks twisted. What was that, a sneer? They hoisted their ivory-looking shockspears, gave the scrimshawed shafts a twist, adjusted settings. Their arms pulled back, launched the weapons. Twin shockspears torpedoed through the air, jetting fire from thrusters at the butts. There was a thud; Wanju and O'Har looked down. Spearheads were buried in the sand, the shafts at an angle, straddled between their thighs, tight to their armored crotches.

O'Har leaped back. "Goddamn, that was close! Goddamn! Jee-zus H. Christ, almost made me a eunuch!"

Wanju stood motionless, the shaft jolting with static pulses that somehow passed through the shielding of his armor. Beads of sweat dribbled down his temples but his voice was precision steel. "Not another move, O'Har. That's an order."

Wanju switched the reflective gold solar filter on his visor to *Clear*. He focused on the Lammeravians' eyes as they reached behind their shoulders, each flipping out another shockspear. A whine shot through the air as their shockspears elongated.

Without moving, Wanju spoke in a low, controlled voice. "Haven't you ever played mumblety-peg in the barracks, O'Har? First one to pull his foot back loses. Since I didn't jump back, they might just let you live. *Might.*"

Red neon ignited in the upper grid of the visor.

INCOMING ALIEN COMMUNICATION

Accept and Translate?

Wanju accepted. A shrill, screeching voice spewed from Wanju's comm, filtered through the translator matrix, converted into intelligible words.

"First setting. You like the rattling of your dangled bearings?"

Wanju sighted the COMM icon. Letters flashed in red, sliding sinuously across the base of the screen, warning him that all speech would now be transmitted in vocal exchange mode, open frequency, without digital encoding.

VOX OPEN

Wanju forced a smile. "It's quite pleasant"—he lifted a leg, stood to one side of the spear—"but I'm not here for recreation." He belted out his words in a command growl. "I am Captain Wanju Bratawoolong. I'm authorized to speak for Stellar Command regarding our rights to this planet we call Primor Five. We respect your greatness as warriors. As fellow warriors, we seek peaceful negotiations with you."

The lead Lammeravian touched a copper disk embedded in the ridged helix of her tympanic membrane. Twisting it, her head bobbed in understanding. She elbowed her comrade, beak curling. "Dangler-of-limp-spear wants the no-kill."

The other rattled ivory claws. "His limp-spear is boneless, but legs and arms are not. Much good crunch on these ones."

Wanju spoke with power. "This world has already been claimed by Stellar Command, through legal filing with the Interstellar Sentients Bureau of Colonization. Knowingly or unknowingly, this makes you trespassers, in violation of Code 73, where the law clea—"

The leader leveled her shockspear at him. "We clutched first. We claim. We stay."

"You were not first—our probe satellite preceded you. You could not have missed its beacon in orbit, nor the continuous transmission loop in Beck's code staking our claim to Primor Five."

She thrust her spear tip toward the sky. "No beings here to challenge our landing! We don't care about stupid beeping buzz-bug in the circling."

"Nevertheless, the interstellar community acknowledges our right to stake a claim on an uninhabited world, and gives us time to bring our colony in. You must certainly be aware of this. While you are in violation of Chapter 456 of the Andromeda Peace Concordat, Stellar Command is kindly offering you—"

"No claw-shake! Andromeda Flock can never understand our heritage, our people, our ways and beliefs. We of the Keyrie Clan see the only way to break the wings of your fighting birds that gobble up the galaxy. War!"

Wanju grimaced—the alien's voice grated like fingernails scraping down a hull. "War comes with being a warrior. But a true warrior sees wisdom in making peace. We have chosen to meet with you to settle this matter peacefully. If you believe you have a grievance, the Andromeda Supreme Court will hear your case."

She hacked and spit. "They do not hear us. They only protect their brood."

"Not true. Many cases have been won by non-member species. If we've violated the law, you will be recompensed. Warriors can be saved this way, both yours and mine. All we ask—"

"No claw-shake! Never again deal with Andromeda and her spineless, treaty signing brood. War! Wars make bones. Bones are food. Our bones, your bones, what does it matter? Wars make bones."

Haven't heard this one before. "Look—we respect your right to feed on the bones of *your* dead. However, this is not the way humans commemorate *our* dead. If you choose to fight instead of leaving Primor, we will not allow you to commit acts that we view as desecrating our dead soldiers. This is non-negotiable."

"Short-heads would rather litter sand with warriors than let their bones sustain the mighty? This is waste of warrior!"

"We appreciate that you may think it waste, but our bodies are ours to do with as we please. Now, let's talk about mining—"

The Lammeravian leader bobbed her molting casque back and forth. "This is why your kind must be cleansed from the universe. You have no glow mirror to offer Xilha; you are blind to the Turning Wheel. You walk in the—"

"Look, we're not going to see eye to eye on this."

The Lammeravian lifted her free hand, clacked her pointed digits against her goggles, flicked the black lenses up. A milky nictitating membrane slid over the silver spheres of her eyes. "What do you mean? Sharp are you as the beak on my face."

Wanju shook his head. So much for universal translators. "Let me speak directly. You try to eat our dead, we vaporize every one of your downed warriors. You hear me?"

The comm screamed in Wanju's ears as their casque plumes fanned out, quivering wildly. "There is no other thinking-way! Unclean one! Here is your short-headed thinking-way!"

Both Lammeravians squatted.

"Uh, Blackjack? They doing what I think they're doing?"

Steaming links of phlegm-yellow excrement plopped in the sand next to their feet. It looked like rotten sausages baking under the sun.

Hell, they didn't come out here to negotiate their retreat, they came out here to pick a fight.

Wanju switched off the open channel, focused on the vid of O'Har. "They're trying to piss us off. Let's get out of here."

"Aww, Captain, I could win this one—I'm full of shit."

"That's bang on, mate." He switched back to open channel as the Lammeravians scooped up their excrement and squeezed it through their bony digits, screaming obscenities.

"We're leaving. Our brigade stands on full assault status; our *wings* primed for attack." *Probably blowing chunder into their stainless-steel punchbowls as we speak, shaking off the cryo-grip.* "Any offensive movement by your forces and we'll swarm over you like flies on a dung heap. Think it over. You have one Primor day, starting *now*."

The leader clacked her beak. "Good. Now we know how to draw the *beenok* from their nest, that we might eat." She pointed a claw at Wanju, her voice a softer screech. "Why you not swarm to the bone-dance when your aerie-ship landed? Why send words, banter words, then you come only one wing?"

Good. They didn't understand human physiology, that there was no way troops could *swarm* fresh from cryo. He sent her barking up another tree. "It is not our way to strike without provocation. We follow the rule of law."

She stared him up and down, studying him closely. "Stupid thinking-way. You lose first sweep. Weak."

"And you pull the tail of a crocodile. We have nothing more to discuss. You have one day to depart. If your rigs dump their payloads—and our scanners will tell us if they don't—we give you our word not to fire on you as you depart."

"*Caw-caw.* This is unbelieving! You steal our home, now you steal our labor? We give you nothing! You turn tail, you take your chances. Starting *now*."

Wanju's voice dropped, ice cold, razor edged. "Warriors keep their word. We agreed to safe passage out for both our parties. We came in peace, we *leave* in peace."

"Our word was no-kill under white pillar." She pointed to the spurting canister. "When white pillar dies, so dies our word."

"We'll hold you to that."

The Lammeravian aimed her shockspear at Wanju's head. "You scan our mother-wing when leaving, you spit in our face. Little birds not go back to master. Knowledge you the drifting in?"

"Understood." Wanju closed the VOX channel. "Come on, O'Har. Head high, ranger. Look sharp."

Wanju did an about face, marched across the flat. His back muscles tightened as his pulse quickened. His eardrums pounded with the rush of blood, but he forced each step to be steady and deliberate. Silence reigned behind, a silence that tiptoed across eternity. Finally, there was a cat-like hiss; the rhythmic clatter of claws. Wanju stopped at the slab's edge, flicked a look back. The Lammeravians loped toward their hovercycles, two shockspears left behind, still thrumming in the sandstone.

"Captain?"

"Yeah, mate?"

"Change your thinking on the Lammers?"

"I'm reminded of a saying—you'll know this one. *Don't throw your pearls before swine.*"

"Confucius?"

The signal canister coughed like a guttering wick.

"Jesus," Wanju said, shaking his head.

"Christ," O'Har said as he cast a nervous glance at the choking canister.

◆ ◆ ◆

The Raptor's VTOL nozzles belched exhaust, lifting the assault craft over the butte. Wanju paused, heart heavy as he hovered the ship midair. He retracted his visor, rubbed his eyes, looked out to the distant cliff. It had a curve to it, and where the rigs had chewed up its face, a giant's bleached skull stared back at him. Grinning. Mocking.

A crackle in his ear. "Jesus, Mary, and Joseph!"

O'Har's image from the turret floated like a will-o-wisp over the console. "Carrier just fed us live feed—surveillance satellite has geosynched over their base. Lammers are rolling *wings* out of their freighter like a mob of angry hornets! We need to get the hell out of here, Blackjack."

Wanju brought up the feed and Core's real-time assessment. Just as he'd suspected, their freighter's hull was cover for their fighter craft, and the top of that cliff made an excellent staging area. Core estimated the freighter's holds were ninety-three percent full: a fortune in refined titanium ore. No way they could call down a strike from the carrier; Core's objectives would never risk annihilating that much ore. And the mining rigs had vanished into bore holes in the cliff. That would take ground troops to clear, which would certainly play into the Lammers' hand.

But the real problem was the mobilization on their plateau. Wanju zoomed in. Lammeravians in battle armor were climbing into cockpits as munitions teams hovered in shuttles, loading ordnance. Core had already crunched the numbers. Rippers vs. Lammers, this was going to be an even match.

Except the Rippers didn't have home field advantage and had just spent six years getting bussed in for the big game. Core hadn't factored the cryonic disorientation of the troops; it had just juiced them up with stimulants. Wanju knew the men, knew their strung-out reaction times. This battle would be a slaughter.

"Captain? They're firing up their ships. They're mounting an offensive."

"I see that, O'Har. Could just be saber rattling, but it doesn't look good." Hell, he knew this mission was going south the moment he read his orders.

"Shouldn't we be leaving now? Core ordered us to report back to the transport ASAP."

"One moment, Sergeant."

Wanju drummed his fingers against the console. Orders. A soldier obeyed chain of command, assuming command didn't have their head up their ass. When command was an AI processor a million plus light-years away from the generals at Stellar Command, that was pretty much a given.

What would his father tell him now, were he alive? Wanju grunted. First thing Dad would say is what the hell was he doing in *Bullamakanka*— bush speak for a place as far in the outback as you could go. Second? That was easy. Same thing his dad had said when Wanju ran from that bully back in first grade at the colony on New Sydney.

Son, sometimes the only thing that works is to stand your ground and use that big stick. You can't hit a bully if you're running.

Wanju gripped the console with both hands, popped it up. He traced the circuitry, a golden spiderweb filled with crystal flies. "Heads up, O'Har. We aren't going anywhere."

"Whaa?"

Wanju found the module he sought, broke it from its socket. O'Har's sphere hovered in his face as he brought the console back down.

"God, Captain, what did you just do?"

Wanju eased back into his seat, tossed the module over his shoulder. "Override remote. I don't want Core jerking us back to base."

"Sir, you see the tacticals, there's no way we can take them alone."

"Who said we're alone?" Wanju keyed open the payload doors on the fuselage; a dozen crystalline stealth drones dropped and soared out across the mesas, flanking them left and right. "We draw a line in the sand. *Here.*"

O'Har had to see the targeting screens ignite in his visor; for once he seemed at a loss for words.

"Those are the new T-38s, Sergeant. Flash as a rat with a gold tooth. I commandeered them before we left base. Merry Christmas."

O'Har's eyes lit up as he cycled through their stats. "Filched 'em, more like."

"Let's not quibble over details."

"Still not enough fire power to hold them back if they mount more than a squadron. And Core will bring you up for court martial for disobeying orders. Out here, it's the long arm of the law."

Wanju cleared his throat. "We had orders to stall for time. So we're stalling. Every minute they spend trying to take us out is another minute for the brigade to mount up. It's their only chance."

O'Har's face continued to float before Wanju, luminous green, lit from all the active drone screens. His eyes glittered sharp as he faced the abyss and gave it a kick in the groin. "Hell, if we live through this, I can just say I was following the orders of my CO."

Wanju felt some of the weight of the world lift off him. "That's the spirit. Think you can figure out your new toys while I send a birdie to brass?"

"Affirmative. And Blackjack?"

"Yes, O'Har?"

"It's been an honor serving with you, sir."

"Likewise, Seamus. Now fire those bad boys up."

"Roger that."

Wanju cleared the console with a wave. He brought up the controls for drone Alpha, had it buzz vertical for a klick, snapped a photo of his Raptor with his entourage of drone wingmen. The image hovered in front of him. He reached out a gloved finger, wrote across it in bold script *Wish You Were Here.* Then he touched the mailbox for Brigadier Karenina.

Poof. Postcard from the edge.

He stared over the horizon, waiting for the Lammers' advance. He called out *battle mix*; music filled the cockpit. It was a collection of chants, songs from the Back of Beyond, tribal droning of the Aboriginals that bled into ancient moans from didgeridoos. Heritage from his father.

Primal sounds from the bush enveloped him. Wanju's mind filled with visions of his ancestors dancing under the stars, their bodies streaked in white. As they stabbed wooden spears into the fire, as sparks flashed and climbed toward the heavens… the warriors captured the rhythm of the corroboree in their hearts, focusing the spirit before the flesh went to war.

The music droned into one unending note, and Wanju droned with it. He swiveled the Raptor, scanning the valley floor below.

Dunes arched in red waves, a turbulent sanguinary sea. Searing winds kicked sandy spindrift from their crests, and he imagined his people, long ago, moving in silent stealth across harsh sands, surviving impossible deserts and insurmountable odds… even a world empire bent on destroying them.

Any way you look at it, whole damn place will be a boneyard in a few hours. War begins where talk ends. We looked in each other's eyes… we just didn't see ourselves looking back.

He took a sip of hydration fluid and focused on the inevitable battle.

Damn bone eaters. You want a fight, and Command has got too much at stake to walk away. And here I am, stuck in the middle of the bowl, going down the gurgler. Well, you might be sly as a shithouse rat, but you're not going to get everything you came here for today. Not if I can help it.

Rangers had one inalienable right, and they sang it every time they marched.

"If I die in a combat zone—"

"Box me up and send me home."

Wanju reached under an armrest, pulled down on some magtape, stuffed a hidden cigar between his teeth. It was against regulations to smoke in the cockpit.

He tapped the self-igniting end.

About the Author

Wulf Moon wrote his first science fiction story at fifteen. It won Scholastic Art & Writing Awards and became his first professional sale in *Science World.* Moon has won over seventy awards in writing, public speaking, and marketing. These include Paramount's Star Trek: Strange New Worlds Contest and Writers of the Future. Moon's stories have appeared in *Star Trek: Strange New Worlds 2, Best of Deep Magic 2, Future-SF, Best of Third Flatiron, DreamForge, and Writers of the Future.* His book *How to Write a Howling Good Story* will be published in May of 2023 by Mark Leslie Lefebvre's Stark Publishing Solutions.

Visit http://TheSuperSecrets.com

Owl

A nocturnal hunter, known for its swift, silent pursuit of prey

Taking Flight on Bone-Shard Wings

by M Elizabeth Ticknor

There is no shame in being afraid of the dark. Darkness is the purview of night, and night is when Owl takes wing. Avoid the liminal spaces between civilization and the primal wilds, the paper-stained alleys and leaf-strewn park trails that so easily isolate you from your fellows.

Beware of Owl, children—and be ever vigilant, for he lurks in places you'll not expect. Watch out for men with strange-stretched shadows, for women with eyes that reflect orange when they catch the light, for children with spindly legs and too-sharp teeth. Owl stretches toenails into talons, strengthening jaws that they might rend flesh like beaks, fletching mutilated arms with bone-shard feathers gleaned from the remains of his victims. His ravenous appetite bloats the stomachs of his hosts to bursting.

Owl is a murderer and a cannibal. Should you give him the chance, he'll rip open your belly, splatter your intestines on the ruddy earth, and pluck out your still-beating heart. Even if he devoured you whole, that would not appease his hunger. Owl is insatiable.

Study Coyote's teachings, children, for it was he who brought us fire, who created death, who taught us how to protect ourselves. Owl's talons may be sharp, but his legs are weak and wanting. He can be tricked. He can be felled from the sky with arrows, bullets, or birdshot.

Be mindful of your hungers, physical or otherwise. We are all of us Coyote's kin, but we are creatures of flesh as well as spirit. Anyone can fall to Owl in a moment of weakness, though it takes time for Owl to fully devour one's spirit. So manage your appetites. Guard against starvation, lest it leave you open to Owl's influence; guard against excess, lest you become easy prey.

People crave a host of different things: freedom, justice, sex, drugs, violence, even pain. The need for affection is vital; touch-starved infants wither and die no matter how well they are fed. The yearning for power is as universal as it is dangerous; far too many fail to resist its siren song. The power-hungry are the most dangerous of Owl's offspring, for they feed not on flesh, but on souls.

Remember, children, that Owl's legs are his weakness. Shatter them, cripple them, strip flesh from bone. Rip the feathers from his arms before he can ascend to the sky. We're all of us at risk when Owl takes flight. In this modern age, it's rare for mortals to have birdshot, bullets, or arrows readily at hand—and, as the descendants of Coyote, our only way to acquire wings is to forge them from bone.

About the Author

M. Elizabeth Ticknor is a neurodivergent, genderfluid writer and artist. She shares a comfortable hobbit hole in Southeast Michigan with her wookiee husband and their twin baby dragons. An avid reader of science fiction and fantasy, Elizabeth also enjoys well-written horror. Elizabeth is a winner of the Baen Fantasy Adventure award; her short fiction also appears in Fireside Magazine, Writers of the Future Volume 38, and an assortment of anthologies by Air and Nothingness Press, Flame Tree Press, and Wordfire Press.

Goldfinch *(Spinus tristis)*

The smallest specimen in our compendium, and a relatively innocuous perching bird, whose males are recognizably yellow or gold in color

Sing Me to Sleep

by J. L. George

When Raven breathed in deeply, she could almost smell the damp earth.

The ground was soft and bright with moss beneath her. Honeyed sunlight trickled slow through the forest canopy, and a cascade of birdsong brought with it the promise of spring. Here, all was well. Outside—

With an effort, Raven dismissed the thought and raised her eyes. She'd be pulled back there soon enough. No sense in dwelling on the real world before she had to dwell in it.

Two birds sat on a branch overhead. Small enough to fit in the palm of her hand, with red masks and bars of bright yellow on their wings. European goldfinches, Ben had told her proudly, when he first showed her the simulation. Raven had been small at the time, but old enough to know Europe was one of the continents of old Earth and to have spent hours tracing its irregular outline on the antique globe in their history classroom. Ben, three years older, obliged her when she begged for the stories he'd learned in his classes, and she dozed off to the sound of his voice and the lulling song of the goldfinches, secure in the knowledge he would watch over her.

Now, Ben lay unresponsive in a sickbay bed, and Raven had lost count of the days since she last slept.

Before the last battle, certainly. Before they lost the war and limped away to this godforsaken corner of the solar system. Before Ben's limp body was dragged from the wreckage of a crashed ship. Raven kept seeing it again in her mind's eye. Twisted metal and sparking electronics. Her heart leaping as she recognised her brother and sinking with a sick dread when she realised he wasn't moving.

Raven laid her hand against the thick trunk of the ancient oak beside her and felt it ripple like a waking beast beneath her palm as its texture began to change. The simulation's menu emerged from the bark, each word settling decisively into place, as though it had been carved by a bored teenager decades ago.

She pressed a few buttons and brought up a memory.

Night in the forest. Darkness fell in one sudden drop, like a curtain across a stage. The birdsong went silent, giving way to the chirping night sounds of insects and, somewhere far away, the harsh bark of a fox. Two dark-headed figures tramped hand-in-hand through the damp grass.

They were so small. Raven was taller now than Ben had been in this memory.

"It's too dark," little-Raven complained. "Where's the moon? Where are the—oh!" She darted from the path as she spotted something in the undergrowth: the tiny green lamp of a glow-worm clinging to a leaf. Her hair fell in a curtain around her face as she bent close. She'd still worn it long, then, and it had felt like a cocoon holding only her and the unearthly miracle light of the glow-worm.

Despite everything, the real Raven felt herself smile, the sick, shaky tension she'd been holding in her chest and shoulders for days starting to melt away.

Bending over the leaf, little-Raven froze and glitched. The real Raven frowned and poked the menu panel.

"Sorry." Helen's voice cut through the forest soundscape, her tone less apologetic than her words. "We need you out here."

The harsh, functional lighting of the space station was disorienting after the simulation. Raven rubbed discreetly at her eyes as Helen led her through echoing grey corridors to the brig, talking nineteen to the dozen. They'd been here over a week and the injured had mostly been treated, but the council was still undecided on what to do. Half voted to surrender and throw themselves on the questionable mercy of Matthias's people, reasoning that they might be the enemy, but there were still rules in war and Matthias would probably follow them. The rest wanted to flee and search for a place to regroup. Tensions were rising, and today another fight had broken out.

"Over a candy bar, of all things," Helen said. Her face screwed up on the words 'candy bar' as though she'd tasted something bitter. Somehow, even on this godforsaken outpost, her uniform was neatly-pressed and her hair tamed into a neat bun. It made Raven feel like a slovenly schoolgirl in comparison. "We lost the war, but our people are drinking like we won, and it's only going to get worse. We can't stay paralysed like this. We need a deciding vote."

Raven held up a hand to forestall her. "Ben's vote. Not mine. I'm not a member of the council."

"He named you his deputy."

"I didn't ask for that." Raven's hands twisted tight together, knuckles paling. "Just wait. He'll wake up, and then he'll vote."

She put from her thoughts what the doctor had told her that afternoon before she logged into the simulation. The resigned expression with which he'd handed her the latest batch of test results, showing no improvement, and the way he'd taken a second longer than necessary to relinquish the datapad, as though handing a pair of scissors to a child he wasn't quite sure was old enough to use them. A part of her wished she hadn't taken it.

Helen strode into the brig and stopped before a cell where two bruised and uniformed figures lounged in obvious inebriation. The other members of the council were already there, ranged in a loose semicircle facing the cell. One of the inmates stumbled to her feet at the women's approach. The other only groaned and clutched his head.

"These are them?" Raven asked.

Helen nodded. "Had to throw them in here to sober up."

Raven looked the standing woman up and down. She stood half a head shorter than Raven, but even drunk, held herself with a fierce readiness. A galaxy of freckles sprinkled her nose and cheeks, and her ginger hair was an unruly mess of curls.

"I know you," Raven said. "Beti, right? You were in Ben's cohort at the Academy." Before Matthias took power and began stomping on the outer worlds; before Ben persuaded them, perhaps uselessly, that they could rebel.

"Yeah. Started the same week." Beti's expression softened as she studied Raven's face. "And you're the sister. You've got the same eyes. How is he? Any news?"

Raven changed the subject. "Helen tells me you fought over candy? Is that true?"

"It wasn't about the candy bar. Not really." Beti moved closer, hands curling around the bars. Her nails were bitten to the quick. "Everyone's on edge. Cooped up, not knowing what happens now... You could help. Give us an update, at least."

A gruff voice cut in. "We're not here for that."

Beti turned to look daggers at the interrupter. Sullen Evan, whose place on the council Raven still didn't understand. His temper was quick, his manner abrasive, and Raven had never met a person who claimed to truly like him, as opposed to putting up with him because his husband was a delight. She was almost sure he'd only ended up with the seat because no-one else wanted the job.

"We need to decide what to do with these wasters." Evan jerked his head at the bars, ignoring Beti's glare. "I say leave them in here, teach them a lesson."

Helen didn't roll her eyes, but Raven suspected it was a close call. "Yes, thank you, we've already heard your thoughts on the matter. Votes for leaving them in here?"

Evan's hand went up, plus that of one other council member, a square, middle-aged woman named Kia.

"Votes for letting the hangover be punishment enough?" Helen raised her hand, and the remaining three followed. Instead of calling it, she turned to face Raven. "Yours?"

Raven huffed. Of course this had been a ruse, an attempt to suck her into the council's wranglings. Why was Helen so insistent on involving her? She was no Ben. "You've already got your answer," Raven said. "You don't need me." With an apologetic glance at Beti, she turned on her heel and made for the door.

As Raven left, Helen's quick, clipped footsteps followed her along the corridor. Raven drew in a breath through her nose. "What?"

"I've heard the doctors talking. They say—"

"I know what they say!" Raven snapped. She went still, willing her hands out of their clenched fists, her tone to moderate itself. "They don't know Ben like I do. He'll pull through. He always does."

Helen was quiet for a long moment. "So far."

Raven intended to go back to the simulation, slip the headset on in her bunk and let the song of the goldfinches lull her to sleep. Instead, her feet took her to the sickbay.

Ben looked so pale against the thin white pillows. They'd shaved his head, something that recruits did to look tough, but that somehow only made Raven more conscious of how fragile he was. She could see all the angles of his skull and kept imagining them caved in like a battered eggshell. He'd been unconscious for days, but the bags under his eyes were as pronounced as if he'd kept Raven company on all her insomniac nights. There was a still, artificial quality to his facial features, as though he'd been coated in polymer.

Raven sank into the chair beside his bed. "It's time to wake up," she told him. "I need you. You always know what to do."

Silence.

♦ ♦ ♦

The eggs were such a pale blue they were almost white, speckled with reddish-brown and small as the tip of Raven's thumb. Five of them sat at the centre of a perfectly round nest. They looked like sweets—like she could pop one in her mouth and the shell would be pure sugar.

"Raven! What are you doing up there?" Ben hissed. Raven flapped an excitable hand at him and pressed her finger to her lips. Balanced precariously on a lower branch, she had to stand on her toes to see into the nest, clutching at the tree trunk to steady herself. The limb creaked as Ben climbed up to sit beside her.

"Look," she whispered. "Real bird eggs!"

The garden sat at the centre of their living complex, enclosed to protect it from the planet's atmosphere and filled with wildlife from old Earth. The gardener had said something about the temperature and humidity being calibrated to match the temperate rainforest native to northwest Europe, but Raven had quickly tuned out the finer details of his spiel, excited to see real animals and living plants.

Ben's eyes went wide—and then he took Raven by the wrist and pulled her away from the nest, lifting her off the branch and setting her gently on the ground.

She swelled with outrage at being moved without permission. "What did you do that for?"

"You mustn't disturb the nest. It might scare off the parents, and they'll never come back, and the babies will never hatch."

Raven mulled this over for a moment, before nodding acceptance. But the thought of having to keep her distance made her sigh.

Ben touched her shoulder. "What's up?"

"I like being with the animals," she said. "It makes me feel... still."

Ben cocked his head. "Is that why you're always waking up at night? You don't feel still?"

Raven shrugged. "I guess so." The living complex kept its lights attuned to a strict circadian rhythm, but she'd never really kept time with it, waking in the middle of the night and sleeping through lessons at school. Their family doctor put it down to anxiety—which Raven understood to refer to the crawling sensation under her skin that made her legs jiggle and her throat close up when she had to speak to new people—but the medication he prescribed only gave her a headache.

This, though. The green smell of plants and silvery birdsong. This helped.

Ben disappeared into his room straight after dinner that night, and when Raven knocked at the door, she found him shuttered behind his headset. She thought perhaps he was still annoyed about the nest and retreated to her own bed in disappointment.

But, a few weeks later, he beckoned her into his room. He'd managed to wheedle a second headset from somewhere and held it out to her as though offering something precious. "Go on," he said. "You'll like it, I promise."

Gingerly, Raven did as she was told, holding still and keeping her eyes closed while Ben strapped the visor into place.

"Okay," he said, at last. "You can open your eyes."

She found herself in a forest of sun-drenched green. A waterfall of birdsong tumbled down all around her, goldfinches darting quick and bright through the trees. Her gaze followed them, entranced.

"They're the same kind they have in the garden," Ben told her. "Now you can look at the nests anytime you like, and you won't hurt them."

"Will they sing anytime I like too?"

"That's the best part. I've been working on the sounds. You know there are frequencies that can make you go to sleep? Slow down your heartbeat and your breathing and make you relax?"

Raven shook her head silently. She hadn't known, but she didn't mind. She liked how Ben talked to her like she knew things instead of assuming she was an empty vessel, the way some of the older kids did.

"Well, they can. I've embedded them in the birdsong, so quiet you don't know you're hearing them. This way, when you can't sleep, you can come in here and it'll help you." Ben's face turned serious. "But don't go messing with the settings. Set the wrong frequency and you might slow your heartbeat down so much you never wake up."

Raven crossed her heart and promised not to touch them. She'd never been quite sure if Ben was telling the truth or spinning a fable to keep her from tinkering with his creation.

Not that it mattered. The birds helped her sleep through every night, and she had no more thought of changing them than if they'd been real.

◆ ◆ ◆

"Raven."

She woke slowly, slumped over the makeshift desk to which she'd retreated after the nurses shooed her away from Ben's bedside. Before her eyes, outlined in blue light, hovered a list of names. The photographs that accompanied them showed young faces, mostly. Bright-eyed and hopeful, as they'd been when they first followed Ben into revolt.

The faces of the dead. It had been her job to compile a list once they'd landed at the outpost and licked their wounds. She'd finished it days ago but found herself scrolling through them again in idle moments. Funny that it should be this list, and not Ben's birds, that finally sent her to sleep.

But something had been niggling at her, right before she drifted off. An itch in the back of her mind and a faint ache in her chest. If she could only remember what it was…

"*Raven*." Helen's voice was sharper this time, and she leaned over to switch off the projection as she spoke. "The doctor's here."

The last shreds of sleep cleared from Raven's mind. "Ben. Is he—"

"No change." Helen sighed. "And they don't think there will be any."

"You don't know that."

"I'm not the one who needs to." Helen's voice grew louder. "Stop burying yourself with the dead, Raven, and start worrying about the living!"

Raven rose to her feet. "Why do you care? Create a new seat on the council. Elect someone else. You don't need me."

"*I care*," Helen snapped, "because my brother's gone too. But do you see me hiding in a fantasy world and pretending he's still alive? I can't do that. We couldn't even retrieve his body." Her hands trembled on the display.

That was it. The thing that had been scratching at the back of Raven's mind before she fell asleep. The ache behind her sternum.

Paul Cole—one of the names on the list, accompanied by a headshot of a young man with Helen's deep-set, serious eyes.

Helen's surname was Cole too.

Without consciously meaning to, Raven found herself on her feet, standing beside Helen's chair. Her voice sounded like a distant echo to her own ears. "Let me show you something."

Helen followed begrudgingly—but even her eyes went wide when they opened on the forest. "This is where you spend your time?" she asked, tracing the veins of a leaf with her forefinger. "It's so detailed."

"Ben programmed it. We were kids at the time, but he kept adding to it over the years. Expanding it, making it realer."

Birdsong, notes tumbling like dust motes in afternoon sunlight. The goldfinches flitted from branch to branch overhead, the bars on their wings glinting in the shade of the leaf canopy.

"Why?" Helen asked.

"I'm not sure why he kept coming back to it. But at the start, he made it to help me sleep." Raven extended a hand toward the goldfinches. One alighted on her forefinger. She looked into the hard black bead of its eye, not quite sure what she was searching for. It looked back for half a second and was gone, darting away to join its fellows. "It's the birds. Their song slows your heart rate. Something to do with the frequencies buried in the recording. Ben once told me…" She trailed off. "It's silly."

"Tell me."

"He told me that I should never touch the settings, because if I got them wrong, my heart would slow down so far I'd die." A rueful smile tugged at her lips. "I never really figured out if that was true, or if he was messing with me. Brothers, hm?"

The birds circled above them once, twice, and vanished into the leaves. Helen's gaze followed them. Her expression, in the dappled shadows, was quite opaque. Raven hadn't thought she was expecting a reply but found herself disappointed.

"Do you mind if I stay, for a while?" Helen said, at last.

"Of course." Still hesitant, Raven moved to her side and brought up the menu on the tree trunk. "Here—this is how you leave."

Helen nodded and copied her movements. Her fingers lingered on the bark like she was touching a loved one's face.

♦ ♦ ♦

Raven went to her bunk, that night. She'd been lying awake perhaps half an hour when a faint sound in the corridor roused her from her thoughts. Socked feet sliding on the bare metal floor, she crept to the cabin door and peered out. The lights were on, which meant somebody had tripped the sensor, but the corridor was quite empty, and the hum of the outpost's generators the only sound.

Perhaps it had just been somebody going to the bathrooms.

Raven retreated to her bunk and pulled on the headset. The sounds of the simulation settled in around her: leaves rustling, insects chirping, the occasional noise of some small creature scrabbling about in the undergrowth. Helen had left and there was no sign she had ever been there, not so much as a footprint in the forest floor.

Raven meandered until she heard birdsong.

Right above her head. She craned her neck and squinted.

There. One of the goldfinches came to a fluttering halt. There was its nest, nestled in the crook of a branch.

She crept closer. Quiet as she could, she shimmied up the trunk, staining her clothes with moss. She stretched and strained to peer in, expecting another clutch of freckled eggs, but started back so that she almost lost her grip when a beak peeked out over the edge.

The fledgling was squat and brown, an uneven scruff of feathers making it look as though it had been attacked by a rogue barber. It moved toward the edge of the nest with an ungainly flap-shuffle and Raven put her hand to her mouth. It was going to fall. She leaned up on instinct, cupping her hand ready to catch it.

"Don't."

This time, Raven did lose her grip. She slid the few feet she'd climbed up the trunk, barely keeping her feet as she landed with an undignified stumble.

Ben smiled at her.

He was taller than her: no longer a child. This wasn't a memory. "Ben?" she said. "What's going on?"

He only tilted his head toward the nest. "How's it going to learn to fly if you keep saving it?"

"It's not real."

Ben shrugged. "That's true. You could fast-forward to when it's an adult, or wind the simulation back to before it hatched. But wouldn't you rather watch it grow?"

The fledgling flapped its wings once, twice, and tumbled from the nest.

It hit the forest floor in an unmoving heap. Raven's heart contracted, and it took all the strength she had not to crouch and scoop it up. Her nails dug into her palms.

The chick righted itself. Flapped again, hopped, and skipped and almost took off. "It's working." She grinned and glanced over her shoulder. "Ben, it's working."

He looked past her. "D'you remember when we were on the run, after we left the academy? Low on fuel and supplies, and we came up on that small moon?"

Raven blinked at the change of subject. "There was a settlement there," she remembered. "Tiny, under the radar." It had appeared first as a cluster of weak, disparate signals on the ship's dashboard. Evan had insisted they should move on—it was old tech, an abandoned craft, nothing they could use.

"You were the one who realised it was a town," Ben said. "Who knows what we would've done if you hadn't found that place?"

"We'd have been fine," Raven said. "You would've thought of something."

"That's what we need now. Sanctuary."

She shook her head. "That place is gone. They all fled when Matthias and his army got near."

"Not that place. Another. I know you can get them there." Ben was still looking past her, eyes on the fledgling as it flapped again, hopped, flew clumsily to a low branch.

Raven followed his gaze, uncomprehending, and turned back to him. "What's that supposed to mean?" she asked, but there was nobody there. Only birdsong answered.

The fledgling made a tiny, peeping sound and took off again. Its clumsy wings worked furiously. Raven was briefly sure it would tumble to the ground, but it made it to the next branch, and the next.

I know you can get them there. Had Ben been talking about the birds? Raven followed the fledgling as it made slow, erratic progress from branch to branch, stumbling over rocks and roots as she kept her eyes trained on the fuzzy little form. She lost her balance, grabbed at a nearby trunk to steady herself, and when she regained her footing, thought for a terrible moment she'd lost track of the chick.

The high, fluid song of the parent birds reached her ears and she spotted them: all three, perched together on a branch of the thickest, most gnarled oak in the simulation.

They didn't fly away at her approach. She looked up at them, her palm coming to rest on the warm bark. "Well?" she asked the birds. "Why am I following you?"

They looked back blankly.

There was movement beneath her hand.

The bark of the tree rippled and changed—but it wasn't the simulation's menu that emerged from its grooves. Instead, there was a set of numbers that Raven's brain took long minutes to process.

Coordinates.

◆ ◆ ◆

She woke late and groggy, tendrils of sleep still clinging to her reluctant mind. It was only when her gaze landed on the time display in the corner of her visor that she shot upright, tearing the headset off her face. At this hour, her alarm should have woken her. Normally, Helen would've been banging on her door to find out where she was.

Her mind felt sluggish and heavy. All she wanted was to sink back into the quiet of the forest and the song of the birds.

The birds.

Suddenly, Raven was wide awake. She knew, with a deep and instinctive sickness, that something was very wrong.

Without even stopping to shove her feet into her boots, she flew down the corridor to the sickbay. Her toes clenched at the cold.

Helen stood at Ben's bedside, an unmoving shadow. The other headset covered Ben's eyes. A heart monitor beeped in time with his pulse.

The intervals were terribly slow.

Slow.

Slower.

Raven snatched the visor from his face with trembling hands and mashed the security button. Only then did she spin to face Helen. "Tell me this isn't what it looks like."

Helen's face was still as a mask.

Something dammed up in Raven pushed free at last, broke past the memories, past, *He's going to wake up,* and aimed itself at Helen. "I trusted you! I let you into our memories!"

"*But* that's all they are!" Helen retorted. "Memories." The mask cracked, and for a moment Raven saw the seething mess of anguish beneath. "Why can't you accept he's gone?"

"No. I have to wait."

Helen blinked. A tear tracked from the corner of her eye to the end of her nose. She seemed to deflate, then; emptied of both her composure and her rage. "I wish there was something to wait for."

Footsteps in the corridor. Evan trailed in after them, swearing and rubbing at his eyes, and a couple of the other council members followed. "What the hell is going on?"

Helen wiped her face. Even now, not a single hair was out of place. "You'll have to ask Raven." Resignation in her voice.

Faces swivelled to look at Raven and she inhaled, slow and shaky. She could tell the truth. Get Helen sent to the brig and stay here at Ben's bedside a little longer. A day, an hour, clutching at grains of sand.

"I vote we leave," Raven said. "And I know where we go."

◆ ◆ ◆

As the council left, Helen reached out. Her hand almost came to rest on Raven's shoulder before falling back to her side. She lowered her eyes and headed out the door.

Leaden-limbed, Raven sank into the chair at her brother's bedside.

When she closed her eyes, she saw the fledgling again. Its clumsy flaps and jumps across the forest floor. Ben's imagined smile in the sunlight. The feeling she'd had ever since the battle—his presence lingering in every room she entered, as though he'd left just ahead of her and was waiting somewhere for her to catch up.

She searched for it now in the silent sickbay. In the still, unoccupied set of his features.

There was nothing here.

She set the visor back in place and switched on the simulation. The beeps began to slow.

About the Author

JL George (she/they) lives in Cardiff, Wales and writes weird and speculative fiction. Her first novel The Word won the New Welsh Writing Awards and Rubery Book Award and is out now from New Welsh Rarebyte. In her other lives, she's a library-monkey and an academic interested in literature and science and the Gothic. You can find her on Twitter at @jlgeorgewrites.

Goshawk *(Accipiter gentilis)*

A diurnal raptor, with sharp eyes and sharper gripping claws, whose prestige and power was considered great enough that only medieval nobility were permitted to keep them

Facts That Lead to My Choosing the Hawk

by Leah Ning

1. Hawks can live for more than 20 years.

This is of utmost importance. It will take time, maybe even ten years, before I see the prince again, and it will not do to train a bird only to have it die before it serves its purpose. I cannot be sure of how long it will take for the prince to tire of my daughter.

2. Hawks are diurnal creatures.

Prince Elias makes his choices at high noon in the village square. This was when he chose my daughter; this was when King Richard, when he was a prince himself, chose the daughters of others, and when his father Walter before him chose still other daughters.

Yes, when Elias chose Willa, the sun was at a perfect zenith. I remember how it blazed heat on the crown of my head, burning my scalp the way Willa's wet face burned in my chest, the way my screams burned in my throat.

The bird must be able to see. Yes, it must be able to see very well, and hawks hunt best when the sun blasts maniac rays down onto the earth.

3. Hawks are easier to tame than eagles.

Or so says every falconer I ask, every book I can find on the topic. An eagle might be better-suited—larger, more powerful, perhaps more frightening—but I must get this right the first time. There will be no more tries after the hawk leaves my wrist, talon-scarred beneath the thick glove.

So I find a goshawk: a blue-gray menace with a striped tail and a hooked beak, and talons strong enough to rend flesh from bone.

4. The maximum weight a hawk can lift is five pounds.

I need not even that. All I want are his eyes, the ones that damned my daughter to his pleasure. I'll not leave him the sight of her, whether he lives or dies. If I could take his hands too, I would. But that requires a sword or an ax, not a bird.

It takes months of training after months of taming, but the goshawk— I name him Liam, what I would have called Willa were she a boy—begins to bring me the eyes of each kill. This done, I allow him to eat, ripping meat from bone with savage yanks, swallowing it down with jerky movements of his neck.

I wonder if he'll want to eat after he brings me Elias's eyes. I suppose there won't be time, since the guards will be on Liam fast. But Elias is the prey Liam will live his whole life for. So who would I be to stop Liam from eating his kill?

5. Hawks love solitude.

In this, Liam and I are alike. I want little to do with those merely mourning the loss of their daughters (of which there are few), and less to do with those living in quiet relief that their daughters still wake in familiar beds and tuck into familiar breakfasts.

I was one of the latter, before Willa turned twenty and Elias grew bored of what he calls his "old haunts." I refuse to be one of the former. I will mourn—I do mourn—but I will not only mourn. To mourn is not enough.

6. Hawks' talons can exert incredible force.

I find this out the hard way. Liam rips through the thick leather of the glove, and I feed him a strip of rabbit to busy him while I put him in his mew.

The blood running down my wrist fascinates me for a moment. I've been thinking, these long months, how best to have my goshawk kill a man. The fastest, sure, would be those talons to the throat, eight quick and ragged slashes through windpipe and arteries.

But is it the *best* way?

I remember the prince's clothing, too clean for a dusty place such as ours, the shine in his boots muted by the short walk from carriage to square center. I remember his furs, splendid white and blinding in that screaming sunlight of noon.

I think, as I stem the flow from my own wrist, of how those splendid furs might run red. How easy to see from wherever I will be in the crowd.

Yes, I will teach Liam to go for the throat.

7. The bond between hawk and falconer strengthens with continued time together.

I thought this only applied to the hawk and not the falconer: that Liam would grow attached to me, and I would remain impartial, the holder of a sleek and feathered weapon. And it was so for a while, especially at the beginning. Hard to love a creature that would as soon have *your* eyes as it would those of a field mouse.

But when it turns that merciless gaze on you as it deposits the jellied eyes of a hare into your ungloved palm? When you become accustomed to its weight on your forearm? When the tender skin of your wrist is marked by its beak the way your belly is marked with the stretches that came from carrying your daughter?

I begin to worry for Liam. To wonder what happens to him after he sets the sharp parts of him about the soft parts of the prince.

There are guards, after all, and they, too, have sharp things, weapons to wield that they'll never grow to love.

I begin to teach Liam to escape. To mistrust humans the way prey mistrusts his shadow on the grass at dawn. The goshawk only blinks at me as if to say he's known this all along, known it as well as I do. I smile and teach him anyway, because he must know that if he is to survive, he cannot return to me.

8. Hawks are territorial by nature.

This becomes especially true when I train him to mistrust others. I can no longer bring him to public places without jesses and a hood to keep him calm. Once, he attacks a man who comes too close, making my heart speed with nerves; once, he attacks a woman who only came to hand me a coin I dropped. I manage to save the woman from the sharp hook of Liam's beak. The man, whose leer and wandering eyes frightened me, leaves with a strip torn from his palm.

This terrifies me and gives me hope in equal measure. This could work. If I can aim Liam like I might aim a true weapon.

9. Hawks can fly for thousands of miles.

This, too, is of utmost importance.

A month ago, King Richard died, and today, my goshawk will commit not just a homicide, but a regicide. And King Elias has not proven himself forgiving.

This will be less of a problem if Liam rips out his throat instead of a strip of his forehead.

I carry the bird to the square, feeling the weight of him, the squeeze of talons through leather, for the final time. This saddens me more than I thought it might. I swallow down the tightness in my throat and move in at the back of the crowd.

This visit is not a choosing; it is an introduction, the new king and his new wife fresh from mourning Elias's late father.

Elias himself steps from the carriage all in black, and there's a moment of dismay: no splendid white furs to spill his filthy blood on.

And then there is a longer moment of deep horror as my daughter steps from the carriage, round with his child, a delicate crown nestled in curls limp with humidity.

My back straightens. She casts her eyes over the crowd, and when they meet mine, when she sees the goshawk, her gaze is every bit as merciless as the bird's. She knows what I mean to do.

I give this power to her: I will not kill her husband until she says so. If she never does, Liam will stay hooded and still. I will live out my days hunting with my goshawk and be happy for it.

Liam's talons give my wrist a brief squeeze.

As Elias begins to speak, Willa nods.

I slip Liam's hood, and those nearest me begin to mutter in nervous tones. I murmur to the hawk while I loose his jesses. He is still, smooth feathered lines angled toward me as I speak. He watches as my eyes sweep the crowd, my heart thudding, and when I settle my gaze on the king, the beat in my chest spikes.

"Kill," I whisper, and as Liam launches himself from my wrist, the soft of his feathers brushes my cheek.

A cry goes up from the crowd. Elias's face turns up. So does Willa's, and so do the guards'; but Liam only circles overhead. There's a collective nervous laugh. A relaxing. The king begins to speak again.

Willa's eyes never leave the goshawk as he dives.

It turns out, in the end, that blood is just as easy to see on pale skin as it is on pale furs. I content myself with that, and with Elias's failure to scream the way I did the day he took my daughter.

After it's done, Liam escapes, blood darkening his toes, wheeling away into the sun the way I taught him.

King Elias does not escape. Unless you can call death an escape, which I do not. Not for one such as him.

I don't escape, either. Not when every eye in the square is turned on me with my leather falconer's glove, the hood and jesses empty on the dirt. Not when the king's eyes, punctured and streaked pink, drop to the dust at my feet.

Later, before I can mount the steps to the gallows, my daughter whispers to me that she's sure she's pregnant with a boy. And she will raise him to be a gentle king.

I go to the rope with a smile on my face, and across the way, a goshawk lights on a rooftop to watch with sharp and merciless eyes.

About the Author

Leah lives in northern Virginia with her husband and their adorable fluffy overlords. She spends her non-writing time drawing, playing video games, and playing piano. Her short fiction appears or is forthcoming in PodCastle, Beneath Ceaseless Skies, Apex Magazine, and Human Monsters, among others. You can find her @LeahNing on Twitter and on her website, LeahNing.com

Draida *(aka "bloodbirds")*

Our final corvid specimen, creatures of nightmare, who call upon the cleverness of crows and the ominous aura of ravens—for whom both "murder" and "unkindness" are guaranteed

Give One to the Soul

by Michael Panter

Crows strangled the sky, black wings beating against the canvas of a night abandoned by cloud and void of star. Some settled on the gibbet, others circled above the glade. All were lost; wretched souls watching and waiting for everything and nothing. To Bree, their caws sounded tortured, like they were screaming for help in a language none could fathom.

Their presence meant she was in the right place, though, if the scrolls could be believed. Some of the texts Bree had found on her journey were older than ink, but all read with the same grave warning: the crows would come, then *they* would come.

Bree shifted silently amidst the cacophony. She was perched like a bird herself, hidden in the branches of a twisted willow tree. Her hair, dyed the hue of summer straw, hung like a braided snake over one shoulder. Cold sweat stained her palms, and the blood in her veins ran strange. Only the deep bitterness in her heart, smouldering like the embers of a forgotten fire, lent her the strength to remain. "Ere a curse is said," she breathed.

A dense mist blanketed the ground, corpse-white and writhing, *alive*, concealing ancient stones dying in a bed of grey-green moss. A full moon hung the sky tonight, and there was power in that, Bree knew.

She adjusted the hem of her yellow cloak, reached to her hip, and fingered the fletching of the arrows in her quiver. It steeled her to do so, better focused her on the task. A lifetime ago her hands had been soft, and that softness had failed her. Now they were gloves fashioned from callouses and scar tissue, tokens of toil and of victories hard-earned.

Three arrows, she had. Three shots, she would need. Three short nooses hung from the gibbet in the centre of the glade, ripe for three necks, and it was the third hour past midnight. A considerable coincidence, some might have marked, but Bree knew no such thing as coincidence. There was only knowledge. There was power in that too.

The escalating fury of the crows snapped her attention back to the glade. Frenzied, they worked their way up to a shrieking crescendo, louder, louder, *louder*. The trees lining the glade began to tilt and sway, whispering amongst themselves as the air grew thick with chill. Bree knew it couldn't be long now.

And it wasn't.

Through the mist *they* came, tall and terrible, gliding from the woods to form a ring around the gibbet. Bree counted nine. Stripped of their earthly disguises, they were pale, appalling things robed in leathery rags, white hair clinging to cracked scalps garnished with festering sores. Obsidian feathers sprouted from necks and shoulders and arms, hideous testaments to a decay untold years in the making. *Draida,* lore knew them as, *the bloodbirds,* sirens of the sky when the world was young and naive. The ages had stripped them of wing and beak, forced them to adapt to endure, but some evils are beyond the cleansing of time.

Bree trained her eyes on the gibbet, counting seconds disguised as centuries as she waited. In truth, she'd been waiting for three years: had devoured a thousand scrolls; trained in all manner of skills; sharpened wits and weapons until she was as finely tuned as the bow on her back. Gone was the timid girl she had been, a mere wretched memory buried without fanfare in the catacombs of her past. Bree was now six and ten, and the monsters of the night had paid the blood price for her ascent to maturity.

Doubts nibbled her resolve, even so. This time her quarry was different. Stakes had served her favourably with the vampori, as fire had with the undead. Silver had dealt with the wolfmen so well that she had enough pelts to clothe a village. Only, they were beasts of a lesser malevolence, and contracts besides. This one was personal. "For the life you will part," she whispered, softly as she could.

The chorus of the crows made it difficult to think, but Bree couldn't properly collect her thoughts even after they suddenly fell quiet. It took her long seconds to realise that something had changed. She squinted; green eyes peeled keenly. She'd always had good eyes, Bree. Her father used to say they were windows to innocence, though that was back before horror had turned them hard.

Something stirred in the glade and the lightest of gasps slipped unbidden from Bree's throat.

Maig ver Gerix, Queen of the Draida, drifted into view, the ragged grey wisps of her gown trailing like eels swimming in her wake. She was as Bree remembered, a dread to look upon, gaunt and haggard and hollow of face. Her lips were the colour of a deep well, drawn up into the cruellest of smiles. Corruption hung on every frosted breath that passed through them. On her right shoulder perched her raven, a monstrous thing, three times the size of any of the crows, with talons that could steal a man's eye from its socket. Its own eyes shone red, burning fire.

Silence.

Bree knew only the pounding of her heart between her ears. She knew what she must do, but not what would come after. Accursed would be the one who would slay a draida, or so the tales insisted. Such troublesome lore was enough to keep even the hardiest of hunters well away. Yet to Bree's mind no curse was more poisonous than guilt, and she'd had her fill of that tonic. She realised tears were welling in her eyes, and turned her fear to fury.

Across the glade, the Queen of the Draida raised her head to the night. "On each the third All Hallows' Eve, we shall convene... we shall feed." Her voice was a rasping keen, like a rusted sword torn too fiercely from its sheath.

"*Feed,*" hissed the others in their ring. "*Feed.*" The crows beat their wings frantically above.

Maig ver Gerix swept her gaze over the gibbet. "On hallowed ground of moss and stone... we take our feast of blood and bone."

"*Blood... bone... blood... bone... Feed! Feed! Feed!*"

The children stumbled into the glade then, three of them, still in their night clothes, swollen eyes shot black as they teetered to the chanting.

"*Feed... feed.*"

Bree recognised them of an instant. The tanner's boy came first, with shaggy red hair that might never have been cut. The widow's twins shuffled behind him on unsteady legs, reed thin and freckled, mouths lolling open. Children of four, five at the most, snatched from their beds, from the warmth of those who loved them the most. Mayhaps they had fought at first, kicked and struggled, screamed as *he* had screamed. Now, though, they were meek creatures snared by song spells, enchanted by chanting.

The huge raven took flight, circled the children once, and eventually came to rest on the gibbet. The crows there fled in haste, scattering to the sky. "*Feed,*" droned the draida, even as the children lurched up three creaking wooden steps to take their places at the gallows.

Maig ver Gerix opened her mouth, exposing the vicious array of her needle-like teeth. "Three vessels clean and pure… we will feed… we will endure."

"*Endure… feed… endure,*" the others intoned.

The children staggered to their nooses without protest. First the tanner's boy, then the twins; sparrows frail and helpless beneath the raven's glare.

The Queen of the Draida smiled. "Keep them whole as life is part… with last breath's sigh, the feed must start."

"*Feed… start… feed.*"

Bree slid deftly onto a lower branch, then down further again, moving as swiftly as she dared. *Three arrows; three shots.* She knew what must be done. *Ere a curse is—*

She stopped short on the lowest branch. The chanting had ceased. The trees were whispering again in its place. *Run,* they seemed to warn. *Flee.* But before she could tell them no, something rustled beside her. She turned. A trio of crows were sharing her branch, unblinking, unmoving, *watching.*

The cackling began then, a shrill sound that hurt Bree's ears. The draida were staring towards the willow, one and all.

Bree unslung her bow and notched the first arrow with a shaking hand. The first shot should have come from the willow, before its target knew to evade it, but that plan was now dying to the sound of wretched laughter. Instead, Bree stepped from the shadow of the tree and into the mist of the glade, frost seeping into bone. Her eyes and her arrow she locked on Maig ver Gerix.

The cackling from the others waned as she advanced. The draida hissed and cringed away at the sight of her yellow cloak, for they could not stand the colour. The books had been right about that, at least.

Three arrows; three shots, Bree thought again. And then what? If anyone had ever killed a draida, they hadn't deigned to say what came next.

Bree pushed the question from her mind, replacing it with the memory of a young boy and his screams as he disappeared into darkness. "Queen of Bloodbirds, I am come for you," she called, hoping she sounded bolder than she felt.

Maig ver Gerix afforded her a barbarous grin, unperturbed by cloak or hair. "*You.*"

The word turned the hairs on Bree's neck to needles. For a moment her courage faltered, and the arm that held the bowstring taut felt heavy and weak. "You know me?"

The Queen of the Draida sniffed the air as if recalling a scent greatly pleased. "The boy…"

The boy. Small hands outstretched, inches from her grasp but an eternity away. "He was my brother," Bree said. "And you took him from me."

Maig ver Gerix sniffed again. "Took him… yes… and *fed.*"

Bree calmed her breathing and adjusted her bow so that the first arrow was trained between the draida's eyes. Its head was yellow gold that glimmered ethereal in the pale light of the moon. It had cost Bree a year's work to have the arrow heads forged. If Maig ver Gerix was troubled, though, she did well to hide it.

"You will do these children no harm this night," Bree spat.

The draida clucked in amusement. Maig's eyes weren't one colour but several as they shifted and changed: now icy blue; now blanched white; now darker than shadow. "We *will* endure," she whispered, words polluted with a strange taint as they reached Bree's ears.

"No," Bree managed, teeth gritted so hard she feared they might break in her mouth. "Tonight, you die."

The crows above erupted in a sudden fever of screams. Maig ver Gerix offered a knowing smile. "Many are they who have tried." The Queen of the Draida drifted closer, her maw opening and her teeth extending to fangs, unnaturally long, too many for her mouth to hold.

Bree flexed her fingers. *Ere a curse is said, give one to the head.* Her first arrow flew.

It took Maig between the eyes with a dull thud. Yet the draida advanced. "Fool girl, none can—"

The second arrow pierced the Queen's breast and buried itself up to the fletching. *For the life you will part, give one to the heart.* It stalled Maig for a moment, though soon enough she was moving again, flexing her claws, eyes growing wider, longer. "*None* can end me."

Bree nocked her third and last arrow with hands trained to think when mind could not. "To make death whole…" She drew her arm back and took aim at her enemy.

The Queen of the Draida spread her arms wide, splaying herself, and howled as she glided forward over the last few feet.

"…Give one to the soul."

Bree swiveled at the last, found the gibbet with her eyes and took aim above it. The raven shrieked, rousing its colossal wings into action.

Too slow.

Bree loosed, and the ghosts of her past gave speed to her deliverance. The golden arrow ripped through feather and blood and bone, and a blackness spewed forth so dense, so terrifying, that Bree was forced to shield her eyes.

When she lowered her arm, all was still. The mist was gone, the crows were gone, the raven was gone, the *draida* were gone. She spun, slowly, but she was alone in the glade save for the three children on the gibbet, now awake and petrified.

Bree gathered them up and bade them follow her. They ceded without question, as frightened children are wont to do.

The journey back to the village was a blur of moving shadows and undulating whispers. Nothing came forth from the darkness to block their way. Bree followed trees she had marked with yellow ribbons, a shell of fulfilled expectation too bewildered to console the calves she herded.

The torches of the village burned bright against the night, two dozen unblinking eyes that watched and waited for nothing and everything.

"Run," Bree told the tanner's boy when they reached the tree-line. And he did, with one hand grasping each of the twins and a fear in his soul he would never truly understand.

Bree watched them disappear. Then she sank to the floor and sobbed until her eyes were sore and her nails were thick with mud where she'd clawed the earth. "I did it… Josiah… I did it."

Her sobs devolved to whimpers, which in turn evolved to a laughter so fierce her ribs began to ache. Accursed would be the one who would slay a draida, so the tales went, and yet Bree felt pure for the first time in three years.

She struggled to her feet and released the bitter residue of her demons with a sigh. Yet even as the breath slipped her lips, she sensed something was wrong. Subtle at first, but flourishing. Her skin began to tingle, and her mouth felt suddenly pinched shut, as though sealed with thick crust. She kicked out but her legs were weightless.

Bree looked to her feet in terror but saw only the forest floor. It was receding. Or she was rising, up, up, *up*, through the trees and then clear of the canopy, out into the admonishing brightness of the full moon.

A murder of crows was gathering in the dark distance, back towards the glade. She could feel them, far off as they were. They were calling. Light as the very air that bore her, she turned to them, overcome with paralysing panic. Wings that weren't hers to command began to beat. *"Many are they who have tried,"* the wind whispered before her ears were stolen.

She fought to reject it, but her strength was ebbing away, along with the essence of everything she'd ever known. Going, going, *gone*. Finally, she screamed, but all that came out was a caw.

About the Author

Michael Panter is an award-winning author from Kettering Town, England with exceedingly high ambitions and a frustratingly low word count per day. In 2018, one of his novellas, *Deathsworn*, won a Watty, Wattpad's highest honour, and his novelette Lilt of a Lark can be found in the best-selling *Writers of the Future* Vol. 38 anthology.

Flamingo *(Phoenicopterus chilensis)*

and

Red-Tailed Hawk *(Buteo jamaicensis)*

Flamingo: A long-legged wading bird, with fink feathers and a long neck, referred to in a group as a "flamboyance of flamingoes"

Red-Tailed Hawk: A diurnal raptor colloquially referred to as a "chicken-hawk," who typically flies to hunt and presumably avoids flamingoes

Felix and the Flamingo

by David Hankins

Felix ruffled his red tail feathers in irritation. Of all the birds to get quarantined with, why a flamingo? Flamingos were idiots! And they stank too. The Candice Lisle Avian Quarantine Center was supposedly the pride of Lincoln Park Zoo, but to Felix it was nothing more than a musty cement room lined with cages. Only the two largest were occupied.

Felix glared across the room at Mateo who stood in his own cage—on one leg—with the satisfied calm of domestication. Felix would never accept captivity. He itched with the need to soar, to hunt with his mate!

The gaping void in his belly gurgled. Four days since the humans disappeared. He was *hungry!*

Felix activated his neural link and tried explaining their situation. Again.

<Look, you dumb flamingo. The humans—>

<It's Mateo, please!> The flamingo's chip-transmission registered as a rich baritone with a pretentious accent. <Honor my Chilean heritage. Just because you're a wild raptor—>

<Red-tailed hawk!>

<—your lack of culturio gives you no right to demean the ancient heritage of the magnifica Chilean Flamingo!>

<Get over yourself. I've heard real Spanish, and yours sucks. You were bred in captivity and hatched right here in Chicago. You've never tasted free skies.> A deep longing for home, for freedom, nearly overwhelmed Felix. He snapped his beak, chirped irritably, and started again.

<Mateo, the humans aren't coming back.>

<Humans would never abandon us! They love us and give us food!>

<They microchipped our brains, didn't like the results, and abandoned us to die!>

<*We're being reintegrated into—*>

<*No!*> Hunger made Felix snappish. He could eat a terrier right now. Or a flamingo. <*It's been four days! At least they left you a bowl of dried shrimp. Did I get any extra rats? No! The humans don't care about us! We're on our own. Now, I can't reach the latch on my cage, but you can reach yours. So stop arguing and get us out of here!*>

Mateo honked and waggled his beak from side to side—as if attempting to jog two brain cells together—then said, <*Very well. If it'll stop your bellyaching. What did you want me to do again?*>

Felix's belly had never ached like it did right now. Nor had his head. He tried to sound calm. <*Stick your long neck through that gap under your gate. Then reach up and pull the lever on your cage door. It's a simple deadbolt.*> Mateo just blinked at him, head cocked.

An entire week of this. He'd been trying to convince Mateo to escape since the day they were dumped at the zoo. Then four days ago the humans didn't return, and Felix's pleas turned desperate. At least in the lab, he hadn't been dependent on this imbecile. He'd had humans to help—

No. Those were the thoughts of domestication.

Mateo's two brain cells must have finally found each other. He settled onto the straw-covered floor and squeezed his head under the gate. It caught for a moment, he honked an *ay, mama-mia!* and then he was through.

<*That's it!*> Felix said. <*The deadbolt's right th—*>

<*Oi!*> a rough British accent interrupted his chip-transmission. <*Sounds like a jailbreak! Need a hand, mate?*>

Felix's head snapped up. He'd never heard another voice in his head besides Mateo's, transmitted through his microchip. They'd been the only birds in the lab. He craned his head in quick jerky movements, looking out the windows. No birds looking in. <*Yes! Help us!*>

<*Right on! Where you at?*>

<*Lincoln Park Zoo! The Lisle Quarantine Center.*>

<*Whatcha doin' there? Eh, no matter. On my way from the cafeteria!*>

Felix screeched for joy. Help was coming! And they sounded competent. Unlike Mateo.

A click and a metallic creak from across the room snapped his attention back to the flamingo. The bonehead had done it! Mateo strode from his cage with a jaunty little dance.

<*Now me! Let me out!*> Felix hopped from his perch and flapped his wings, bouncing around his cage's straw-covered floor.

Mateo marched across the bare cement and looked down upon Felix, his head cocked once again in that infuriating non-expression.

<*The deadbolt! Pull the deadbolt!*>

Mateo bobbed his head from side to side, his way of saying no. <*I suppose I shouldn't expect manners from a wild bird.*>

<*What?*>

<*Manners, courtesy, couth! All week you've pestered me, but never once did you say por favor.*>

<*Please? You've waited all week for…please?*> Unbelievable! Felix screeched at the nitwit outside his cage. <*Fine. Please. PLEASE! Let me OUT!*>

Mateo chortled and pulled the deadbolt with his beak. Felix threw himself at the gate. It popped open and he flopped into the room. Free! He was free! Felix couldn't fly properly—the scientists had clipped their wings—so his flight turned into a happy hop across the cement.

The entry door clicked open and both birds jumped and turned. A brown rat the size of a terrier sauntered in, bulging with muscles and walking on his hind legs like a human. A leather satchel swung by his side.

Hunger burned every thought from Felix's head. He was a starving predator and dinner had just waltzed in.

Dinner stared at him wide-eyed and mumbled aloud, "Bloody Hell!"

Felix's hunting shriek bounced off the walls and he shot across the room. The rat dodged and Felix's talons snagged the satchel's strap. He swung onto the rat's back and pecked at its spine. The first peck missed and the second pierced the swinging satchel. The rat twisted and squirmed.

"Get off! Ya bloody bird! Get offa me!"

Felix lost his balance, fell to the cement, and yanked at the satchel in his beak. Something inside tore and the taste of cold fish flooded Felix's senses.

Food!

He yanked chunks of fish from a foil pouch. He'd never tasted anything so good.

The rat shook loose of the satchel and more pouches spilled onto the floor. It scrambled back and pointed an accusing claw at him. "That's my dinner! Give it back!"

<*Mine!*> Felix screeched again and spread his wings, protecting his kill. The rat's paws went up, held out like a placating human.

"Okay, okay. Bloody law of the jungle outside the lab. I was lookin' forward to that tuna fish." He huffed and eyed Mateo, who was running in circles and honking. "Don't take too long, mate. It's gettin' dark. You're not the only predator in this zoo, and the humans left most of the cages open."

♦ ♦ ♦

Felix was finishing off the third tuna fish pouch when Mateo finally calmed down. The flamingo's mood shift wasn't gradual. More like flipping a switch from panicked to pretentious. He waddled up to the rat and craned his neck downward.

<*Do you know where the humans went, rato?*>

The rat's muzzle split in a furry grin that revealed sharp teeth. "They ran away. The Rat War pushed 'em outta Chicago!" He spread his paws. "This is our land now. Welcome to Ratatopia!"

<*Rat…atopia?*>

"Yeah. All us rats with neural implants got organized, escaped, and started a war against humanity!" His beady eyes sparkled. "And we're winning!"

<*But humans are our friends.*> Mateo's phony Spanish accent slipped, and he shifted from foot to foot, looking distressed.

Felix gulped the last of the tuna and ruffled his feathers. <*Get it through your thick skull, Mateo. No more humans. We're on our own.*>

"As it should be, mate!" The rat exuded self-satisfaction. "I'm Bruiser. Got brought over from McCartney Labs in London for the chipping experiments. Stayed for the war." He chuckled. "What's yer story?"

Given an opportunity to talk about himself, Mateo's mood brightened. <*I am Mateo, Chilean flamingo of impeccable breeding. The savage who assaulted you is Felix.*>

Felix prodded at the pouch, digging out scraps. <*We're neurally implanted too. But for some reason, the humans deemed our experiments a failure and dumped us here for 'reintegration.' Speaking of which…*> Hunger muted, Felix turned and hopped through the open door.

Fresh air that smelled of new spring growth and freedom washed over him, despite the fenced enclosures and low buildings. A shiver shook Felix and he gazed up at puffy pink clouds in a deep blue sky.

Sunset. A predator's favorite time. Starlings susurrated overhead, sending a pang of longing through his chest. He missed soaring. He missed...so many things.

It had been over a year since the humans had taken him. His mate probably thought him dead. He still dreamed of Her, though his dreams had changed since he'd been chipped. Things had names now. Birds shouldn't assign names to things. Especially not human names. Things had scents. Sounds. Textures.

That was how he remembered Her. Golden eyes and a piercing cry overlaid with the wild smell of sunshine on Her feathers.

Someday he'd soar again. He would find Her.

Mateo pushed through the door, breaking Felix's reverie. The flamingo honked excitedly then bolted down the sidewalk. Spindly legs made his pink body waddle like a goose while his head stayed perfectly level.

<*Where are you going?*> Felix asked.

<*Family! I smell flamingos!*>

Bruiser shot out of the Lisle Quarantine Center after Mateo. "Hold on, mate! Not that way! You tryin' ta get eaten?" Bruiser bounded after the flamingo and yelled over his shoulder. "Come on, Felix!"

Felix ignored the rat and leapt into the air. He needed to fly! To return home! He pumped his wings, struggled, but clipped feathers refused to gain lift. He hit the ground—hard—and screeched at the top of his lungs.

He was grounded. The feathers would grow back, eventually, but until then—

A terrified honk from Mateo and a cat's warbling snarl snapped Felix's gaze to the now-empty sidewalk. A shiver crawled down his spine. Mateo wouldn't last one day in the wild.

Felix bounded down the sidewalk with an awkward hopping, flapping motion. He rounded a corner and froze.

A gray lynx crouched on the trail, its back to Felix. It had thick paws, black-tufted ears, and a twitching tail. Mateo and Bruiser stood frozen before it, backed against one of those small flatbed carts that humans drove around parks. The lynx stalked forward.

Felix gave his hunting screech and the lynx's head snapped around. He flapped as hard as possible and arced over the cat's head. It swatted at him but didn't leap. He landed between it and the others, spread his wings, and screeched again. <*Mine!*>

The lynx growled, ears back, hackles rising.

There were scrambling sounds behind Felix. "Into the driver's seat, stretch! I'm steering!" Felix half-turned his head, keeping one eye on the lynx, which lashed its bushy tail.

Bruiser and Mateo were in the cart. The flamingo looked uncomfortable in the driver's seat, sitting sideways to let one spindly leg dangle under the dash. Bruiser stood by the pedals, placing Mateo's foot. "Push here to go, here to stop. Oh, man, I've always wanted to drive one o' these!"

Mateo craned his head upside down to look at Bruiser. <*I don't understand.*> Neither did Felix, but he had bigger problems.

The lynx stalked forward, each step a precise announcement of inevitable death. Felix screeched again, wingspan blocking the sidewalk, and refused to step back. The cat would leap the second he showed fear or weakness.

"Where's the…ah ha!" There was a click and then the cart leapt forward. Bruiser jumped to the steering wheel and yelled, "Come on, Felix, let's ride!"

The cart sped away. Felix leapt into the sky and the cat lunged for him. It missed, and he flapped furiously after the weaving cart. His wings burned with effort, and he tumbled downward.

He hit the flatbed with a thump, talons scrambling for traction. They caught an attached metal ring. He flapped his wings for balance. Bruiser cheered, and the cart swerved violently forward. Felix looked back.

The lynx bounded after them.

<*Faster! It's gaining!*> Felix's breath came fast, his heart beating like it would burst out of his chest.

"More 'go' pedal, stretch!" Bruiser clung to the wheel with all four paws, shifting his weight left and right to steer.

<*It's Mateo!*> The flamingo gave an indignant honk and the cart skidded to a stop. The lynx bounced off the rear bumper and tumbled aside.

"Wrong pedal!" Bruiser slapped at Mateo's neck. The flamingo dodged and pecked the rat's head. "Ow!"

The cat surged to its feet, shook its head, and snarled. Its warbling hunting cry filled Felix with adrenaline. He needed to fly!

<*Go-go-go!*> he screamed, wings flapping uselessly as he clutched the metal ring.

The cart jumped forward then skidded around a corner and bumped into the grass. Felix held on but slammed onto his side. Stars danced in his vision and he gasped for breath.

<Where'd you learn to drive, you maniac?>

Bruiser threw a furry grin over his shoulder, leaned left, wove them through a flower bed, then back onto the sidewalk. "Top Gear reruns on BBC! Pedal to the metal!"

<It is!> Mateo honked.

They passed through the zoo's north gate, lynx loping right behind them. It leapt with a snarl and slammed into Felix. He screeched, scratched, and pecked with all his might. They rolled into Mateo's seat in a snarling tangle of claws and talons. Felix bit an ear, tore clean through it, and the cat caught his wing in powerful jaws.

"Hold ooooooooon!" The cart hit a bump, leapt into the air, then dropped out from under them. The lynx shrieked, releasing Felix, and they tumbled downward.

The splash took Felix completely by surprise. Murky water enveloped him, dark and heavy. His talons caught something soft and he latched onto it. Fur. The body beneath him jerked aside. Too powerful for Bruiser. The lynx. Felix thrust his head forward, bit deep, and tore. Again. And again. He savaged flesh with his talons. Blood filled the water before he broke the surface and let go.

Felix gasped for air, beak open wide. How did ducks do this? He started to sink again and spread his wings across the surface. The lynx surfaced several yards away and swam for the shore. Mateo floated serenely beside him, head high. Bruiser paddled in a circle and yelled at the lynx.

"That's right! You better run, ya plonker!" Bruiser stopped swimming long enough to shake a fist. The lynx limped from the water, blood streaming down its right shoulder. It eyed them and mewled before padding back to the zoo.

♦ ♦ ♦

Felix paddled with a new appreciation for waterfowl. Mateo drifted past, head cocked to the side.

<Do you need help?>

Felix huffed, almost said no, but swallowed his pride. He cawed gently. <Yes. Por favor.>

Mateo's head bobbed in a pleased manner. <Grab my tail feathers and I'll drag you to the flock.>

<Flock?>

Bruiser yelled as he paddled furiously toward the far shore. "Are ya blind? There must be a hundred of the pink buggers!"

Felix blinked and looked around. Indeed, near the pond's far end was a flock of flamingos. Bright pink mottled with white against the shore's cascade of green. He bit gently onto Mateo's tail feathers and allowed himself to be dragged across the pond.

They soon reached the flock, who honked and clucked like geese. Heads twitched from side to side in unison. How did they do that? These birds weren't microchipped, so Felix couldn't speak to them mind-to-mind, but he understood their body language. Cautious of him but welcoming of Mateo.

Bruiser was another matter. He climbed onto the muddy nesting ground and the nearest flamingos hissed at him.

The drenched rat held up both hands. "Not lookin' for a fight, pinkie. Just wanted distance from that soggy moggy tryin' to eat us."

Felix pulled himself onto the mud and shook his wings. Water flew. <Thank you, Bruiser. You saved us with that cart.>

"Well, saved meself. You was just an added bonus." His tone was light, joking.

<I...I'm sorry I tried to eat you.>

"No worries, mate! Law of the jungle. Speakin' of which, I gotta run. There's a war on, and I don't wanna miss it!" The rat plodded through the flamingos, who split to give him a wide berth.

Felix shook himself again—he was soaked!—and Mateo honked at him, all pretense of a Spanish accent gone from his chip-transmission. <You placed yourself in danger. For me. Why?>

Felix looked for somewhere dry to stand. He failed and ruffled his feathers. <Couldn't let you die in your first five minutes of freedom.>

<Yes, well. Flamingos are not without gratitude. You are one of us now. Welcome to the family, mi hermano!> He honked, and the flock joined in, bobbing their heads excitedly.

<Wait, what?>

<You are an honorary flamingo, Felix. Please, join our flock!>

Felix almost said no. Red-tailed hawks were solitary creatures. They mated for life, but the idea of a flock was anathema. Yet Mateo's offer touched him. It rang of...friendship.

<Okay. But only until my feathers grow back. And don't expect me to strut around all pretentious-like! Hawks don't strut.>

<*Perhaps. We shall see.*>

Felix spied an oak tree on the shore and plodded through the mud. He walked as tall as possible, trying to keep his feathers clean. It was *not* a strut, merely practical.

The sky darkened and the Flamingos settled in for the night, standing one-legged with their beaks tucked under a wing. Felix perched on a high oak branch and gazed northward. A hawk's piercing cry echoed through the night. It wasn't Her, but it stirred the longing in Felix's soul. He gave a soft chirp in reply.

He would find Her again. In time. But for now, he had a family—a crazy family to be sure—that accepted him. This was a safe place, among friends, where he could rest and recover.

And then he would soar!

About the Author

David Hankins was recently named a Writers of the Future winner for Volume 39 (April 2023). He writes lighthearted speculative fiction from the thriving cornfields of Iowa where he lives with his wife, daughter, and two dragons disguised as cats. He suffers from incurable wanderlust and—through some glitch in the bureaucracy—convinced the U.S. Army to fund his travels for twenty years. As a retired veteran, David devotes his time to writing, traveling with family, and finding new ways to pay his mortgage. His stories can be found in DreamForge Magazine, Factor Four Magazine, and elsewhere. You can find him at https://davidhankins.com

Peacock *(Pavo cristatus)*

The male of the "Peafowl" species, marked by royal blue body feathers and the eye-spotted "tail," which can be fanned in a brilliant and seemingly powerful display

…such displays appear less grand after significant postmortem decay

The Boy He Wove

by Ryan A Cole

Pradesh had learned much in his years as a bone-knitter. He knew how to strip the life-thread from a corpse, until the milky white fibers settled into his fingertips. He knew how to keep it from seeping back into him, from warping his own tired skeleton to mush. And better yet, he knew exactly when the thread should be woven—when his cuticles crackled, and his knucklebones crunched, and it felt as if his wrists would bend up to his elbows if he let himself sneeze, or look away, or even breathe.

But above all, he knew this: Never trust a flesh-knitter.

Scammers, the lot of them. Tricksters and thieves. First, they befriend you. Then, they turn the whole damn province against you, burning your shop into a pile of timber and salting the earth so nothing can grow—not the weeds for your supper or the bones for your power—and digging up all of the bodies you had gathered from a lifetime of service, and stashing them all in the walls of a workshop that was miles away from what was meant to be your grave.

That was what he got for putting faith in someone else.

Pradesh had been dead for a few weeks now—or dead in about every way that could matter. Ninety-nine percent of him was in that workshop. All that remained, all that the mob had forgotten to steal, and that Kathavi, the knitter, had missed in his threadwork, was one tiny bone. One measly toe. Not so convenient for seeking revenge. Nor, for that matter, a miles-long journey. Sure, he was present through his earth-bound spirit, but the most he could do on a physical level was tap one end of his body on the ground, roll in the dirt, and creep like a worm through the piles of ash, the shattered glass jars, the splinters of table.

Tap, stretch, tap. The language of his new life. The voice of a toe bone without any mouth.

Lucky for him that he had someone who would listen.

"Papa?" Anang's voice carried from the doorway, the burnt leaning planks half-collapsed on themselves. The boy, his arms wrapped around a wad of gray blankets, stumbled through the foyer. "I finally found what you've been looking for," he said.

Pradesh tried his best not to cringe at his son's appearance. The mismatched eyes—one black and one green—both of them sagging and too close together. The lumpy, bald head, all patchy and scabbed. The cheekbones, jagged as the spindle on the mantle. And most obvious of all, and most egregious: the skin. Anang, from the moment of his flesh-knit birth, had been sewn with whatever Kathavi had on hand—be it the feathers of a hawk, the scales of a viper, the sandpaper feet of a psoriatic chicken. He was the product of a secret, revolutionary alliance, of bone and flesh-knitting as they always should have been. The child Pradesh had always wanted, always dreamt of.

And now, thanks to Kathavi, the scourge of the province.

Peering past Anang to the pile of blankets, Pradesh tapped the tip of his toe in the dirt. "Human?" he said in the code they'd devised.

Anang cocked his head. "What was that?" he said.

"Is it *human*?" said Pradesh, now frantically tapping. "A man or a woman?"

Anang didn't answer, but he slowly unwound the folds of the blanket. Both of them leaned in, eager to see.

"A child?" said Pradesh. "It's so small." *Tappety-tap.*

But Anang shook his head, and as he reached into the bundle and extracted the pile of mud-smeared bones—the bones Pradesh hoped to soon call his own—Pradesh stopped tapping, and he grimaced at the gift.

"It was all I could find," said Anang with a smile. The most disgustingly sweet curve of purple, scabby lips. A smile he hadn't seen in quite some time.

And Pradesh didn't have the heart to make it disappear. "It's perfect," he lied. "Here, help me put it together."

♦ ♦ ♦

The skeleton, they learned, was anything but perfect.

"What is it?" said Anang as the two of them fiddled with the dozens of bones that were scattered around them. Some were as short as Pradesh was wide, many as thin, and most were as light as a plucked down-feather, and surprisingly hollow; their echo felt empty. Which gave him his answer.

"It's a bird," said Pradesh—*tap, tap*—in the dirt. "But what kind, I'm not sure."

What appeared to be the pelvis was squat at the hips, the legs short and stubby, the vertebrae stretching a foot above its chest. There was a tailbone significantly thicker than the rest, which looked to have evolved to pull a heavy train of feathers. A suspicion confirmed, soon enough, by Anang.

"It was buried by the granary on the other side of town. I almost didn't see it, the grave was so deep."

The granary. Where each year, the wild peacocks gathered. Where they picked at the barrels of poorly-stored crops.

Pradesh would have sighed if he still had breath. Would have gone, by himself, to Kathavi's own workshop, where the knitter had stockpiled all the town's dead. Would have found himself a body he knew how to use.

But this would have to do. Better to be trapped in a bird than a toe bone.

"Stay back," he said—*tap, tap*—against Anang, while the boy's scaly eyebrows scrunched up in concern. They tugged at the heart Pradesh didn't have, made the marrow in his toe-bone body prickle. Strange, how one look could say so much.

"It's alright," said Pradesh. "It'll work, I promise."

Or rather, it had to. Otherwise, they wouldn't have a way to Kathavi. And without him, Pradesh would never rescue his skeleton, never hug his son again, never smile at his smile. If Anang could be believed, the bones were all there. He'd made Kathavi promise to keep them intact. And Pradesh knew well how persuasive the boy could be.

Resting his chipped enamel shell on the spot where the bird's tiny vertebrae connected with its skull, Pradesh cleared his mind. He tried to tap into the bird's latent life-thread, to draw on the milky, white primordial essence that served as a glue for this plane of existence. When he found it, it slipped, eel-like, through his grasp. But he caught it at the tail. Steadily yanked it. Drew it from the calcium and into the light.

Carefully, he unspooled the thread around the vertebrae.

Allowed a spark of hope.

And then he started to knit.

He wove each bone to the base of the next, the marrow-core stretching with a snap-crackle-hiss. Bending and breaking and melding as needed, 'til the bones had been tied and the creature in front of him looked as it had in the moment of its death, without any flesh. Before letting go, he made sure to tie his own toe into the mix. A tiny, white speck, indistinguishable from the rest—a vessel for his spirit. No one, including Kathavi, would notice.

Pradesh stood up on a pair of rickety legs. He wriggled the claws on his four-toed feet. And he extended the featherless bones of his wings, feeling at last that he could go where he wanted, do what he wanted, say (a bit better than before) what he wanted.

"Thank you," he said, though it came out as a squawk.

His son's scabby face split into a grin. Anang put a leathery hand on Pradesh.

But he didn't pull away. Not now, not ever. The two of them, finally, had what they needed. And now, there was only one place left to go.

◆ ◆ ◆

Pradesh hadn't known what to expect as a peacock. He'd assumed a pair of wings would feel like arms, that the curve of a beak would remind him of lips. What he hadn't prepared for was the dizziness, the vertigo. He liked having eye sockets (sans actual eyes), but having one hole in each side of his head made it difficult to focus. As he jostled along in the crook of Anang's arm, and they swept through the fur-lined door of Kathavi's workshop, he offered silent thanks that he didn't have a stomach. It would have long been emptied.

"We're here," whispered Anang, as if Pradesh didn't know. As if he could have forgotten the red-clay walls, the reek of rotten sinew, the layers of old bear skins and sheep fleece and feathers that were ready to be woven onto someone else's body.

He hoped, if they were lucky, *his* would be that body.

"I'm busy," called a sad-sounding voice around the corner, where the hallway curved into the heart of the workshop.

"Too busy for me?" said Anang, voice shaking. Wielding the hurt they had chosen him to wear, and which would whittle the most at Kathavi's broken conscience. Pradesh had heard rumors of the man feeling guilty.

The Boy He Wove

Kathavi poked his head around the skin-draped wall, and he ran a dark hand over the scar on his neck where Pradesh had once knit his broken collarbone to health. Back when they were friends. When they wanted the same thing.

His beady eyes bloodshot, he gaped at Anang. The boy he had made, and then betrayed, and then abandoned. "Anang?" The name a whisper. "What—what are you doing here?"

"I need your help," said Anang.

Kathavi's eyes glistened, transported to the past. To the pitchforks, the fire. The lies that Pradesh would come after their loved ones, turning their broken, buried bodies into playthings. A collection of one that would inevitably grow.

Anang, unsteadily, shuffled up to Kathavi. He held out Pradesh. "I found this in the graves that were by the mausoleum."

Kathavi ran a quick, discerning eye over Pradesh, the milky white thread that bound the bones together. "It's one of his creations."

"Yes, but from *before*."

They both knew the painful implication of that word.

Kathavi reached out, gently poked at Pradesh. Ran his calloused fingers on the cold, flattened wing-bones, the unclothed ribs, the elongated neck. It was all Pradesh could do to not reach up and bite him. "I can't," said Kathavi, "it's still too dangerous. The townsfolk are angry. If they see that I've clothed one of *his* abominations, they might come back for more." Kathavi gritted his teeth. "I won't give them any more reason to hurt you."

Which was what they'd expected Kathavi to say. Out of fear, or self-interest, the man was a coward.

But Anang was prepared. He lay one patchwork hand on Kathavi, and he made his voice crack, let his eyes start to water. "Please?" said the boy, who wasn't really a boy. "I want something of my own. I don't have anything else."

And maybe it was luck, or the sickly-sweet way that Anang's lips twisted, but Pradesh saw a change in the flesh-knitter's demeanor. "Fine," sighed Kathavi. "For you, I will try."

There it was again, an irresistible smile. Anang leaned in and gave Kathavi a hug. "Thank you," he said, and laid Pradesh on the workbench.

Kathavi just grumbled. "Now go," he said, "before anyone sees you. Come back tomorrow. I should have it done by then."

With that, Anang slipped like a shadow from the workshop, leaving Pradesh alone with the man who had killed him.

◆◆◆

The real work began later that evening.

Pradesh: wings splayed face-up on the workbench, tail-bone clicking impatiently beneath him, eye-socket trained on the flesh-knitter's needles.

Kathavi: looming overhead, chewing on his lip as he mumbled to himself. "Would the crest go here? Should the plume go there? Are the feathers of a peacock more blue or green?" He examined the nooks and the crevices of Pradesh, determining where—or rather, *how*—to clothe him. Apparently, peacocks were not the man's specialty.

"Where are my bones?" Each word a squawk. "Where did you hide them, you thief!" *Squawk-squawk!*

But Kathavi ignored him. The voice of a peacock meant nothing to the knitter. "Will you stop wriggling?" A fist on his vertebrae. Pickle-thick fingers clamped around his neck.

And Pradesh had nowhere to run, to hide. Helpless, he let the flesh-knitter study him, biding his time. Hoping he didn't take notice of the way that the claws of his right foot glowed a bit brighter, how the stitch of the thread caught on one of his toes.

Kathavi ran an impatient hand on Pradesh. Over his pelvis; his thin, knobby knees; down to his right foot, tapping in a frenzy…

Pradesh squirmed away. "Let go of me!" *Squawk!*

Kathavi leaned back. He wiped at the sweat on his liver-spotted forehead. Rummaged in the hides and the feathers and the scales that were stacked on the workbench, waiting to be woven. "Peacocks," he muttered. "I don't have any peacocks." Then, even softer. "Miserable creatures."

That's right, thought Pradesh. *Miserable for* you.

Suddenly, Kathavi pushed away from the workbench. "You wait here," he said to Pradesh. Then he slunk away through the door of the workshop, presumably to find a live peacock to steal from. Which shouldn't be difficult—he was a master at stealing.

The door clicked shut.

Pradesh, once again, was alone.

But not for long.

The door to the workshop slowly creaked open, and Anang, limbs dragging on the floor, poked in. Just as they had planned.

Pradesh waved him over. "Untie me!" he hissed.

His son did so, and in the moments they had before Kathavi returned, they desperately searched for Pradesh's human bones.

♦ ♦ ♦

"This is pointless," said Pradesh as he riffled through the last of the crates by the workbench. He slumped on the floor. "Kathavi must've burned them."

Anang, on the other hand, wasn't deterred. "Papa?" he said. "I think you'll want to see this."

Pradesh waddled over; he peered into a section of crumbling wall where Kathavi had attempted to smear it in plaster. Where the tip of a fingerbone jutted into the lamplight. A human fingerbone. Maybe *his* fingerbone.

Pradesh dove head-first into the wall. Bone-wings scrabbling, beak tip chomping, bits of the once-packed clay flying everywhere. The deeper he dug, the more skeleton he found, pieces of it falling into a pile on the floor.

"You wonderful boy!" yelled Pradesh—*squawk-squawk*! "You wonderful, beautiful, precious boy!" Anang grinned back, both of them digging. Both of them flushed with hope, and excitement.

And both unaware of the man in the doorway.

"Anang," said Kathavi. "What are you doing?"

Half a second of silence, when the world stopped moving. Pradesh: his wingtips buried in the wall. Anang: his overlong fingers caked in clay. They glanced at each other, glanced back at Kathavi, and knew their chance at deceit had ended.

As quickly as it had stopped, the world started moving.

Kathavi let go of the feathers he was carrying—a seafoam green with cerulean edges—and he dove at the wall. "I should have known it was you, I should have known you'd come back!" Voice carved into a sharp, bitter blade. "But there's nothing you can do. The boy is mine. Anang is *mine.*"

Pradesh did his best to back away from Kathavi, but the strength of a bird wasn't that of a man, and he felt his neck crunch as Kathavi's grip tightened.

"The bones!" yelled Pradesh, pointing to the wall. To Anang still beside it, watching them in horror. "Grab the rest of the bones!"

But the boy, eyes wide, backed up into a corner. Fear and indecision writ large on his face.

Pradesh felt his hope start to fade at that retreat. But he couldn't give up, not here, not now, when his chance at a real life, a *family*, was in reach.

He may not have had brute strength on his side, but he had something else. Something wispy and white.

He unspooled the life-thread from one of his wings. Watched as the stitches binding them dissolved. And as the filaments sizzled, and his vertebrae crunched, and the whiplash threatened to grind him into dust, he fastened the knot.

And he threw it at Kathavi.

The man recoiled, holding his chest. He yelped as the knot unraveled and spread, knitting his bones to unnatural angles. Clavicle twisting up to wrap around his neck, ribcage bending out to cradle his elbows. Bone by bone, he picked apart Kathavi. Bone by bone, he fastened the stitches. And bone by bone, he gave Anang another chance to snag what they had come for. But the boy still huddled, quivering, in the corner.

Kathavi fell, whimpering. He struggled with the sutures, but the thread wouldn't move. His skeleton held. Both were immune to his flesh-knitting magic.

So, he threw it at something that he knew would obey.

A greasy black thread whipped out at Pradesh, pulling a mountain of feathers over his eye-sockets. Tiny quills stabbing him, crushing him in seafoam green and cerulean. Pricking his beak, his skull, his wings, until all he could see, all he could taste, was the recycled skin and the freshly plucked feathers of the peacock Kathavi had left to obtain. Pradesh began to drown in his newly clothed flesh.

"Anang!" he yelled, but it came out jumbled. The flesh-thread filling his beak was too thick, the feathers that were clogging his throat too heavy. Desperately, he grappled for his own knitting spell, and he pulled until Kathavi was howling on the floor. Both of them writhed and fought and screamed.

"Stop!" Anang's voice. The first thing he'd said since Kathavi had returned.

But neither of them stopped.

Anang knelt by Pradesh, and he rested a warm, scaly cheek on his skull. Petted his smothering blue-green crest. "Please," said the boy, "please, Papa, let go."

"I'll only let go if *he* does," said Pradesh. "If he gives me my bones."

"*Never*," hissed Kathavi, his eyes squeezed shut in pain.

But Anang was unrelenting. He crawled over to Kathavi. "Papa can stay as a peacock for now." Dark tears left oily tracks on his cheeks. "What if he left, and he didn't come back? Would you promise to give him his feathers and skin? Just please, don't hurt him, he's all I have."

Kathavi kept groaning as his body came undone.

Pradesh kept a hold on the man's stitched-up bones. Ready to break him, to kill him, to win. His anger white-hot, his knits wrapped tight. He wasn't convinced he could let go of either.

But faced with the fear in Anang's mismatched eyes, Pradesh knew one thing: he had to at least try. His love for his son trumped everything else.

Stubbornly, he loosened the knots on Kathavi. Let go of the thread, until the filaments dangled like droopy white worms.

Anang knelt quietly next to Kathavi. He whispered in his ear. One by one, the feathers fell away, and the black thread choking Pradesh dissipated.

Both on the floor, they glared at each other—Kathavi bent into a misshapen ball, Pradesh in a pile of keratin and sinew—and even with all of the hurt they'd inflicted, they knew, deep down, that they had something in common. Something worth more than a chance at revenge.

Anang stood between them: a living, breathing barrier. He smiled, his cracked teeth snagging on his lips. "Please," he whispered. "No more fighting."

And faced with that smile, Pradesh couldn't say no.

♦ ♦ ♦

Later that evening, when Kathavi's bones were set and Pradesh—for now, at least—was a newly clothed peacock, complete with a coat of cerulean feathers and a fuzzy green crest on his bumpy-skinned head, he sat with Anang at the threshold of the workshop. "Now what?" he said—*tap, tap*—like before.

"We shouldn't have come here," said Anang, his eyes glassy.

Pradesh had a hunch that there was more left unsaid, that the last few weeks—of hiding and scheming—had taken its toll, and that Pradesh's stolen body was the least of their worries. And yet, it was the one—the *only*—thing he had focused on.

"You're right," said Pradesh. "I was selfish, and…" What else was there to say? "I'm sorry."

Anang leaned into him, warm against his wings. Even though the boy didn't nod, didn't speak, he hugged Pradesh tighter than he ever had before. As tightly as Pradesh had always hoped a son would.

Bones, in that moment, were a trivial thing. He had all that he needed, all that he wanted. He nuzzled his beak in Anang's scaly arm. And for the first time in weeks, he let himself smile.

About the Author

Ryan A Cole is a speculative fiction writer who lives in Virginia with his husband and snuggly pug child. His work has appeared or is forthcoming in: Writers of the Future, Vol. 37; Ember Journal; and the anthology Mother: Tales of Love & Terror by Weird Little Worlds Press. He is an Associate Member of the SFWA, an Associate Editor at PodCastle, and a First Reader at Diabolical Plots.

Find out more at www.ryancolewrites.com

Harris's Hawk *(Parabuteo Unicinctus)*

A medium-sized, brown bird of prey, sometimes referred to as a "wolf hawk" due to its species' tendency to hunt in packs

Cheer Hawks and a Side of Murder

by Crystal Crawford

On a muggy mid-spring evening in downtown Tampa, just blocks from the moonlit bay, three Harris's hawks descended toward a dim back alley behind a rundown strip mall. The shops were closed for the night, all lights off but one—the back porch light of Madame Sava's Emporium.

Tory was the last hawk to land. By the time her talons hit pavement, the others had already shifted. The alley soon contained three cheerleaders, half of Morrison Academy's varsity squad. They were dressed in variations of black leggings and dark, oversized sweatshirts, their attempt at blending in.

Tory tried the shop's backdoor. It was locked. A handwritten note was taped to the door: *Back at 9pm.*

Jillian, the squad captain, smoothed her long, blonde ponytail, then turned a disgusted stare on the girl next to Tory. "That was gross, Meredith." She planted her hands on her slender hips.

Meredith stretched one arm across her chest, working out the kinks from flying. She was stockier than Jillian, thighs and arm muscles honed by lifting at the bottom of the pyramid. She blew her asymmetrical bangs—dyed black this week—away from her eyes and shrugged. "I thought we decided not to talk about what happens in hawk form, *Jillian*. It was a mouse. I was hungry. Deal with it."

Tory suppressed a shudder, remembering how the bones had crunched, and sighed. "C'mon, guys. Can we focus? Madame Sava should be here any minute." Bickering was nothing new for Jillian and Meredith, especially since the arrangement with Madame Sava, but the last thing they needed tonight was to draw extra attention—Tory's red hair and lanky height did that well enough on its own. She pulled the hood of her sweatshirt up over her ponytail and leaned against the alley wall.

"Let me talk when she gets here. It's my money," Jillian said, her shrill voice also sounding mouselike to Tory. "Do *not* screw this up for me. We're almost out of time to undo this before it's permanent, and I will *not* go to prom as a hawk."

Tory checked the time on her watch, then dropped her head back against the wall of the shop. "Fifteen after. If I'm out past ten o'clock again, I'll be grounded for eternity." She tapped her fingers on her thigh. Prom was the least of Tory's worries. If her foster parents found out about *any* of this, she'd be far worse than grounded; they'd kick her out. She couldn't afford to navigate all the rules and stress of another new place. Not with finals coming up. She had already repeated eleventh grade the year her mom got sent to rehab. She was *so close* to graduation, to proving she was more than the high school dropout everyone expected her to be. She couldn't get held back another year.

Meredith fidgeted with the sleeves of her sweatshirt. "She said she was coming, right?"

Jillian huffed. "She'll be here."

A large, dark shape smashed into the ground just beside Tory.

All three girls jumped back and screamed—then screamed again as they realized the shape was a person.

Jillian took a tentative step forward. "Where did they come from?"

"I think they fell from the sky," Meredith said.

The girls looked up—nothing but moonlit clouds hung above them.

Tory crept toward the limp form. "Hello? Are you—okay?" She nudged the person's shoulder with a sneakered foot. The body flopped onto its back.

Glassy eyes stared up at her from Madame Sava's lifeless face.

◆ ◆ ◆

Tory dug Madame Sava's keys from the corpse's pocket (accompanied by less-than-helpful squeals of disgust from Jillian and Meredith), and the girls carried the body inside the shop. Now, with the yellowed light of the old desk lamp in Madame Sava's back office illuminating those vacant eyes, the full reality of what they were staring at sank in.

Tory never should've agreed to this plan in the first place. Jillian had promised the strange stones she'd gotten from Madame Sava were a harmless way to gain an edge for nationals, but life was never that easy. *Winning will look great on scholarship applications!*—that had been the pitch that sold Tory. *It's no big deal,* Jillian had said. *We'll get enhanced speed and agility for a couple weeks, and as a bonus, we can shift into hawks whenever we want until the spell wears off! It'll be awesome, trust me!* But if Tory had learned anything in this experience, it was never to believe Jillian when she said, *Trust me, it's no big deal.* The fine print on contracts with shady emporium dealers, it turned out, was a very big deal. No one had mentioned that if they didn't return to Madame Sava to break the shifting curse before the deadline, they'd be stuck permanently as hawks.

And now she was staring at a corpse.

"You guys." Tory stared up at Jillian and Meredith across Madame Sava's body. "What are we going to do?"

"Call the cops?" Meredith stepped back against the wall, putting distance between herself and Madame Sava's body.

"And say *what*, Meredith?" Jillian always masked fear with aggression at competitions, Tory knew, and she was doing the same thing now. Her voice turned mocking. "We're totally innocent, we swear! We were just harmlessly loitering in a back alley in the dark when a body dropped down on us from the sky!"

Meredith hugged her arms to her chest. "Well, it's true!"

Jillian barked a harsh laugh. "Would *you* believe it? I know I wouldn't."

Cold fingers of dread raced down Tory's spine. Forget being kicked out—arrest for murder would be *way* worse. "Maybe we leave. Pretend we were never here."

Meredith gaped at her. "Are you serious? We can't just leave a dead body! Besides, what if there are security cameras, or—or our fingerprints are on the door or something?"

Tory stared at her. *Fingerprints.* Tory had grabbed the keys, opened the door, turned on the lamp. Her fingerprints would be on everything.

Jillian planted her hands back on her hips. "We can't leave. We need to figure out how to break this curse. Besides, if there are security cameras, we're screwed, anyway. They'll have seen us shift."

A deep voice came from the darkened front area of the shop. "There are no cameras."

The girls shrieked. Jillian and Meredith grabbed onto each other and ducked behind Tory.

"Who are you? How did you get in here?" Tory said.

A tall man in a long, dark coat stepped into the office doorway. "Lesson number one: never speak freely until you're sure you're alone." His smooth, deep voice seemed to fill the whole shop, carrying a hint of a Southern drawl. He was middle-aged and handsome, in an old-timey movie kind of way, with a clean-shaven face, dark eyes, and thick, black hair slicked back with gel.

"Lesson one for *what?*" Tory stepped back into the other girls, eyeing the door to the alley. Could they make it?

"Your new job." The man gave them a cold smile. "You, my three lovely hawks, are going to help me solve this murder."

◆ ◆ ◆

The next night, Tory, Jillian, and Meredith landed in the shadows outside a convenience store five blocks from Madame Sava's Emporium. The man had told them to go to school like usual, to keep appearances, but by fourth period, Tory's stomach had officially reached the level of knots that made keeping lunch down impossible. She'd spent the rest of the day in the nurse's office, scrolling her phone for any reports on Madame Sava. So far, there was nothing, but that had just made Tory's anxiety worse. This entire situation was a landmine, waiting for one false step to set it off. They didn't even know this man. Now, sneaking out of her house after curfew to meet him in a dark parking lot just felt like the next wrong turn in a hellish Uber ride Tory had never wanted to be on in the first place.

Tory shifted to human form alongside Jillian and Meredith. "I don't trust him," she said.

Jillian whispered back. "Of course not. He's probably a psycho. But he knows we were there, Tor. And he knew what we could do. If anyone besides Madame Sava has info on how to break this curse before the end of the week, it's him. We play along, find out what he knows—and if he gets creepy, we fly away and turn him in to the cops. They'll believe our word over some middle-aged psycho. Easy."

"Easy?" Tory glared back at her. "You mean like 'Just a little extra agility and speed for Nationals, Tory. It's no big deal. It'll be *easy*'?"

"Like you weren't ecstatic when we won!" Jillian narrowed her eyes at Tory. "Don't act like some kind of victim, Tory. No one *made* you do this. You and Meredith signed that contract just like I did, and we won, just like I promised. But if you're so picky about how I got it done, maybe you should've come up with your own solution!"

Tory threw her hands up. "We are turning into *hawks*, Jillian. Hawks, forever! This is the exact opposite of a solution."

Jillian leaned toward Tory and gave her a cold glare. "We're *all* stuck with this, and I'm trying to fix it. Help, or get out of my way."

"We should've just done steroids," Meredith muttered.

Tory kicked at a loose bit of gravel. "We never should've done *any* of this."

"On that, my lovelies," the long-jacketed man said as he appeared from the shadows, "I agree entirely. Now let's get to work."

He clapped his hands, and all four figures vanished into the shadows.

◆ ◆ ◆

Tory stumbled as her feet hit concrete. Beside her, Jillian screamed. All three girls now stood on the oil-stained second floor of an abandoned parking garage, a shorted-out fluorescent light flickering above them.

"How—how did you—" Meredith stammered.

The long-jacketed man stood in the shadows a few feet away, watching them. "Surprise pounce, flush and ambush, and relay," he said.

Tory gaped at him. "What?" Jillian and Meredith cowered behind her.

"The three main tactics Harris's hawks use for cooperative hunting in the wild. One of the rare species of raptors that actually *do* cooperate to hunt. When they land, they even stack on top of each other sometimes—like cheerleaders." The long-jacketed man narrowed his dark eyes at the girls. "Stop your bickering. You will work together from now on. Understood? Or our deal is off."

Tory returned his stare. "We never made a deal."

"You do what I tell you, and I don't turn you in for murder. That's the deal."

Jillian stepped forward. "We'll take it."

"Jillian!" Tory spun toward her.

Jillian looked at her and shrugged. "What other choice do we have?"

The man smiled. "Indeed."

Tory turned to him. "I don't agree to anything. Not until I know what you want us to do."

The man met her stare. "Basic surveillance. Fly over a few places, see what's happening, report back. Do it all in hawk form, and no one will suspect a thing. You're not a native species, but most people don't look closely. In fact, working together, you could have it all done by the end of the night."

"By tonight?" Meredith asked.

The man nodded. "Scout's honor."

Tory scoffed. No way this man was a Scout. "What kind of places?"

"Local business owners' places, mostly. Just a quick peek at their homes or shops, to see if anyone's talking. Someone must know something. Just land on a windowsill or roof, and your hawk ears will pick up any conversations inside, no problem. Then report back to me."

Tory stared at him. "That's all?"

The man grinned. "That's all."

Tory glanced at the others, who nodded their approval. "Okay, I guess we'll do it."

"Excellent." The man's grin widened. "Your first target is just around the corner from here."

"Wait!" Jillian stepped forward. "We'll do it on one condition."

The man froze. "And what would that be?"

"You help us break this hawk curse when we're done. I don't want it anymore."

The man's eyes narrowed. "And you think I have the ability to break it?"

Jillian pulled her shoulders back and stood tall. "Yes."

The man's smile returned. "Very well. Deal."

He clapped his hands, and all four figures vanished.

◆ ◆ ◆

The first two locations the man sent them were empty and quiet. As they swooped toward the dockside auto shop that was their third target, Tory saw a blonde, broad-shouldered man wearing a crocheted hunter-green sweater—like something Tory's late grandmother would've made—slip in through the shop's back door.

Jillian glanced back over her wing at Tory and Meredith then banked left, descending toward the roof of the building.

Wind tickled Tory's feathers as she followed Jillian's turn. Flying was actually kind of awesome, now that she'd gotten over the terror of morphing into a bird. Permanent hawk-form was definitely not in her life plans, but she'd be sad to lose the flying.

Tory landed in hawk form on the roof next to the others and listened. Heated voices sounded inside the shop, clear as day. With her keen hawk senses, Tory could hear the men's steps, their clothes rustling as they walked or fidgeted, even their breaths.

"This is still too soon to meet. I said to lay low," said a raspy male voice. He sounded like a smoker.

"Screw that. I'm getting out of town. I need my cut." This voice was smoother and higher-pitched, but still male.

A third voice, deep bass with a Jersey accent. "Not gonna happen. Finish the job."

"That crazy hag attacked me! What was I supposed to do?" said the higher-pitched voice.

The smoker's voice again. "You were supposed to bring them *here*, Saul, not drop a body in front of them! What if they go to the cops?"

Tory tensed. Was he talking about *them*? She glanced at Jillian and Meredith and found their wide hawk eyes staring back at her.

The Jersey-bass voice raised in volume. "The buyer wants the girls *and* the stones. If we don't make that meet with every bit of that, it's on *my* head. Finish the job!"

The higher-pitched voice growled, "Fine." There was a rustle like hands rummaging through objects in a drawer.

"Not that one," the first man said. "That's the one that *causes* the shift. You need the one that un-hawked the hag."

Jillian's feathers slicked, then her wings shot open. She launched herself over the edge of the roof.

Crap! Tory rushed to the edge and peered over.

Jillian perched unsteadily on a strange metal contraption attached to the side of a dusty shop window, trying to keep her body out of sight while she craned her head to look in the window.

Beside Tory, Meredith shifted to human form. "Jillian!" she whispered. "What are you—"

A red light on the contraption flicked on—just as a metal cage sprung up around Jillian.

"Gotcha!" Jersey-bass yelled, yanking open the window to reveal a broad-shouldered, green-sweatered man. A wall of grease and sweat smells slammed into Tory as he grabbed for the cage.

Tory screeched and flung herself at his face.

A bearded, red-haired man rushed up and yanked the cage in through the window.

Tory pushed off the sweater-man's head with her talons, gouging his scalp as she used him to gain momentum toward the red-bearded man who reeked of cigarettes.

A third man—bald and wearing a grease-spotted t-shirt—rushed toward them, brandishing a crowbar. Meredith swooped in, diving at his face. Baldy let out a high-pitched yelp, and the crowbar clattered to the floor.

Tory crashed into the hair of red-bearded man who ran with the cage, digging her talons in. He screamed and flailed, trying to dislodge her.

Jillian's cage went flying.

It crashed hard to the cement floor and popped open.

Jillian darted out, feathered chest heaving.

Tory's heart lurched at the angle of Jillian's wing. It was broken, for sure.

Jillian blinked wide eyes, then made a mad hop-dash for the table—which held a flat, red-marbled stone, just like the one Madame Sava had used on them.

Tory swooped in as the bald man lunged for Jillian, battering him off.

Then Meredith screamed. "Tory!"

Tory spun.

Meredith was back in human form, with the green-sweatered man's arm around her throat. He held a flat, blue-marbled stone to her chest.

A large hand crushed into Tory's back. She gasped.

"Got you," the red-bearded man snarled in his smoker's voice. "Toss me the stone."

The green-sweatered man holding Meredith tossed it one-handed, and the red-bearded man pressed it to Tory's fluttering chest. She shifted to human form instantly. The bearded man slammed a knee into Tory's back, holding her to the ground.

"Here," he grunted, tossing the stone over Tory to the bald man.

Tory shifted her head to see that the bald man had Jillian. Jillian let out a series of airy, painful shrieks as he crushed her to the floor with one hand, then pressed the stone to her chest too.

Jillian flashed into her human form, sobbing, her lower arm at a horribly wrong angle.

"Tie them up," the green-sweatered man said. "Then load them in the truck." He tossed the bald man his keys.

The lights in the shop flickered, then went out. "I wouldn't do that," came a deep, Southern drawl from the shadows.

Then the sound of a single handclap.

Tory suddenly found herself next to a beat-up pickup truck in the parking lot behind the shop, with Meredith swaying beside her. Jillian sobbed at their feet.

"Go, run!" the long-jacketed man's voice shouted. A rectangular, shimmering gap appeared in mid-air, the size and shape of a mail-slot, and keys shot out at Tory from the rift, which immediately snapped shut again.

Tory stared, then snatched the keys from the ground and turned to Meredith. "Help me get her in the truck. Hurry!"

♦ ♦ ♦

Turns out, when you show up at a hospital scraped up and covered in grease with your sobbing friend holding her broken arm, people ask a lot of questions. Jillian had been taken to see a doctor, while Tory and Meredith had been separated into private rooms to wait for their parents. They'd given a rushed version of their story when they arrived at the hospital, but since they were all minors, the police officers were waiting to question them further until each of their legal guardians had arrived.

Tory sank into the plastic-covered armchair next to the hospital bed in her room and clutched the paper cup of awful coffee a nurse had brought her. She tried not to worry about what Tom and Laura would say when they showed up as her "parents." She was out on her butt, for sure. They'd have her back in state custody before sunrise.

The door flung open, and Tory's foster mother rushed in, still in the floppy shirt and sweatpants she always wore to bed. "Oh, Tory!" She stared at her for only a moment, then folded her into a hug. "I'm so glad you're okay."

Tory stiffened.

An officer entered the room. "Are you ready?"

Laura pulled back and brushed hair from Tory's face. "I told the officers to speak with you as soon as they could." She moved over to sit in the chair next to Tory's.

Tory nodded, dread settling in around her heart. So this was it—the beginning of the end. Who was she kidding? She'd been spiraling toward this end all her life. Her family had always been screw-ups.

The police officer across from her had her hair gelled into a bun so tight it looked headache-inducing, but her smile was kind. "Run me through this again. You and your friends were at Madame Sava's shop to return something."

Tory scraped her fingernail on the outside of her paper coffee cup and tried to return the smile. "Yes." This was the story she and Meredith and Jillian had rehearsed in the car, the closest to the truth they could get without being locked up for delusions.

"And while you were there, what happened?"

"We… found a body."

The officer jotted something on her notepad, then looked up. "Right. And did you report it?"

Tory swallowed. "No." She forced herself not to look at Laura. She couldn't take the glare of disappointment she knew would be there. "We wanted to, but… a man showed up. He threatened us."

She continued through the story, staring straight ahead at the officer, answering every question as honestly as she could without mentioning hawk-shifting or shadowy teleporting.

"This man who made you help him track down the murderers, does this fit your memory of him?" She held up a sketch that looked vaguely like the man, but years younger, fatter, and without the coat—exactly how she and the others had decided to describe him on the drive over.

"It… could be." Tory nodded. Protecting the long-jacketed man was the least they could do, after he'd saved their lives.

The officer nodded, then flipped her notebook closed. She smiled at Tory, then turned to Laura. "You can both go. If we get any leads on the man who threatened these girls, we'll let you know right away."

Laura nodded. "Thank you."

As soon as the officer left, Laura moved to kneel in front of Tory. "You look exhausted. Tomorrow, you can stay home from school, if you need to—we'll figure it out. Are you sure you're alright?"

Tory gaped at her. "You're not mad?"

Laura smoothed Tory's hair. "Well, honey, we'll have to talk about you sneaking out. And you really should have told us what happened, right away—but everyone makes mistakes, Tory. We know you were scared. You did what you thought you needed to, at the time. We're just glad you're okay."

"Tom too? You're not... kicking me out?"

"Of course not. I know it's hard for you to trust, but I called Tom, and we both agree. We're here for you, Tory—always. Even after you turn eighteen, if you still want us."

Tory didn't know what to say.

Laura smiled, then stood and reached down for Tory. "C'mon, let's get you home. I'll make you some hot chocolate before bed."

◆ ◆ ◆

The next morning, a knock sounded on Tory's front door, followed by Laura calling up the stairs.

"Tory? Are you up to a visitor? There's a detective here to see you."

Tory's nerves went off like fireworks. Had the cops found a lead already? And if so—what did that mean for her and the others? She dragged herself out of bed, threw her messy hair up into a quick ponytail, and hurried downstairs.

But when she saw the visitor waiting for her on Tom and Laura's floral loveseat, her stomach plunged to her toes.

The man in the long jacket sat, legs crossed, holding one of Laura's teacups. He took a sip, then smiled at Laura. "Thank you, this is delicious." He set the teacup down on the coffee table, then turned his smile on Tory. "Why don't we step out on the porch to talk?"

Tory followed him outside. As soon as the door closed, she turned to him.

"What are you doing here?" she whispered. "You can't possibly be a real cop."

He laughed. "I'm a P.I., actually. But I am here on official business, in a sense. I'm a regular consultant for the police, and I offered to follow up on some leads for them."

Tory lowered her voice even further. "Who were those men at the shop?"

"Dealers—rare species, mostly supernaturals. The cops got a *very* helpful lead about them this morning." He smirked. "They're already in custody. Three fewer scumbags to worry about, around here."

Tory stared at him. "That's... really a thing?"

"Supernatural trafficking? Yes." He scowled. "Unfortunately. I'm sorry you and your friends got mixed up in it, and I'm sorry I put you in danger. I needed your skills to verify I had the right men, but I thought for sure if something happened, I could move fast enough to keep you safe."

Tory met his eyes. "You did keep us safe." A short laugh escaped her. "And thanks to you, Jillian won't have to go to prom as a hawk. That stone thing at the shop cured us."

The man laughed. "Well, I'm sure that's a relief for her."

Tory smiled. "You have no idea."

The man glanced at the door. "So, you graduate in a few weeks, don't you?"

Tory hesitated. "Yes." Where was this going?

"As an apology, of sorts, I have a summer job offer for you and your friends—one that would even look good on college applications. I've already spoken to your foster mother at the hospital, and she approved it if you're interested."

Tory narrowed her eyes in curiosity. "Go on."

"Our network could use some good P.I.s. We'll train you. Though officially, you'd be my assistants until you come of age."

"Your network?"

"We supernaturals look out for our own. It's a legit job, Tory. With above-average pay. Though of course, no one outside our network knows about the supernatural aspects. I've talked to Jillian and Meredith too, and they're on board if you are."

Tory shook her head. "But I'm just a *below-average* teenager. I'm not a supernatural. I'm not even that great at cheerleading. That's what got us into this mess."

"This *mess* ended up catching three creeps and protecting a lot of people, Tory." He slid two flat, marbled stones from his pocket and pressed them into Tory's hand. "Don't underestimate yourself." He smiled, then stepped off the porch onto the front walk. "Tell Laura thanks for the tea."

◆ ◆ ◆

On a muggy summer evening in downtown Tampa, just blocks from the moonlit bay, three Harris's hawks descended toward a dim back alley behind a rundown strip mall. The shops were closed for the night, all lights off but one—the neon *Varsity P.I.* sign in the front window of Madame Sava's former Emporium. Below the glowing letters hung a logo of three hawks, flying in a V formation.

A man in a long, dark jacket was already inside waiting for them.

About the Author

Crystal Crawford writes YA fantasy (and a smattering of other genres) in Florida, where every natural body of water hides something that could eat you, and if they don't get you, the weather might. She lives with her husband, four kids, and her one-eyed cat, who have supported her dream of writing and drinking far too much coffee. When she isn't writing, she enjoys napping, reading, playing video games, watching shows with her family, and recording secret singing videos in her closet, though most days you'll find her doing laundry and homeschooling the kids.

Secretary Bird *(Sagittarius serpentarius)*

A diurnal terrestrial raptor native to sub-Saharan Africa, whose powerful downward kicks earned a scientific name that translates to "the archer of snakes"

Forget-Me-Not and Morning Dew

by Yelena Crane

Ignore my slicked-down feather-mane, my stilt-legs that kick with power five times my weight, my wings that rip through air—I am a man. I will be man again.

A spell gone wrong, and now my sentience wastes beneath plumage, scorching in the savanna sun.

Blackest Crest and Longest Lashes strut ahead of me on their fine legs. Those aren't the secretary birds' real names. What's in a name when the air is rank with pheromones? When I try to mimic them, my own footing is unsure. I've never had legs so thin and hollow before. Two days less human, and I'm still all kook.

There's a strong impulse to *hunt hunt hunt* and *eat eat eat* I must ignore. The more I let the raptor instincts take over, the more I lose myself. There are four things I must remember above all else: bushwillow branches, forget-me-nots, fresh morning dew, and the magic words.

A pattern of vibrations tells me the others were successful in flushing out food. From their stomps, I can tell the prey is small and slippery. A snake. The emptiness in my stomach pulsates. A reminder I want that meat. I want everything that moves within stomping distance. My gullet has no discrimination against bug, reptile, or rodent; it wants only to be fed. It repulses me, the things I've eaten and enjoyed.

"Wait for me!" The bushwillow branches I'd been gathering fall with a *thunk*. "I'm coming just now!" I don't know if my thoughts translate proper into bird-talk because the others only speak to me through the hammer of their feet on the cracking clay.

Forget-Me-Not and Morning Dew

It's kief how the world becomes sepia from my kicked-up dust when I run all knobby-ankled to catch up. They greet me with nature's music of beak-ripped flesh.

"Eish, leave some for me!" The puff adder is colors I've no words for and couldn't see before with human eyes. Colors as delicious as the meat.

Blackest Crest has the snake's head, plus some, hanging from her beak. She'd have swallowed it entire except Longest Lashes is at the other end. The snake's tail still has some whip of life in it.

Food strengthens the contractions in my gut until it's all I can think of. Calculations whir in my birdbrain that I don't quite understand—a notion I'd been busy before with something important.

The fussing over who gobbles down more of the hisser distracts me yet again. Reminds me I won't likely see any morsel of that sweet flesh. All that energy running here, wasted.

A snake that big means rodents nearby. The landscape is flat as far as the eye can see, and my new eyes see far. The sound is soft when I hear it, wind brushing against stalks except there is no wind.

Prey.

I fight the impulse. There's bushwillows in the distance I need to get to. My wings pump and I'm airborne. Flying toward them feels like flying toward my humanity. From this distance, the view is almost worth it. The horizon's near bare except for buttons of acacia trees scattered over clumps of dirt. Scarves of waterholes peek from the dust.

A kite's up ahead on the hunt. I know I can get what it's chasing faster on the ground. I land, ready to trample, forgetting why I ever made so much effort to fly.

The kite, who'd been here first, don't welcome my presence.

"Yoh!" The arrogance of birds still shocks me. "It didn't have your name on it," I say. If he don't like the competition, he's in the wrong field of work. "How about we make a jol of it?"

There's a prattle on the ground only scampering food—that don't know it's food—makes. It'll have to do for club music. My wings dance, flashing open and closed so fast the lizard and kite don't know where to focus.

Stomp go my feet, before my mind can think it.

The kite's all wings again, trying to outmaneuver me from the heavens. Failing. Shame for the old bru, running on South Africa late-time means leaving on an empty stomach, because the lizard's already caught between my stocky toes. The kite won't get mercy from me. It flies off, chirping insults and skindering untruths about me to the clouds.

The meat's warm and raw as air when I swallow it whole, warm still when I cough up a pellet of bones. Lizard's not man food, I think, looking down at the forbidden sausage. There are three things I must remember above all else: bushwillows, morning dew, and words.

I'm all mouth, gathering branches and grass when Blackest Crest swoops down close. "Can you understand me? Can you help?" I ask.

She angles her head left, angles it right. Silent except for the ruffle of her feathers.

"Where's Long Lashes then?" I ask.

No answer.

Better I don't know, that I don't entangle myself in the lives of these birds. Better except there's her scent again and a newer instinct taking hold of me, a whisper, for now, saying *mate mate mate*. I don't remember a woman ever being so irresistible as she, a crest so iridescent.

Now is not the time for such thoughts. I've paid for each hour as a secretary bird with memories of who I used to be. Hours I spent collecting ingredients. I'm running out of time if I let distraction delay me.

There are two things I need: bushwillow branches and the magic words.

♦♦♦

My pile is almost ready, wide enough to bed a human body since I don't know if the spell will also transport me back to my flat in Johannesburg or change me here. I'm willing to take the risk. Man has survived worse than savanna with secretary birds. I'm searching for one last branch when there's an unexpected shadow overhead. It's Long Lashes, giving chase. I don't realize what toward, until it's too late and he's landed on my day's work.

"Stop!"

He's kicking faster than I can run. By the time I'm close enough to shoo him off, the long, elegant branches I walked kilometers to find are broken and scattered chips. Long Lashes don't even notice me.

"Why?" My nictitating membrane swallows up my tears so I can't even get a good cry. It makes me more furious. I follow after Long Lashes to force an answer out of him even though the only answer can be he thought there was food inside.

His feather tail is a beak's reach away and I take the bite. "Ears clogged? Yebo or no?"

Long Lashes croaks hoarsely, stomping his feet backward at me. I don't know what it is we're doing, until we're flapping wings and take the fight skyward. I kick him for destroying my hard work. Kick because I fear the pile wouldn't have turned me back anyway. Or worse, the man-me was never real and I'm a secretary bird born, raised, and gone crazy. All the frustration and anger works down into my legs. Into my beak when I croak in rapid bursts, not saying anything, just making noise.

I don't know what I've done or how tired I am until Long Lashes plunges down from one thousand meters and it's all my fault. I've murdered my own kind—no, not my own.

I'm human, damnit.

It's easy to trace Long Lashes. When I find him, he's in a bed of short grass and looks nothing like himself. He's two crooked legs, a bloodied chest, and a bashed-in human skull. "Long Lashes?" It's him, I can smell it from a kilometer away. I'm poking softly at him. "Please be alive. I'm sorry, so sorry." He doesn't move. I'm a murderer in truth now, a killer of my own kind; of two. I take in his human form again and wonder if any birds are real or man's fantasy for flight.

Standing over Long Lashes's corpse, I pray for forgiveness, though I'd never been a praying man. I pray death's not the only way to reverse the spell. There's no way to even get Long Lashes proper buried, my talons aren't built for scooping up clay or rocks.

Bushwillow branches and special words, I must not forget. Will secretary bird croaks do? They must. For me and for Long Lashes.

♦ ♦ ♦

It's just after all the morning dew is dried and instead of hunting, I'm spitballing rhymes that do nothing but make me hungry. Blackest Crest takes to the skies and offers pleasant shade when she blots the sun. For the first time since we've met, she's undulating and croaking. Without meaning to, my wings flap up and I join her. Midair, our talons clasp. The air's thick with her perfume and the music of our wings flapping in courtship. "Were you human once too?"

I'm forgetting one important thing, words.

I remember! The words find me in the sky with Blackest Crest, interspersed with the strong impulse to *mate mate mate*. "O beautifulest of birds, beautifulest of creatures. Notice my slicked down feather-mane. My stilt-legs. My wings. Pick me."

About the Author

Yelena Crane is a Ukrainian/Soviet born and USA-based writer, and incorporates influences from both her motherland and adopted home soil into her work. With an advanced degree in the sciences, she has followed her passions from mad scientist to science fiction writer. Her stories appear in Nature Futures, Daily Science Fiction, Third Flatiron, and elsewhere.

Follow her on twitter @Aelintari and https://www.yelenacrane.com/

Fethrian

A nomadic species of sentient winged humanoids, whose typically drab feathers and sharp eyes help them to hunt at night

His Glowing Feathers

by Akis Linardos

Cold wind blew through the window holes of Azu's tree hut, stinging the wounds on his wings as he counted the freshly plucked feathers strewn on the floor.

Eighteen.

Like all Fethrian, his wings draped over his arms like a cape, but *his* bore unique marks—clusters of fluorescent feathers that formed six peacock-eyes along the coverts. In the night, they glowed like shining aquamarines. Azu took a deep breath and pulled another feather, pain jolting his wings. Blood dripped from its stem.

Nineteen.

Through the window hole, Azu's nocturnal eyes saw the Forest of Kem hued like the stain of blueberries in the twilight. Above the trees, his best friend Remi glided forth on his wings, his yellow scarf fluttering against the wind. Remi had the wings, face and fluffiness of an owl, the paws and size of a cat. When standing on his hind legs, he could reach up to Azu's knee.

Remi entered the hut. "Hey Azu, you'll never believe what I..." He clacked his beak nervously at the bloody feathers on the floor. "*Scat!* What are you doing?"

Azu pointed to a honeycombed bone atop his hay bed. "A death threat this time. Woke up to find it there."

"Was it Leyka? Or that self-important buffoon, Grom?"

"Everyone."

Remi's ears drooped. "Azu..."

Azu crouched and gathered the feathers he'd plucked. "I'm not wanted here. I'm a freak. A glowing freak in the dark."

"Oh, Azu, you're not a freak. You're unique. No other raptor is like you. It's not a bad—"

Azu flew down the hut—cringing at the ache of his wings—toward the crevice at the tree's base, where he'd tucked his supplies.

Remi followed, hovering above him. "Azu, what happened?"

"Blundered another hunt. Prey saw my wings and escaped. Everyone slept the day on empty bellies because of me."

Azu strapped his pouch belt around his waist, securing inside his own feathers, a bundle of deer-sinew string, his box of tar, and jerkies he'd smoked a fortnight ago. His knife's handle protruded from his belt's sheath.

"All I've ever wanted," Azu said, "was to fit in. To be respected as a hunter."

"It's just one night. I'm sure they will cool off."

Azu slung his bow and quiver along his back, then stormed down the hill.

"Where are you going now?" Remi asked.

"Nefta's shrine. I'll give her my feathers as an offering."

"Nefta's—are you *mad*? That's on the other side of the forest. You're in no condition."

Azu spread his wings. The cold wind struck the fresh wounds like icy daggers. He doubled over.

Remi latched on his shoulder, light as a feather bundle, claws pricking Azu's shoulders. "You need to rest. You cannot—"

"Your claws hurt."

Remi retracted his claws. "You cannot fly with these wounds."

"I'll walk."

"Azu..."

The trailing voice of his friend stung, but Azu had to go. The moon shone blue only once every thirty years. And that was ten nights away. Only then would Nefta grant wishes. Would She find his motive pure and remove his glowing feathers or smite him for his selfishness? He didn't know, but he had to try.

◆ ◆ ◆

Deep in the Forest of Kem, the cold wind stung the scabs on Azu's wings, and leaves crackled beneath his feet. To his nocturnal eyes, the forest was coated in a shade of blue. Ruins spread amidst the trees, granite pillars dressed in ivy with gray orbs etched on their peaks. It'd been three nights since he left home with Remi.

In a bush by a headless statue, a pair of leaves jerked. No, not leaves. Ears. A jackrabbit! Any Fethrian would miss it, but Azu's eyes were the sharpest in any tribe he'd been. His redeeming quality as a hunter.

Before he could nock an arrow, however, the rabbit turned. Aquamarine reflected in its pupils momentarily, and it ran away.

In his mind, Azu heard his father's sharp, accusing voice, *"Of course it got away. It saw your feathers. You're a glowing peacock, a failure of a hunter."*

Remi landed beside him, folding his wings as he slurped the lizard off the claw of his right paw. "Don't sweat it, jackrabbits are hard to digest."

Azu eyed him, pouting.

Remi slurped on. He looked at Azu. "Oh. Do you want some?" He pulled the scaly thing from his mouth.

"I'm good," Azu said, walking away.

Remi winged up from the ground, gliding on Azu's shoulder. His claws dug into Azu's skin. "Oh, come on, Azu. I mean the moon has been so bright. It was—"

Azu flicked a finger on Remi's paw.

Remi pulled back his claws. "Sorry. Seriously though. I'm even having a hard time myself and—"

"Will you be quiet?" Azu said.

Ahead, a whirring sound echoed behind a crumbled wall. One of the pillars moved. The orb at its peak emitted blue light.

Azu crouched. Remi jumped down from his shoulder.

"What the hell?" Remi said.

"Golem of Nyx."

"Golem of what?"

"They used to make these things in Alun Tor, five hundred years ago. Street patrol."

The pillar moved. Its whole form came into view, a giraffe made of white stone crawling with moss, its long neck embellished with arabesque patterns.

"How the hell is it still moving?" Remi asked.

The pillar twisted. The orb turned in its socket, revealing the traces of an eyelid. Azu crouched further down, pressing his fluorescent feathers against the ground. The automaton moved toward them in slow calculating steps.

His Glowing Feathers

"It saw me," Azu said.

"No, it hasn't. Stay still, it's patrolling, nothing to fear."

Closer. The giraffe's neck moved like a shark's fin through the long grass.

"We have to run," Azu said. "It will see my wings."

Remi unsheathed his claws and dug, covering Azu's wings with dirt.

"Stop that," Azu whispered.

The pillar stopped. The red eye looked down at them. It gleamed, and the wind rippled around it with a wailing sound.

Remi froze, standing on his back legs, dirt dripping from his paws. Azu leaped out, pulled Remi along, and bolted to a sprint.

A glimmering red beam struck the ground where they'd stood.

Remi flew. Azu ran, wings shifting painfully behind his shoulders. Sounds of whirring cogs and wood snapping followed. Red flashes blazed the forest. Vegetation burned where the rays hit.

Remi floated ahead, throwing backward glances. "There's a cliff ahead. Watch out!"

The foliage cleared. Azu reached a precipice, overlooking a patch of barren land made silvery blue by the gibbous moon. He halted, feet scraping the dirt. Below was gravel, a drop greater than two oaks.

He glanced over his shoulder. The pillar rushed at him, red orb wailing.

Azu jumped, wings fully spread to glide. The scabs cracked, searing pain jolting his muscles. A blue shaft of light passed over him. Remi rushed down, clutching Azu's shoulder, cupping his own wings to slow Azu's fall.

Azu's feet touched the earth, and he toppled over in a flutter of feathers, elbows scraping on the gravel. A cloud of dust dried his tongue. Something tickled inside his throat, and he coughed violently.

Remi floated down. "Are you alright?"

"I feel like I just swallowed pebbles."

On top of the escarpment, the golem stood. The blue orb dimmed before it vanished into the trees.

"That was close," Remi said.

"Too close. Can you check where we are?"

Remi nodded, soared upward, and returned moments later. "If we stay along the length of the escarpment, we'll be back on track before night's end. Then it should be straight to the Elderwood."

"Great," Azu said, walking toward the escarpment.

"How are the wounds?" Remi asked.

"Terrible."

"What were you thinking anyway? That was the dumbest thing you've ever done."

"I had to jump; the golem was catching up."

"Not that, you imbecile. The plucking. Were you planning to pluck yourself bare?"

"Let's not talk about it now."

"Oh yeah, great, shut the gates again. Don't let me in. You're an egotistical fool. And this whole quest is stupid."

"No one forced you to come."

"Someone has to keep an eye on you, lest you have another plucking fit."

Azu smiled. "Thanks Remi."

Remi fluttered his wings. "Cotton-headed fowl."

They reached the forest at the escarpment's edge by late twilight. Gnarled roots stretched along the ground and lianas hung from trees like a snake infestation. Sweat coated Azu's neck, inviting the chilling wind to the root of his feathers. A lump had formed on his left wing.

Remi floated above him, gliding between the branches. "How are you hanging on?"

"I'm fine," he said, cringing at the hoarseness of his voice.

"Sure you are."

"What do you want me to say?"

"Let's find a place to camp for the night. I'll bring you some lizards. You can char them up with a nice warm fire."

"I said I'm fine!"

"You're a proud cockatoo is what you are!"

Azu's brain buzzed. He swallowed, tasting the ache in his throat. A butterfly with bright red wings fluttered by. He remembered his mother's words.

"*Rare colors are the most beautiful, Azu. The butterfly tells the world: Here I am, shining in the dark night. I'm not afraid.*"

The butterfly blurred. Shadows creeped from the corners of Azu's vision and engulfed the world.

"Azu! Hey, Azu! Wake up!"

Remi was a fuzzy form. Why did everything turn sideways?

"Wh-what happened?" Azu said.

Remi placed a paw on Azu's forehead. "*Nefta's wings!* You're burning with fever. Come, there's a house behind that thicket. The roof is mostly caved in, but it's dry enough. I need you to walk. Can you do that?"

Azu forced himself up on wobbly legs.

"That's it," Remi said. "Easy now."

Shadows threatened to swallow the world again and Azu shook his head to keep them away, focusing on the next step. Ground. Grass. Stairsteps. Floor. Bed of hay.

Soft paws touched Azu's head. "That's it, lie down. Your head here. There."

Remi climbed onto his chest, his fur so warm, suffused with earthy scents. Through the buzz, Azu heard Remi's chest vibrating with the sweet cadence of life, sending a message to the core of Azu's being: *Get well my friend, I'm here.*

♦ ♦ ♦

Azu stood alone in a dark forest, unable to peer through its shadows. From the moon came a figure, wings like midnight winter, a face pale and severe. His father.

"You killed her. You're a freak! That thing saw your feathers. It's all your fault!"

"No."

"Leave. Never tell anyone I'm your father!"

Tears streamed down Azu's face like liquid snakes. He was immersed in a dark sea, and from beneath, the abyss looked back at him—blue eyes in the blackness. He looked up, his father a thinning shadow on the face of the moon.

"Please, father, don't leave me here."

Azu awoke, covered in sweat. His head buzzed still, prickling at the temples. Through a ruined roof, he saw a single star remaining in the dawning sky. A bonfire warmed him, scented with roasting meat.

Remi approached, swinging a charred lizard over Azu's mouth. "Alright. I'm not taking no for an answer this time. I even charred the skin so it's crispy as you like it."

Azu swallowed his spittle, feeling a prickly lump in his throat. "I had jerky left in my pouch."

"Not any more you don't. You probably lost it when you fell from that cliff. Now open the gates to Rhondo."

Azu sat up, trying a bite of the reptile. Stringy texture. Rough on his sore throat.

"Picked you some berries too. If your stomach can handle them."

Azu nodded.

"How's the pain?"

"Better. I'll be fine tomorrow."

"I think you'll be fine when you let go of silly thoughts."

"Silly?"

"What are you trying to achieve, Azu? You're going to travel all the way to Nefta's shrine to say, *'Hey goddess, remember those wings you gave me? Well, they don't quite work for me, how about we try something else?'*"

"You don't know what it's like."

"No, I don't. For me, having you has always been enough."

"Fethrian *need* to hunt."

"Says who?"

"It's what we do. Should I be relying on you and your lizards? I can't do this anymore. Every time I find a new pack, I think it will be different. But it's always the same. I'm always a burden. Even now I'm a burden to you."

Remi shot him a sharp glance. "You're the reason I'm alive."

Silence.

"Remi…"

"Hm?"

"Thank you."

Remi looked away. "Stop saying that, you idiot."

They reached the Elderwood the following night. They could tell by the trees, whose pinecones glistened purple under the starry sky, and the nightingales, whose song was the heartbeat of the forest. Rain had come and gone, leaving behind a scent of rich, wet earth.

Remi slumped onto Azu's shoulder. "I don't know how your legs are still working when my wings are totally spent. I just—"

A wolf's howl sounded from the direction of the trees. Azu pulled his bow out.

"I thought there were no wolves at Kem!" Remi said.

"We're on the other side of Kem now," Azu said, picking up the pace.

Bushes swayed in the wind, and Azu jerked, bow nocked, aiming at every flutter of a leaf.

A howl came from the right. Another answered from the left.

"I don't like this. I don't like this one bit," Remi said.

Azu spread his wings. He tried flapping them, and it was like pushing through sand.

An abrupt bush-rustle. A shadow jumped from the right, and Azu loosed an arrow. The wolf cried out. Two more emerged from the thicket. Azu folded his wings tightly and ran.

Remi flew ahead, glanced backward. "*Scat!* Three of them!"

Azu nocked another arrow.

"Three inches to your left. Now!"

Azu flicked a wing open, using the force of the wind to twist full circle, gritting his teeth against the pain. In the blurry second of his spinning, he glanced the outlines of three canines. He fired. A wolf yelped and dropped in its tracks.

"Two left, keep it up. *Scat!* River ahead!"

A waterfall poured into a river, cutting through slippery rocks. Azu pulled another arrow against the bowstring, flung a wing open and spun as he vaulted backwards over the river. Two wolves leaped at him hungrily—one's jaws agape inches from Azu's legs. Azu released the arrow, gutting the wolf's throat with a wet gurgling sound. The beast splashed dead into the water.

Azu curved his shoulder, flinging the quiver forward as he landed on the other side of the river. The other wolf bounded past and spun around. Remi descended, wings flapping, clawing the canine's eyes. The wolf snapped its jaws, catching the yellow scarf around Remi's neck and shook its head violently. Remi's head slipped through the scarf and he hurtled away. He crashed against a boulder by the waterfall.

Remi dropped limp onto the gravel, a wing draped over his body like a bedsheet.

"*No!*"

The wolf moved toward Remi. Azu leaped, cupped his wings protectively around his friend, blocking the wolf's approach.

So this is how it ends.

But nothing happened. Azu peeked over his shoulder. The wolf was growling low, eyeing him warily, then it turned and raced away into the woods. Azu's gaze fell on the waterfall. It seemed that a great beast with six radiant eyes looked back at him. But when he folded his wings, the beast in the waterfall shimmered out, and all he saw was his own reflection in blurry liquid lines. There was no beast, only his wings. They had scared the wolf.

Azu cradled his friend, found the scarf—torn where the wolf had bit it—and wrapped it around Remi's neck to keep him warm. He found a hollow tree trunk, nested inside, and pressed his temple against Remi's fluffy chest, searching for his gentle heartbeat.

It was still there.

The night stretched long, and as Azu faded to weary sleep, he kept whispering a prayer.

Please, Nefta, don't let Remi die.

♦ ♦ ♦

The first rays of sunlight burned through the trees. It had been three nights since Remi fell unconscious, and Azu stayed by Remi's side to keep him warm. Hunger panged his stomach, but he found little more than tart blackberries nearby.

A flutter of feathers and wheezing. "Azu…"

Azu leaned closer and whispered, "Remi, are you okay? How's your head?"

"Like it's been rammed against a wall."

Azu laughed. "It was. But it's a hard one to crack."

"So hungry…"

"Stay here. I'll go get you something."

Azu pressed his lips against Remi's fluffy scalp and went hunting under the sun for the first time in his life.

In the river he found flint and stone to carve a single arrowhead. He snapped a tree branch, cut the stubs, peeled the bark, and cut a slit on one end. Using tar and string from his supplies, he fastened the arrowhead into the slit, spun the arrow, and left the river behind.

Through the woods he reached a clearing, where the daylight itched and pricked his eyes. A deer—blurred by daylight—grazed idly. Azu nocked his arrow, soared upward, clenching his teeth against the pangs of pain hitting his wings. He closed in on the deer with the sun on his back, hoping the sunlight would outshine his glowing feathers, obscure his presence. Sweat beaded his forehead, watery eyes blinked rapidly. He moved closer—so close he couldn't miss—and released the arrow.

It found its target.

Returning to their crude camp with chunks of the tender backstrap, Azu gathered pine needles and dry twigs for kindling. As dusk came, he glimpsed an orange flash on the western hill.

Azu made a fire by the hollow tree and cooked the meat on a stick.

Remi's eyes cracked open. "I dreamt of a squirrel with thick juicy thighs. What are you doing?"

"Preparing breakfast," Azu said. "Bagged a deer. I'll cook these extra pieces—they'll last us a few nights."

"How long was I asleep? A week?"

"A few days. I think I saw the glow of Nefta's shrine. We're very close. On time for the blue moon." Azu sliced a piece of venison, handed it to Remi. "Gather your strength for tonight."

"Did you kill the *scat* that threw me?"

"No, the wolf ran away."

"Ran away?"

"Yeah. In fact, we don't have to worry about wolves again. I found a way to—"

"Azu! I can't move my wings!"

Azu turned. Remi hoisted himself up with his two front legs, wings limp on either side like a brown cape. "I can't. Azu, I can't even move my back legs. I can't feel them at all. I can't feel anything below my chest!"

"No," Azu said, rushing to his friend. "No, no, no."

Azu placed his hand under Remi's belly. Soft, fragile. Cold.

Remi whimpered. "I-I can't feel them."

Azu's own legs felt numb. "Nefta will fix it. Don't worry, Remi. Come, lay on my arms, I'll carry you to the shrine. There."

As Azu comforted his friend, his father's words creeped into his mind. *It's all your fault.*

♦ ♦ ♦

Remi's gentle purring vibrated on Azu's chest as he carried him up the western hill. Nightingales sang to the clear night sky. The blue moon shone dimly, painting the tree barks in a cold hue. A sound of rushing water came as he crested the hill. A smell of wet earth. A steadfast susurrus of prayers.

A waterfall poured down a basin into an enormous reservoir. In the middle, a statue with radiant orange wings protruded from the water, painting the lake like lava, the granite around like molten rock. A dozen Fethrian bowed, their wings stretched out in pious fervor. Azu recognized some. Members of tribes that had kicked him out. But it didn't matter anymore.

Remi mumbled, "Azu…"

"It's fine, Remi."

Azu put his friend down gently on a grass bundle. Between the bowing Fethrian, a feminine figure walked. Inky black feathers enveloped her like a gown, cowling her face. The priestess of Nefta.

Azu stepped into the reservoir and walked toward the statue. He bowed low, spread his wings wide, feeling the cool waterfall spray. He prayed his thanks to Nefta, for his life and Remi's, for the trees and the night skies.

The water rippled. He shivered. The priestess stood before him, redolent with rosemary and sage. A crone's voice spoke.

"You who come to the shrine on the night of Nefta's Flight. If you wish a boon, offer something of value to the goddess. Remember: without sacrifice, nothing is granted."

Azu bowed his head lower, and the priestess left, taking the chill with her. Azu whispered his prayer.

"Nefta, hear my plea. Let my friend fly again, heal his broken legs and wings, for which I bear the fault. You can have my bow and quiver, the tools of my hunt. My pride."

He submerged his bow and quiver in the shallow lake.

"You can have my own feathers, plucked in a fit of shameful rage."

He scattered his feathers over the bow.

Nothing happened.

Time flowed onward and Azu repeated the prayer until the cold seeped from the water to his legs, shivers shaking his whole body. The nightingale song and the susurrus of prayers surrounded him. But the goddess remained silent.

"If I didn't appreciate your gifts, it was because I was a fool. Forgive me. Please don't let Remi pay for it."

The blue moon dimmed. Nefta's Flight would soon end, along with Azu's chance to get his wish.

"Mother, can you hear me? Are you there, nesting in Nefta's garden?"

Azu swallowed.

"I wish you were here now. Remi is important to me. I put myself in front of a wolf to save him, just like you did for me. My feathers saved someone, Mother. Please, if you can hear me, whisper a word in Nefta's ear."

A silvery veil trickled over the blue moon. Time was almost up.

Azu glanced over his shoulder. Remi watched him, beady eyes curious, lifting himself partially on his front legs.

Azu saw the forest, painted in that hue of blueberry stain, the pinecones shining purple, the nightingales leaping from branch to branch. The night so beautiful.

He shut his eyes.

"Please, Nefta, heal my friend. Do this and—"

Azu's voice broke. He drew a deep breath. What is given to Nefta may never be taken back.

"Do this, and you may have my eyes."

A soft breeze touched Azu's eyelids. A voice spoke to him, its cadence like drizzle on a lake.

Noble soul that fears not the darkness. You who would sacrifice everything for another. Rise. I have taken less than what you were willing to offer. Your eyes will still guide you, but now in the daylight, not the night. Fare thee well, my humble hunter that shines so bright.

The orange glow dimmed. Nefta's presence vanished. Azu glanced over his shoulder. Shadowy branches swayed under gray moonlight. The forest was dark and scary.

He could no longer see into its shadows.

A fluttering of wings. Remi glided toward him. "Azu! I can fly! I can feel my legs again!"

Azu caught his friend in an embrace. "Thank the goddess."

"Azu... What did you offer Her?"

"Nothing important. Let's go."

"What about your feathers?"

"Why pester the goddess with such things? Let's go. We'll build ourselves a new home. I... will need your help though."

"Anything, Azu. What do you need?"

"I can no longer see in the dark."

Remi's ears drooped. "Oh, Azu…"

"It's fine. Really. I hunted in daylight while you were unconscious. I can do it again."

"What about your wounds? You still can't fly. Maybe the goddess can fix them?"

"She's gone. Don't worry. It's all right." Azu placed Remi on his shoulder and waded out of the reservoir. As he stood on solid ground, he opened his eyes wide and looked to the moonlit path that had brought them here. "I'll walk."

ABOUT THE AUTHOR

Akis is a genre writer trapped in the body of an AI scientist. Trying to explore as much as he can of this unlikely reality, he has lived in four different European countries throughout his research career. His fiction has been published or is forthcoming at Apex Magazine, The Maul and Abyss&Apex. Find him on Twitter @LinardosAkis

Kestrel *(Falco tinnunculus)*

A small breed of diurnal raptors in the falcon family, whose name is derived from the French *crécerelle*

Falcon's Apprentice

by Jody Lynn Nye

"Marie-Jeanne!" Father called.

Marie-Jeanne bound the last cord around her soft boot top and tied a firm knot, then rushed out of the door of the mews into the cold spring air. Her brown braids danced on the shoulders of her gray woolen smock.

Father looked impatient, his thinning black hair even more disarrayed than usual. He leaned on his crutch for strength. The Comte de Velay, a bulky man who would have made two of Father and Marie-Jeanne combined, loomed over the much shorter falconer. His broad, bearded face was set in a grimace. On his wrist, killer talons gripping the leather gauntlet, stood Mistinguette, the valuable young kestrel on which both Father and Marie-Jeanne had been lavishing endless attention and care. The huge white bird turned its head toward the sound of her flapping footsteps. Her fierce eyes were covered by the embroidered blue leather hood.

It seemed that the blindfolding had not been enough to keep the kestrel from striking. Blood ran down the side of the Comte's face. A gouge the shape of Mistinguette's beak almost beside the liege lord's eye told the tale. Marie-Jeanne ran for the box of clean lint and the earthenware jar of Frere Benedict's salve that they kept in a chest just inside the door.

"You told me she would be ready by today! Why is she not enchanted for obedience?" the Comte demanded, as Marie-Jeanne stretched her meager height up to wipe away the blood and dab the green paste on the wound. He hissed at its contact, but the pain would subside in moments, as the holy salve healed swiftly. Nothing would be left but a tiny scar.

"As I have explained, my lord, to instill obedience in a falcon is to damage its natural instincts toward hunting," Father said, bobbing his head humbly. No matter how many times he had told the lord that, it did not remain in de Velay memory. "It must keep its wild tendencies. If it becomes too tame, it sees prey animals as its equal, not its inferiors. She is ready, I swear to the good God."

The Comte thrust the bird back toward Father. "If it bites me again, I shall strangle it, whether it is worth two hundred livres or not!"

"Perhaps, then, it should not go out today," Father said, gently touching the kestrel on the backs of her legs to make her step up onto his gauntlet. "I will get your goshawk Remy ready for you."

"No! His grace the Bishop of Mende joins me on the field today. He brings his own falconer and his white gyrfalcon. I want to show him I have as fine a bird as he. The kestrel comes."

"Yes, my lord," Father said, in resignation. He thrust Mistinguette toward his daughter.

Marie-Jeanne accepted the bird on her unprotected arm and withdrew well away from the Comte's reach. She cooed calming words in the kestrel's ear and stroked her soft, speckled breast feathers. Mistinguette's wings bated slightly, then settled into place. The kestrel liked her, though its way of showing it did was kind of painful. Marie-Jeanne tried not to cringe at the sharp talons' grip poking pinpoint holes in her skin through her woolen sleeve. She didn't dare cry out, or the Comte might decide the hunting bird wasn't worth his time after all. Father was the one who knew all the enchantments to communicate with and guide his charges, not she. He and the journeymen were vague when she asked them what the training entailed. Someday she would learn all of the secrets of falconry, but she had not yet!

"Prepare it to depart," the Comte said, grandly. "That and the minor birds for my sons and the ladies. We leave at first light. Coneys are running wild across the barley meadows. It should be a good day's hunting."

"Yes, my lord," Father said, his head keeping time with his words. "I am not yet fit after my fall during the last outing, my lord. Er, may we not await my son Emile's return? He ought to be back today after bringing your kindly gift of the white merlin to the Bishop's palace at Chartres?"

"You have other apprentices," the Comte said, dismissively, without a care for Father's injury, though Marie-Jeanne knew that his carelessness was the reason for it. "Send one of them."

Father hesitated. He and Marie-Jeanne knew that though they had been trained in the spells and cantrips of falconry, none of the young men in his employ dared get near Mistinguette.

"My daughter will go," Father said, projecting an assurance that Marie-Jeanne was sure he didn't feel. "She will do well."

"That girl?" the noble asked, his disdainful gaze searching her from her thick brown braids down the heavy woolen smock and hose to the soles of her worn leather shoes. Like Father, she was small-boned, and looked years younger than her fourteen summers. "I have seen her running in the fields like a wild animal herself. Has she ever aided on a hunt? There are dangerous creatures out there that also hunt rabbits."

"She will do well," Father said again. "Only wait here a moment while I kit her up."

Limping on his crutch, he dragged Marie-Jeanne into the mews.

"Shoes tied? Yes," he said, pulling bags and boxes down from shelves on the wall opposite the falcons' perches. "You'll need a hat for the sun and a bag for the kills. You're strong. You can carry plenty of coneys and small game birds. Let the men take on anything larger. Wear a heavy cloak. It looks as if it might rain. Draw the falcon under cover with you. Her temper will fray if she gets wet."

"Why me?" Marie-Jeanne asked, although she took her cloak down from the wooden peg on the wall. "The day is fine. I could gather strawberries for Mother. Or mushrooms. I know where there are morels."

"I need you to go. Today is not a day to run free. Do your duty!"

"Send Simeon or Pierre. They have experience."

"Mistinguette will not behave for them," Father said simply.

"Father, this is the season of La Bête!" Marie-Jeanne protested. Stories of the terrifying shaggy, fanged beast that was part boar, part wolf, who tore apart the unwary and unholy, had kept her up at night after many a bonfire party. "I heard that she was spotted again in Gévaudan, and left a body torn apart, but with no blood in it."

"You know the comte does not believe in such legends," Father said. "Perhaps the bishop's prayers will keep the monster away." He shook his head and ran a knobby knuckle down Mistinguette's feathery breast.

"The best defense you have is here. Follow her lead. She will guard your life."

"So, have you heard the latest rumors, my lord?" the comte asked his honored guest as they trotted along together. "La Bête has struck again, it seems."

"Pah!" the clergyman said, waving a gorgeously gloved hand. Clean-shaven, the bishop had a long, narrow face with high cheekbones and a thin, pointed nose with arching nostrils that made him look disapproving even when he smiled. "The court of inquiry is already looking into it. The man who was killed was unpopular and rumored to have cheated many of his customers. You will see, it will turn out to be one of those. No supernatural beasts stalk here!"

"But, my lord bishop," put in Comtesse de Velay, "there have been many incidents of brutal killings, including innocent children, all torn apart as if by a beast."

The bishop crossed himself. The rest of the party followed suit immediately.

"We fear the wolf and the boar for a good reason, my lady," he said. "One does not have to look to Satan. Those poor children might have fallen afoul of a real beast. And we are far from Gévaudan."

The nobles' huntsmen and servants shook their heads, careful to keep their skepticism out of sight of their lords. The bishop might be anointed by God and protected by divine hands, but the rest of them feared what Satan might have set loose on Earth for the rest of them.

Marie-Jeanne had no time to tremble or look around for the fabled man-killing monster. In the trail of the nobles on their great horses, she sat astride a donkey saddled with nothing more than a couple of flour sacks padded with straw. She had to admit how fine her lord looked in his red hat and surcote, astride the steady chestnut stallion that was almost as red. The horse's saddle looked large enough to sail on and glinted with silver. The saddlecloths were embroidered with the crook and sword symbol of Velay. The bishop had the wheatsheaf of Languedoc on his garments and his dark bay horse's trappings, but in gold and surrounded by a shield to show his status as the overlord of the province. The ladies and gentlemen all looked so impressive in their silks and fur-lined cloaks. Servants leading or riding beasts of burden carried baskets of food and jugs of wine for an open-air feast when the sun reached its height. A pack of fine hounds milled around them, yelping to one another in excitement. Marie-Jeanne was both honored and terrified to be in their number.

With every bounce on the rough road, Mistinguette's claws tightened on Marie-Jeanne's wrist. Even the thick gauntlet she now wore to protect herself from the kestrel's talons only blunted the points, not the fierce grip. She would have bruises, she knew it. The thought of punishment by her father and the hope of a gift of money and a share of the kills from the Comte or the Bishop were all that kept her from slowing down so that the hunting party would disappear out of sight. On her back flapped the enormous leather bag to hold prey. At her hip, she had a small creel containing the lure that would attract Mistinguette back should she stray after being flown. It was baited with pieces of pigeon, which were beginning to stink in the growing warmth of the day. The kestrel could smell the meat and tried to climb down from Marie-Jeanne's glove to get at them. Only the hanging jesses in the girl's fist kept her from getting away.

Spring in the Languedoc came earlier than it did to most of France. Tiny, yellow-green leaves festooned the dark brown branches of beech trees. The oaks still stood proudly naked, their shaggy, gray-brown bark silver in the slips of sunlight that penetrated through the thick forest. They were making for the barley fields, where the growing grain had already attracted pests. While the hunt would cut down on the number of rabbits, it would also trample a good portion of the crop. Father's friends grumbled, saying they did not know which was worse. Flies swarmed to her sweating flesh. With one hand for the reins and one for the kestrel, she had to ignore the itchy bites.

"Ho!" called the hunt master. Marie-Jeanne kicked the donkey to hurry it to join the rest of the group. As soon as she could stop, she scratched her bites. The donkey lashed his tail to rid himself of the flies.

They had paused on the outskirts of a field, next to a small house. The farmer and his family bowed and scraped apprehensively. The farmer's wife offered small beer to the hunters to refresh them after their ride. The Comte made a face, but he didn't spit it out. If the bishop had not been nearby, he surely would have. It was too early in the year for new wine, and peasant beer often tasted bitter.

True to the report, brown rabbits ran to and fro among the bright shoots of barley. The Comte grinned.

"My lord bishop, would you care to make the first strike?" he asked.

The bishop bared his big white teeth. They made him look rather like a hare himself.

"I shall. Robert! Bring me Matilde!"

The bishop's falconer sprang off his small brown horse and presented himself at his master's saddlebow. He held up the shimmering white gyrfalcon to his lord. Before the Comte could make a similar cry, Marie-Jeanne clambered awkwardly from the donkey's back and dragged it behind her as she hurried to present Mistinguette to his gauntleted wrist. With a quick swipe, she removed the kestrel's hood. She got a grudging glance of approval for her pains. So far, so good. All she wanted from the day was not to disgrace herself or her father.

"Smooth and easy, my lord," she said. "She's had as much jostling as she can take."

"I know, I know!" the comte grumbled.

The bishop lifted his hand to the sky. The gyrfalcon needed no more urging. She opened her great wings and rose up like an angel toward the blue heavens.

All the smaller birds in the field scattered like ashes in the wind. The rabbits continued their frolicking, unaware of death hovering above. The white falcon held in the sky for a moment as if she was painted there, then dove straight for the biggest, plumpest coney. An audible crack sounded as the gyrfalcon broke its prey's neck. The huntsman jumped down from his horse to retrieve the dead rabbit and present it to the bishop.

At the shock of the feathered killer, the rest of the herd scrambled for safety. Little was to be found, as the rest of the party released their hawks in pursuit. Smoothly, the Comte raised his arm and loosed Mistinguette into the air. She floated away like a leaf. Lady de Velay sent a kiss after her favorite merlin. The tiny bird arrowed after the lead rabbit, veering off just as the beast leaped into a hole at the field's edge. A dozen of its kin followed it, vanishing like drops of water down a drain.

At once, the dogs went after it, digging at the dirt and warbling like out of tune choristers. Marie-Jeanne smiled. The rabbits would be miles away in a minute, vanished along the endless corridors of their warren.

"Heel, sirrah! Heel!" The huntsman called in the dogs, who had caught nothing. But Mistinguette fluttered her pale wings on the air, and dove into the barley, halfway across the field. She didn't come up again.

"A strike, by Jesu!" the Comte said, with a laugh. "Go get it, girl."

"Yes, my lord!" Marie-Jeanne said. With a look for apology at the farmer, she sidled into the young grain.

It didn't do to charge in upon a kestrel with its kill. One had to approach the bird carefully. Marie-Jeanne neared the row where she heard the sound of satisfied peeping. She parted the stalks of grain. Mistinguette looked up at her with fierce eyes, standing on the belly of the rabbit she was disemboweling.

"Now, now, my chick," Marie-Jeanne said in the most soothing voice she could. Father always said that hawk magic began with eyes, hands, and voice. She began to stoop low and eased a gloved hand toward her charge. "Come to me, then. You'll get your treat. Let me have the rabbit." She felt in the lure pouch and brought out a chunk of pigeon flesh. "Look here! This is for you."

She extended the gobbet of meat toward the fierce beak. Mistinguette snatched it from her gloved fingers, leaving a gouge in the leather. Marie-Jeanne took the kestrel onto her wrist and hastily stuffed the rabbit into her bag. Flowing blood was said to attract La Bête. She glided out of the barley field and presented the falcon to the Comte.

"A fine catch," the bishop praised him, as Marie-Jeanne displayed the dead coney. "A bit smaller than mine, though." The huntsman took charge of the prey, handing it off to one of his apprentices. Marie-Jeanne curtseyed and drew back.

The Comte smiled, showing his teeth through his beard. "The day is young." He hefted the falcon so that her wings flipped. "She will catch many more fat rabbits for me today."

Mistinguette shrieked in protest at the mistreatment.

"Hand to her strings, my lord!" Marie-Jeanne cried, alarmed. "She's going to bolt!"

Her warning came too late. Before the comte could grab for the jesses, the kestrel shot away from him and flew into the nearest treetop.

"Come back here!" he bellowed. "I swear, I will kill that hawk! Get her, girl!"

Marie-Jeanne pressed her lips together. No word of criticism must escape them, but he knew how flighty the kestrel was! Keeping Mistinguette in plain sight, she went out into the open and took the lure from her bag. On a twelve-foot cord, the leather bag had been made to resemble a flying dove, but years of being stooped upon by countless birds of prey had torn it into a figure more like a blackened hedgehog. Still, the hawks recognized it and came to it, most of the time. Marie-Jeanne played out the cord and began to swing the lure in a wide circle. Mistinguette's head went up. She saw it, of course she did, but the stubborn kestrel hunkered down again, clinging to her branch. Marie-Jeanne sighed. If only she knew the chants and spells that would bring the kestrel to her wrist!

A keening wail rose from the forest behind them. All the horses and donkeys bucked or danced at the sound. The huntsman plowed in among his dogs, cuffing them to make them stop howling at the mournful noise. Marie-Jeanne froze. The lure dropped to the ground.

"What in hell was that?" the comte demanded.

"Some poor beast being torn by a wolf," the bishop said, with an expression of disapproval at the noble's blasphemy. "Nothing to do with hell at all, my good comte."

"Very well, then," de Velay said, sulkily. He did not like to be corrected, even by Holy Mother Church. "Let us go on with our hunt."

But the cry had alarmed Mistinguette. She lifted from the branch and fluttered into the woods. The bishop laughed.

"Curse it, let her go!" the comte barked. "She's of no further use to me. I have better birds."

Marie-Jeanne knew better. Once out of sight of his illustrious company, he would demand that Father reimburse him the price of the costly falcon, meaning that the family would work for years with catastrophically reduced pay. It would be a horrible way to reward Father for sending her on her first hunt.

"I will find her, my lord," she said, gathering up the lure. De Velay waved her away impatiently. Marie-Jeanne marked the direction that the kestrel had flown, and ran after her, hoping to spot a glimpse of her white feathers against the dark trees.

The lure was of no use among the undergrowth of the forest. Mistinguette had not yet learned to come to her name. Without Father's cantrips for finding and trapping, all Marie-Jeanne could hope was to find the kestrel on a low branch and coax her back onto the glove.

The forest was usually alive with the sounds of birds and small animals, but it was eerily silent that day. Marie-Jeanne could not help but think that the terrifying cry had silenced them all with fear. Her own heart beat hard against her ribs. What if La Bête was real? What if it came upon her in the woods all alone? Would anything be left of her to tell her grieving parents what had become of her? Her blood ran like ice in her veins.

Behind her, the rest of the hunting party had carried on. The nobles shouted encouragement at their birds as they flew after rabbits and pheasants that the dogs flushed from cover. Soon, their voices died away in the distance. Marie-Jeanne crossed herself, hoping that she would not become lost. She had scavenged in the forests for mushrooms and nuts all her life, but usually in the company of friends or siblings, one at least who knew the way home.

A reassuring peep sounded from far ahead.

"Mistinguette!" Marie-Jeanne called. "Come back, chick!"

Another peep, as if in answer, gave the girl a direction, at least. A well-worn deer path led her that way. She pushed aside branches, scaring a squirrel up the nearest tree, where it scolded her as she passed. More peeps made her turn left, then right, then right again, stepping over humped roots and avoiding the piles of scut left by animals.

"I'm coming, chick!"

At last, the plaintive sound seemed to come from above her. Marie-Jeanne looked up. Mistinguette clung to a branch high over her head. The girl held up her wrist and the lure.

"Come down to me, chick!" she called, keeping her voice soothing.

The kestrel rose a handspan, then dropped back, scrambling to clutch at the branch. She tried again, swung upside down, and flapped hard to right herself. Marie-Jeanne realized with horror that the kestrel's jesses were caught. If she struggled too hard, she could break her neck.

The thought of Father shamed and impoverished struck Marie-Jeanne with shame. She had no choice. Fastening the big leather pouch tight to her back, she found a handhold and pulled herself up against the stout bole. She felt for a toehold and boosted herself up another foot. The first big branch was still over her head. One long stretch with her right arm, and she managed to hook a hand over it. The gloves kept her from skinning her palms on the rough bark.

Mistinguette's flapping and calling became more frantic. One long feather, dislodged by her struggles, floated down past Marie-Jeanne's head.

"Don't struggle, dear one!" the girl pleaded. The kestrel could do herself a mischief, perhaps even break a wing! "Oh, how I wish I could tell you—all you need to do is sit calm!" That was unlikely. Mistinguette would probably tear her face in her hysteria. What would Father or one of the boys do? She had seen Henri, the eldest journeyman, soothe an eagle from insane fits to cooing affection with a few soft words. Not that the bird was tamed, far from it, but she had never understood how he had done it. When she asked, the boys put her off. Did they seem... embarrassed as to how they had learned to communicate with the hawks? In all the years since Father had let her begin to handle the birds, she had been bitten, screamed at, battered by wings, soiled upon, scratched, and coldly ignored by them. What more could they possibly do?

It didn't matter. Her duty was clear: save the bird then go back to face whatever punishment the comte chose to subject her to for not controlling it. He was not a bad man, only impatient. If she was successful, he would calm down. She'd receive no money, but at least Father would not be the loser on the day.

A warm stream rained down on her unprotected head. Marie-Jeanne touched the liquid and looked at it. White and pasty. She groaned. The bird had soiled on her hair! Stifling her resentment, she gritted her teeth and felt for the next handhold, and the next. Mistinguette was upset. She understood. Suddenly, a mad golden eye glared at her. Marie-Jeanne recoiled just in time from a strike by the deadly beak.

"There you are!" she said, in the same tone Mother used to talk with babies. "Hold on, my chick. I'm here. I'll help you."

Mistinguette couldn't understand her, or didn't believe her. The kestrel swung upside down, bating and flapping helplessly. Marie-Jeanne pulled herself up to the branch above the falcon, and gently drew her up by the tangled jesses. The kestrel shrieked, a sound that penetrated the girl's ears like a spike.

Mistinguette fought hard. She beat her powerful wings, trying to take off through the treetops. Marie-Jeanne held on, keeping up the stream of calm nonsense words, all the while desperately hoping she wouldn't tumble off the narrow branch.

"There, there, my chick. You're fine now. Look at what you've done to your feathers! So untidy. You don't want anyone to see you like that, do you? No, of course not. Let me smooth them down. You'll feel much better when you're neat."

As she spoke, she gathered the wild kestrel into her lap, petting and petting at the skewed feathers, patting them down into place. Mistinguette panted, her beak half open. Marie-Jeanne closed the heavy cloak about them both, enveloping them in a tent of wool. It smelled familiar and comforting to her. She hoped the kestrel found it so.

Gradually, the kestrel stopped struggling. Marie-Jeanne's hands found her crouched in her lap, in the hollow formed by her smock's skirts. Mistinguette scratched with one foot after the other, making herself comfortable. She fixed the girl with a searching look, then very deliberately hunched down, her tail feathers held high.

She's going to soil again, Marie-Jeanne thought, in despair. *Mother will make me wash all my clothes in the brook.*

But no white stream issued from the falcon's backside. Instead, Marie-Jeanne felt a warm spot in the bottom of her skirt. When Mistinguette rose, a small white sphere lay where she had been crouching. An egg!

"Well, aren't you the clever girl?" Marie-Jeanne exclaimed. Father would be pleased. The kestrel was old enough to produce eggs! They would have to find her a mate. She reached for it to put it in the lure bag. The shell was still soft. It deformed slightly against the glove leather.

The kestrel jumped up on her wrist and nudged at the egg.

"You don't want me to take it? Why not?"

Mistinguette looked up at her, then rolled the egg toward Marie-Jeanne.

"You...want me to have it?"

The kestrel shrieked. She bent down with her beak open, then looked up at the girl again. Her meaning was clear. Marie-Jeanne gasped.

"You want me to *eat* it? Father would be furious!"

Mistinguette nudged the egg again. Marie-Jeanne raised it to her mouth.

"No, I ca—"

She had no time to finish her protest. The falcon shoved the small sphere into her open mouth with its hard, little head. Marie-Jeanne almost vomited. The shell tasted bitter and salty. It was very small, though, about two inches long. She might be able to swallow it whole. But, ugh, the shell collapsed and broke on her tongue! The slimy insides, all still hot from the falcon's body, filled her mouth. She gagged, ready to spit, then she caught Mistinguette's eye. For once, it was patient, waiting and watching.

Suppressing her disgust, Marie-Jeanne swallowed once, twice, and the mouthful of slime and shards went down.

"There," she said. Her voice sounded weak in her own ears. "Happy? Now, may I take you down so that the comte does not wring both of our necks?"

Mistinguette peeped like a new-hatched chick and climbed up from the woolen skirts to take a post on Marie-Jeanne's right shoulder.

The girl could not believe her eyes. The kestrel understood her!

It peeped at her again, as if to tell her to hurry. Marie-Jeanne didn't hesitate. She tied the hanging leather jesses to the neck of her cloak and turned to face the trunk. Slowly, she felt her way down. It seemed years before her foot crunched onto the fallen leaves and twigs at the base of the tree. Marie-Jeanne sighed and dusted her gloves together.

Then, she winced.

"I don't know which way is home," she said. "I followed your calls. I turned this way and that, and I can't really see where the sun lies. We could be lost in here for days!"

Mistinguette almost chuckled as she trod on Marie-Jeanne's shoulder. She took hold of a lock of the girl's hair in her beak and tugged.

"What, you want me to go that way?"

Another tug.

Marie-Jeanne trembled at the notion that a miracle was occurring. A beast that could understand the speech of men? Or…was this the secret that the falconer's apprentices refused to share? Had they eaten an egg that made them bird-kin? She must ask Father, but first, she must return home safe and alive.

She turned in the directions the kestrel indicated. To and fro, to and fro, Mistinguette guided her, not even protesting or crying out when Marie-Jeanne tripped on a root or raised her arm to swat at biting flies.

The forest was still quiet, but it was a waiting silence. The animals sensed some kind of danger. Could it be La Bête? Marie-Jeanne drew her belt knife. She walked faster through a small clearing, feeling eyes on her back. The villagers complained of wolves in the woods. Had she rescued the falcon only to be eaten by a beast?

Snuffling noises broke the silence. Marie-Jeanne heard them off to her left and diverted to avoid the source. A musky odor filled the air. It could be her imagination, but her senses seemed keener than before. Every leaf had a sharper edge. Every smell had intensified so much she might have had her nose pressed to everything she passed. Sounds, too, reached deeper into her ears, creating a landscape in her mind. This was magic, then. Marie-Jeanne felt the sort of awe she experienced during mass, of something so great that her poor small brain could sense but a dust mote of a distant mountain.

A sudden burst of sound and smell erupted before her. Marie-Jeanne stumbled backward and fell against a tree, moments before a great gray boar hurtled into the clearing, no more than twenty feet away from her. Its tiny eyes had a mad glint. It saw her and bared its teeth. The sharp, pointed tusks at the sides of its mouth gleamed. It pawed the ground like a bull. She couldn't fend it off with only a knife. If only she knew some of Father's protective spells!

"Jesu preserve me," she prayed, clasping her hands together. "Oh, God, I will be dutiful!"

The boar lowered its huge head and charged toward her. She was doomed.

An earsplitting cry erupted in her right ear, rising higher and higher until she feared her skull would split. Marie-Jeanne dropped to her knees. The boar, whose approach threw clods of earth up on both sides, stopped so suddenly its front legs buckled. Mistinguette shrieked her hunting cry again, louder than ever. The boar charged at them, but a yard from Marie-Jeanne, it rebounded as though it hit a stone wall. Marie-Jeanne gasped. The boar scrambled up, bellowing angrily, but it hurtled out of the clearing, avoiding them in a wide arc.

She stared at the kestrel. Mistinguette tilted her head and chuckled again, as though to say, "It was nothing, really. You could have done it yourself."

Marie-Jeanne shook her head. Magic. The world was full of wonders. She had so much to learn.

In between steering her toward home, Mistinguette let out her hunting cry any time an animal approached them. Marie-Jeanne tried to imitate the sound, but the kestrel sounded as if it laughed at her efforts.

"You must give me a chance to learn," she told the bird, sternly. "No one has ever told me what it was really like to be falcon's kin!"

They emerged from the forest by the barley field. The farmer and his workers were doing their best to repair the damage done by the hunting party. By the position of the sun, more than two hours had passed since the falcon had flown away. Marie-Jeanne sighed. She could discover no sign of the comte and his guests but footsteps and hoofprints. If she was lucky, perhaps they had stopped to dine, and she could retrieve her donkey. Otherwise, it would be a long and a disgraceful walk home. She wished for some of that promised feast, even a crust of bread and a sip of watered wine.

"A raw egg is hardly a meal," she pointed out to the kestrel. "Too bad I didn't keep the coney. I could have cooked it for us." Mistinguette peeped in reply.

At least the path was dry. Marie-Jeanne trudged up a gentle hill, following the broken branches left by the party. She hoped they weren't far ahead.

A distant murmur met her enhanced hearing. That was the comte and comtesse, and the bishop! She had found them!

With an apology to Mistinguette, she began to trot down the hill. A strange smell met her nostrils. So strong it made her eyes water, she knew it wasn't dog, horse, or human.

As she looked down the road, she saw it: a beast the size of a large man, but on all fours, with thin black fur over gray skin. It could have been a boar bred with a she-wolf. Marie-Jeanne's heart wrenched. La Bête! It held the entire hunting party at bay.

"Spread out, men," the comte said, his voice amazingly calm. He had his arms out to his sides, his sword in one hand and a dagger in the other. Two men lay on the ground. At first, Marie-Jeanne thought they were asleep, but one of them had no head. "Keep it from charging the ladies. Madame," he said to his wife, "ride hell for leather. Go home and summon all the men-at-arms!"

The comtesse turned her horse this way and that, looking for a way around. Any time she moved, La Bête growled at her, making as if to charge. With a wrench of the poor beast's head, the lady kicked her steed. It leaped into a gallop. La Bête sped after her. It was fast as lightning.

A page in red livery sprang into its path.

"You shall not harm my lady!" he cried. The horrible beast cannoned into him. With one bite, it severed his head then plunged its jaws into his heart. The men charged at it with their hunting weapons. Like a whirlwind, La Bête tossed one after another onto the ground. The comte brought his sword down on its spine. The blade bounced off as if it had been a stick. La Bête jumped onto his chest and opened its jaws.

"No!" Marie-Jeanne screamed. But instead of the word emerging, a deep-throated scream came from her lungs, rising higher and higher into the sky. Mistinguette added her shriek.

In a heartbeat, the beast sprang off the comte's body and hurtled toward the girl. Marie-Jeanne didn't know where the courage came from, but she found herself running at the monster, her arms wide as if they were wings. She screamed and screamed, feeling herself fill with power. The kestrel kept up her cries as well, creating a veritable wall of sound into which La Bête hurtled. And fell.

It rose to its feet, looking shaken but angry. Marie-Jeanne saw its face clearly for the first time. Its teeth were as long as her fingers, and its tiny eyes gleamed with evil.

"You monster!" Marie-Jeanne shrilled. "Foul beast of Satan! Die! I will break your neck! Die!"

La Bête charged her again and again and again. It could not penetrate the kestrel's spell. Marie-Jeanne faced an impasse. If she stopped screaming, it would devour her, and destroy the comte and the others. She glanced at Mistinguette. The kestrel kept up her cry, keeping her safe, keeping them all safe, but for how long?

By now, all the hawks had joined their voices to Marie-Jeanne's. Seeing hope, the comte rallied the hunting party. They mustered all their weapons.

"I'm sorry, girl!" the comte called. He dropped his hand, and the huntsmen loosed quarrel after quarrel at the monster. The arrows bounced off the invisible wall, but also from La Bête's hide.

"It is an unholy monstrosity," the bishop declared, regaining his wits at last. "Robert! Bring me Matilde!"

With a puzzled look, his huntsman ran to him, bearing the crying gyrfalcon. From a saddle pack, the bishop took a small bottle. He uncorked it and put it into Matilde's talons. The gyrfalcon looked as confused as the hunter, until Mistinguette raised a call higher and shriller than ever before. Matilde lifted from the bishop's wrist and flew over La Bête. It dropped the bottle on the beast's head.

Holy water poured down the black-furred creature's body. Where it touched, it left red runnels like fire. La Bête leaped in the air, trying to catch the gyrfalcon, then it rolled on the ground, keening in pain.

"At it, men!" the comte shouted. He led the charge at the monster, with all the men, horses, and dogs behind him.

Despite its agony, La Bête sprang up. With one final snarl at Marie-Jeanne, it galloped into the undergrowth. Cracking branches and threshing footsteps disappeared in the distance.

Marie-Jeanne dropped to her knees and let her voice die away. Mistinguette leaned over and chucked her in the cheek with her head, as if to say, "Well done."

"Well, then," the comte said, swinging out of his saddle and striding to her. Unlike his usual bluff self, he looked abashed. "It seems that not only the falcon, but the falconer is full of surprises. I apologize for doubting your father when he said you would do well. You have done more than well, child." He held out a hand to help her up.

"Thank you, my lord." Marie-Jeanne discovered that her voice was no more than a hoarse croak. Mistinguette peeped.

The comte smiled.

"Say no more," he told her. "I think we've all heard enough from both of you for today. I see why I cannot control your falcon. I'm not enough of a wild creature. But it seems it takes one wild spirit to defeat another. You and your kestrel shall ride with me again. I have more to learn from you."

"And I from her," Marie-Jeanne said, stroking Mistinguette's soft speckled breast. "So much more."

ABOUT THE AUTHOR

Jody Lynn Nye lists her main career activity as 'spoiling cats.' When not engaged upon this worthy occupation, she writes fantasy and science fiction, most of it in a humorous bent. Since 1987 she has published over 50 books and more than 170 short stories. She has also written with notables in the industry, including Anne McCaffrey and Robert Asprin. Jody teaches writing seminars at SF conventions and is Coordinating Judge for the Writers of the Future Contest.

Find out more at http://www.jodylynnnye.com

About the Publisher

Mike Jack Stoumbos is the lead editor and founder of WonderBird Press and the creator of the Unhelpful Encyclopedia series.

Murderbirds is WonderBird Press's debut anthology—the first of many, with more installments in the Unhelpful Encyclopedia series and several other projects on the horizon in the coming years.

WonderBird Press is primarily focused on speculative fiction anthologies. Many of the stories in this and upcoming volumes will be humorous, hopeful, or "feel-good" tales within the scifi, fantasy, and horror genres. As an author of optimistic space opera and an educator himself, Mike Jack wants to contribute more uplifting tales appropriate for teens as well as adults to a fiction landscape that often leans toward the bleaker side.

With each new anthology, Mike Jack plans to draw on the talents of authors actively working and growing in the speculative fiction communities. Most of the authors in this volume are part of at least two of the author support groups mentioned in the acknowledgments. About half of those involved are former Writers of the Future winners, many of whom were in the same Writers of the Future Workshop cohort as Mike Jack.

WonderBird Press does plan on expanding to feature book launch events and promotionals for indie authors, workshops and materials for growing writers, and eventually opportunities to publish novels and series—once again with a nod toward hope and humor whenever possible.

The Press is still in its early stages. Find out more as we grow by visiting https://www.mikejackstoumbos.com/wonderbird-press

◆ ◆ ◆

We Hope You Enjoyed *Murderbirds!*

If you had fun reading these stories—if they made you laugh, cry, gasp, or all of the above—please leave a positive review and rating where you purchased this or wherever you recommend books. If you want to make an author smile for a week, mention their story as one of your favorites in your review. It's a small extra step, but it makes a big difference for indie presses and new publications, including paving the way for future projects.

Speaking of which, we have more Unhelpful Encyclopedia volumes waiting in the wings.

♦ ♦ ♦

Coming Soon from WonderBird Press

Murderbugs!

The swarm is already gathering…

Made in the USA
Middletown, DE
06 April 2023

27964950R00135